A LITTLE MERCY

By

Celeste Charlene

Sep 2, 2015

Chaz,

May God Almighty grant you mercy.

Celeste

Jer 43:14

This is a work of fiction, and is produced from the author's imagination. People, places and things mentioned in this novel are used in a fictional manner.

To Kathryn Page Camp, my faithful friend and critique partner. Thank you.

CHAPTER ONE

Liz slid out of the taxi with the other travelers. The six-hour trip left her drained and grungy, but she didn't have time to clean up. She needed to shop at the African market before it closed for the noon rest.

She took a short cut through the seafood aisle and lingered a moment to breathe in the tantalizing aroma of frying fish. Then she stiffened her spine before wading down the next shopping lane, which was always strewn with garbage. The stench brought tears to her eyes. She waved her hand to keep the buzzing flies from landing on her face. Then she picked up her pace to reach the adjacent aisle of shops.

Customers shouted salutations across the crowds. The shoppers pressed in and shoved her forward. Everyone talked to friends and caught up on the local news. People paced. Buyers bargained. Sellers settled on prices.

Stopping at a little table, she bought mangoes, papayas, and bananas. Then she headed to a booth that sold office supplies. When she spotted an open box of ink pens, she picked up one and took off the cover. A couple of the merchants sold used pens that were out of ink, so Liz tried writing with it. This one worked.

The ebony-skinned trader rubbed his palms together. "The pen is one hundred francs."

"Will you sell me two for one-hundred and fifty francs?"

He nodded and handed her another one. "Give money."

After testing the second pen, she reached for her coin purse as several women shrieked. Liz turned to the cries.

Shoppers screamed, leaped out of the way, and darted in every direction. A giant naked man glowered and stomped toward a teenager with a baby clutched to her chest. People scattered so he had an open path to the terrified girl.

Liz sprinted toward the teenager, stopped in front of her, and faced the goliath. Sometimes the shock of her white skin among the Africans frightened people, but a gigantic fellow like he was, wouldn't scare easily. His defiant glare sent shivers down Liz's spine. She would try to distract the crazed man long enough for the girl to get away.

Saliva dribbled from his lips as he growled loudly. With both his hands, he lifted his blood-covered machete. Sweat poured off his face, down his chin, and onto his glistening chest. The powerfully-built fellow didn't take his eyes off Liz as he raised the blade higher over his head.

Her heart beat faster. His bloodshot eyes riveted her to the ground as he stared fiercely down on her. Shudders ran up her backbone.

Lord please help.

Taking a deep breath to stay calm, she pressed her shaking arms to her sides. A hush fell over the horde of onlookers as everyone stood still. Silence filled the air. Her pounding heart beat like an African war drum. A sudden movement might prompt the livid man to lower the blade.

Liz held her ground.

Confusion flittered across his tattooed face. He shook his head as if to rid himself of one of the insects on his cheeks. Lowering the machete to his side, the crazed fellow roared and twisted away from her. He hadn't gone more than a few steps when the market policemen seized him.

Taking a deep gulp of air, Liz pressed her hand on her chest. Feeling a little dizzy, she staggered backward.

Someone caught her by the shoulders and steadied her. She turned to the side and looked up into the tanned face of a handsome man and mumbled, "Please excuse me. I'm sorry for stumbling into you."

"You didn't." The crinkles around his piercing blue eyes deepened. "I was trying to catch you before you fell."

"Thank you." Her heart raced again, but this time it was fueled by the good-looking gentleman before her.

He whispered, "That crazy man was about to lower his cutlass on your head."

"I know." Her breath caught. "When I saw that terrified girl with the child, I had to do something."

"Did you think you could stop him?"

"It was impulsive, but …"

A security officer interrupted her. "Did that lunatic hurt you?"

Liz turned to the cluster of market police. "He didn't harm me, but how are the girl and the child?"

"They are fine. That crazy man killed his wife. His family bound him with chains to a tree. He broke his bonds and ran to the market after slaughtering several animals. You are lucky. That murderer almost cut your head in two." The officer made a slicing motion.

Liz shivered and looked around. Then she realized her backpack was gone.

The tall stranger held up her bag. "It slid off your shoulders when you tripped, so I grabbed it."

"Thank you." She reached for it. "I thought it may have been stolen in the commotion."

He extended his hand. "I'm Andrew Thomas." His Midwestern accent gave him away as American.

She took his hand. "Elizabeth Connor, and you're the first American I've met in this market."

"This is the largest shopping center in the city. They have almost everything for a price." Andrew pulled out his handkerchief and wiped sweat from his face. "We met two years ago when you boarded a flight north. I was the pilot. You were the only woman on the plane, and I invited you into the cockpit."

"You have a good memory."

He put his handkerchief back in his pocket. "You told me about Jesus, but I wasn't ready to listen."

She lifted her hand to her unbound hair and wrinkled her forehead. She always wore her hair in a neat chignon while traveling in public transportation. Where was her hair clip?

Liz looked down. Andrew looked at the ground. Everyone around them looked at the dirt.

He asked, "What are you searching for?"

"My barrette. It must have fallen out when I ran." Liz had to look demented herself with her uncombed hair blowing around her face.

"I don't think you'll find it in this crowded place. Do you have another one?"

"Back at home." She ran her fingers through her curls and shoved them behind her ears. "I remember that conversation we had in the cockpit. You tried to warn me that the country was dangerous and suggested I return to the States."

"Did you?"

"No, I didn't want to give up and fail God. Staying here was a challenge, but the Lord carried me through some frightening situations."

"Just like the one today in the market?"

She lowered her voice. "Maybe we can talk later, but not here."

"Where?" He asked.

Staring down the lane, she slapped her cheek. "Oh no! I'll probably be arrested."

Then she turned her back on him and ran down one of the passageways.

CHAPTER TWO

Andrew raced after her. He scanned the crowded market. No police officers chased her. Why was she running? No one pursued the attractive lady.

She ran faster than any female he knew, but he was a fast runner himself. It was easy to keep her white arms in sight in the market, but hard to keep up with her. She darted in and out and around people like a bush rat escaping a wildcat. Every head in the market had turned to them as if he and Liz were the main attraction.

Andrew was a cautious man, and impulsive women made him nervous. He'd make an exception for her because she was brave and beautiful. At the last booth he caught up with her as she was rummaging around in her sack. She lifted her sparkling eyes at him, and he was lost in the pools of green.

"When I saw the girl in trouble, I dropped these two ink pens in my bag before paying for them."

Andrew's voice teased. "I'm surprised this trader didn't send the police after you."

"I thought he may have called the law, which is why I ran all the way here."

She turned to the merchant. "Please forgive me for not paying you."

"No problem. I watched you save girl."

Liz dug around in her backpack. "My coin purse must have fallen to the bottom of my bag."

"Let me pay for the pens." Andrew reached into his pocket.

"No, thanks. I found my money." She lifted a plastic sack out of her backpack.

The bulging bag broke. Mangoes, papayas, and bananas fell out, leaving pieces of torn plastic dangling from her fingers.

Andrew grabbed the bananas before they hit the ground. He thanked God for his quick reflexes. Bending over, he picked up the papayas and handed them to her.

As she crouched to collect the mangoes, she bumped into him. "I'm sorry. Markets are so congested. It's hard to turn around."

Holding some mangoes in his hands, he stared at her lovely face. "I believe these got away from you."

She put them in her backpack and pulled out her coin purse. After paying the merchant, she turned to Andrew. "I apologize for running off like that, but I didn't want him to think I had stolen his pens."

His breath quickened. She was caring and courageous, and had stared down the crazy man, who was twice her size. It was foolish and irresponsible, but it worked.

"I've been trying to keep up with you. You said that we might talk later, and then you ran off."

She moved away from a group of Africans bartering for goods. "You can see that I wasn't trying to get away from you. Let's get out of the way of shoppers." She stepped between two stalls where the venders sold bolts of cloth.

As she pulled out her umbrella, a hairbrush fell to the ground. She turned to get it, but he picked it up and handed it to her.

"Thank you." Liz clicked open her umbrella. "The sun gets hot around noon."

"Yes it does. Everyone is hurrying to go home and escape the heat. They eat and take a nap. Would you like to go somewhere for lunch?"

"I didn't get breakfast this morning, so I'm hungry." She slapped dirt out of her skirt. Then she ran her fingers through her hair. "I'm not presentable for a restaurant."

His brows deepened as he rubbed a spot on his grease-stained shirt. "I'm not too clean either." He removed his Oregon Trail Blazers cap and beat dust out of it and then brushed his short hair back with his fingers.

"I spent all morning in a bush taxi with the windows open. The breeze blew dirt on me, so I'd like to clean up before we go anyplace." She swiped her hand across her face, but smeared the dirt rather than wiping it off.

He wanted to offer his handkerchief, but it, too, was dusty. "Can you get freshened up in the restroom at the restaurant?"

She giggled. "I haven't agreed to eat, yet."

Andrew bowed. "Miss Connor, will you join me for lunch?"

Her green eyes twinkled. "I'd enjoy that."

A gust of wind lifted the golden-brown curls that framed her heart-shaped face. He could scarcely take his eyes off her. "You look lovely. Besides, the restaurant doesn't have a dress code."

Moving farther out of the line of shoppers, he stepped under a colossal umbrella that covered the next stall. "There's a European restaurant called 'The Falls.' I'm the only American on the team, but the Canadians said no one has come down with typhoid fever or amoebic dysentery from the food." Andrew reached for her bag. "May I carry this for you?"

"Yes, please."

He slung the bag over his shoulder. "I fly for HOW, the Health Organization for the World. After I became a Christian, I wanted to serve in some way." He turned the corner. "My truck is parked near the main entrance of the market. Would you like to ride with me?"

Liz grinned. "Unless you want to join me in a bush taxi."

"Don't you think using that transportation is testing God?" He led the way down a narrow opening toward the main gate. "Many taxis aren't roadworthy and some drivers don't have licenses."

"Bush taxis are the only way I have for reaching my mobile clinics. I'm trusting God." Smiling, she turned to him. "Let's stop for a minute so I can get my sunglasses from my bag."

"They're on your head."

She reached for the glasses but twisted them in her tangled hair. The sunglasses hung from a weird angle. He gently unwound the strands that held them and handed the glasses to her.

He suppressed the urge to run his fingers through her long curls to straighten the messy style, but she looked so vulnerable. Andrew didn't want to change her expression or her appearance.

"Thank you." She took the sunglasses. "How long have you been here in Tamago?"

"A year, and I'm surprised I've never seen you." Taking the keys from his pocket, Andrew walked to the passenger side. After unlocking the door, he opened it, and cupped her elbow to help her up onto the seat. Then he handed her the backpack.

After putting it next to her feet, she reached over and unlocked his door.

He pulled it open. "How often are you here in the city?"

"I've been coming one or two weekends each month to purchase medicines and supplies."

He climbed into the driver's seat and inserted the key in the ignition. "When we talked in my cockpit, you thought you'd be staying in a grass hut without running water and electricity."

"I live in a mud house with two solar panels that provide power."

"Where's the village?"

"It's called Gotulga, and it is three hundred miles from here."

"Are you the only American there?"

"Yes"

Andrew smiled. If Liz was the only American in a rural village, it would be easy to find her. On the other hand, she was the most spontaneous female he'd ever met. What if she moved to a distant village to save people from an epidemic or was transferred to another country?

He had found her again and couldn't lose her.

CHAPTER THREE

Hunger gnawed at Liz's stomach. Her mouth watered at the thought of eating a tasty meal, but she hated going into a nice restaurant when she was so filthy. As she brushed more dust off her clothes, she glanced at Andrew who was coated in as much dirt as she was.

"I'm giving a health lecture at the university auditorium this evening, so I brought nice clothes to change into." She smiled.

Andrew downshifted to drive around stopped vehicles. "It's a casual eatery and you're fine. Besides, if I let you out of my sight again, you might disappear."

She giggled. "You make it sound like I'm a spirit."

"I tried to find you two years ago in the airport, but you had vanished. Then I had to search for my co-pilot who'd also disappeared."

"Did you find him?"

"Yes, he'd been taken to another room for questioning." Andrew stopped at a red light. "It was the first time he'd flown in Africa and the officers were double-checking his credentials."

"What happened to the African pilots?"

"The authorities didn't want them to fly government insurgents out of the country who might have absconded with the nation's funds, so those pilots were imprisoned during the military coup."

"How did you get a job with the African airlines?"

"The new military regime advertised in the foreign embassies that they needed neutral pilots to fly passengers on their commercial airlines within the country."

Liz pulled her hair away from her face and wished she had her hairclip. "Did you respond right away?"

"Yes. The American airline I worked for had already left Tamago because it wasn't safe. I was without a job and thought I could help."

"Wasn't it dangerous signing up with the military government?" Her eyes watered from the stench of heaping garbage that lined the roads.

He shifted gears and slowed. "One time after I landed, two warring tribes surrounded the plane and started fighting. They jumped on the wings and smashed windows, so I prayed. The armored tanks arrived and drove the fighters off." Andrew turned down a side road. "That made me realize I needed God in my life. I asked Him for forgiveness of my sins and trusted Him as my Savior."

"I'm glad you did."

As they drove over a bumpy stretch of road the motion jolted her up and down in the passenger seat. "I wish they'd repair these potholes."

Andrew reached behind her and tugged her seatbelt free from its holder. "Fasten this. That's another thing. Taxis don't have seatbelts."

She pulled the belt around her and buckled the clasp. "That's true, and this cushioned seat is much more comfortable than a metal bench welded to the back of a van."

He stopped the truck.

"What's wrong?" She asked.

"The sign says, 'The Falls,' but it points down that dirt road and doesn't look right."

"There's no other road, so let's try it."

Andrew turned onto the path. A half a mile later, he stopped in front of a locked iron gate. "This is strange. The restaurant exists and it's open because someone I know ate there yesterday."

Liz scrunched up her face. "Maybe an old notice pointing the way fell down in those grasses. I'll get out and look."

"I'm coming with you." Andrew stepped out of the truck as Liz jumped down from the passenger side. She went to the back of the vehicle and he met her there.

Liz whispered, "Do you hear that?"

"I don't hear anything. We're the only ones here, except that herd of giant forest hogs over there. I've never seen that many in one place." He pointed. "I recognize those creatures by their large, pointed ears."

"I hear a crying baby." Liz turned her head left and then right. "Those animals aren't dangerous. They're mostly herbivores."

"Hogs can be scavengers if provoked. The leader attacks with his tusk if he suspects his family is in danger."

Liz walked into the nearby bushes of the large field and stood still. She moved her head trying to hear the cry again. It sounded like a cat screeching, so she started jogging toward it.

An enormous hog darted out from a thick cluster of elephant grass. He led the pack straight toward her.

She kept running into the herd.

***

Andrew hadn't heard a baby cry but raced after her. The bright sun was hotter than usual and the heat must have been responsible for Liz's delusion. Why else would she dash like a crazy woman into a pack of wild hogs?

Her initial rush toward them must have incited their wrath because the big, black animals stampeded the ground like a herd of buffalo. Liz kept racing toward the attacking beasts.

He had to reach her before the hogs did, so he took a gulp of air and increased his pace. His heart lurched when she tripped, but she immediately regained her balance and picked up her speed.

Andrew breathed a sigh of relief when at last she turned away from the herd. A moment later, she swerved again toward the pack. His heart plummeted. She sprinted and wavered like a person who had lost her mind. The tusk of the giant leader was aimed right at her. He couldn't let her be gored or trampled to death, so he ran faster.

When he was close enough, he reached for her hand. He missed but caught her wrist and tugged her away from the stampeding beasts. As they jogged together, Andrew loosened his grip. Then she twisted out of his hold and turned back into the herd of charging animals.

He screamed, "No, Liz!"

Her impulsiveness was about to get them killed, so he screamed again. "No Liz, come this way!"

Andrew's chest pounded like the hooves of the wild hogs stampeding the ground, but he turned back into the path of the angry herd with her.

Then he saw it. A black baby's fist rose and fell, not far in front of them.

Hoping to reach the tiny infant before the herd did, Andrew caught his second wind and raced ahead of Liz. The wild beasts closed in on them. His heart pounded faster. He scooped the child up in his arms, spun around, and grabbed Liz's hand. He yanked her out of the path of the herd just as she leaped away from it. The beasts dashed past them. She kept pace with him as if she ran a five-hundred yard dash every day.

With one hand he pulled the baby closer to his chest, and with the other he maintained his hold on her. Then she tugged her hand out of his and lifted both sides of her mid-calf skirt to sprint faster.

He headed to the passenger door of his truck. The hogs stopped and stood at the edge of the field as if they were afraid to walk on the gravel. Andrew turned and helped Liz inside the vehicle. He handed her the child and slammed the door.

He was about to run around the truck and get into the driver's seat, but the giant leader of the pack crossed the gravel and crept closer toward him.

Slowly, Andrew inched backward as the massive hog waddled closer. The beast, like a bull, stomped his feet in the dust and lowered his head, getting ready to charge.

CHAPTER FOUR

Andrew's heart thudded louder as the enormous hog kept his head lowered and growled.

The truck door squeaked open behind him. Liz called. "Andrew, jump!"

He turned and took a couple quick steps. He leaped into the passenger seat as Liz tried to move out of it and into the driver's seat. Her skirt caught on the old-style gear stick and held her in place.

Andrew squeezed his long frame into the small space but was practically on top of her. He twisted back to close the door and slipped on Liz's backpack on the floor. His body slammed forward. He reached for the back of the seat, so his weight wouldn't land on the baby snuggled between them.

She crunched closer to the driver's seat as he raised his leg away from her and rolled over onto his back. He collapsed on the narrow space to the right of her in the passenger seat.

When he'd caught his breath, he started laughing at Liz, who was still trying to disentangle her skirt with one hand and hold the baby in the other arm. He reached over and unwound her skirt, so she was free to move into the driver's seat.

His breathing slowed as he looked out the side window. "That gigantic hog is still there."

Then they both started laughing. Liz laughed until tears ran down her face. The green of her eyes grew larger. "We saved the baby."

"We sure did. Two years ago we escaped the perils of a military coup d'états." He shook his head. "Today you faced a crazy man, ran away from a herd of forest hogs, and rescued an infant. Do you always live on the run? Or is your life one impulsive race away from danger?"

She laughed and laughed. He could listen to her little girl-like giggle every day. Turning to her, he pulled leaves out of her hair.

Liz lifted her thick hair away from her face. Using the back of her hand to wipe the sweat, she spread more dirt across her cheeks.

He took out his dusty handkerchief and gave it to her. "I'm not sure this will help."

"Can I use it for the baby?" She asked.

"Do whatever you like with it."

Andrew rubbed his palms together several times but they were still dirty. "When I invited you for lunch, I had no idea we'd stop for an African safari and rescue a baby."

As if on cue, the infant wailed. Liz set the noisy bundle on her lap and opened the filthy, wet cloth. She didn't seem to notice the stench, but it gagged him. Andrew hadn't paid attention to what soaked and covered the large rag wound around the child.

"Open my bag, take out the bottle of water, and pour a little on this handkerchief." She handed it to him.

"How long do you think she's been there?" He pulled out her bottle of water and poured some on the cloth.

Liz stretched the foul rag out to examine the naked infant. She picked up a dried piece from one of the folds. "This is the child's umbilical cord." She tossed it out the open window. "She's a newborn and must have been abandoned shortly after her birth because she hasn't been bathed."

"Is that what the stench is?"

"It's a mixture of afterbirth, blood, and urine, but it might be a wild animal's wastes." Liz ran the damp handkerchief over the infant's head. "This cloth is black already and I've only wiped off her face."

"What do you need?"

"Look in my backpack and take out the roll of toilet paper. Unwind a handful of tissue, pour water on it, and give it to me."

She took the soaked paper from him and started washing off the crud from the infant's body. "I don't see a blemish on her. She's a perfectly formed little girl."

He handed her a fresh wad of dampened toilet tissue. Taking it, she washed away more filth. He opened his trash bag to throw away the smelly pads and then poured water on another one which he gave her.

After cleaning the rest of the infant's body, she ran her fingers again over the baby's features more closely.

Liz arched an eyebrow. "I don't see any injuries."

As she finished checking out the baby, a couple of drops of water splashed near the infant's mouth from the wet tissue. The child made sucking movements.

Liz beamed. "That's a good sign. Take the spoon out of the side pocket of my bag."

"Do you always carry a spoon with you?"

"It's better to eat food with it than with dirty fingers."

She positioned the child in the crook of her arm. "Pour a little water into this spoon. I'll feed her a few drops at a time. She probably hasn't had anything since she was born. If that's true, she's in remarkably good shape. Infants are extremely resilient. I don't see any unusual abnormalities on her to cause someone to desert her. She doesn't have six toes, a cleft lip, or a club foot."

"So why was she left in a field with wild beasts?"

"Babies are discarded in the city for different reasons than in the villages. I read in the newspaper that a university student dumped her infant in an outhouse because she was on a special scholarship and wanted to finish her education."

"Isn't leaving a child in a field or a toilet illegal?" Andrew kept pouring water on the spoon, which Liz put to the child's lips. "Wouldn't it be more humane to take the newborn to the hospital and leave her there?"

"Yes, that would have been better, but the mother might have been too frightened to do that. Chances are the police investigate abandoned infants. They might have found the mother and thrown her in prison." Liz tilted her head to the side. "Can you look in my bag for a purple housecoat?"

"Do you carry everything in this backpack?" He lifted out the robe.

"I carry everything but the kitchen sink and wish I had one now to give her a proper bath. With my daily trips to villages I never know where and when I'll be stranded so I try to be prepared."

"I'm impressed. I thought you were impulsive and disorganized." Andrew lifted the robe by the shoulders. "What do you want me to do with it?"

"Spread it open on your lap."

He stretched the gown out and draped it across his thighs and legs.

"Fold it in half keeping all of it on top of your lap." She looked down at the infant. "Put the water bottle away. I've given her enough for now."

Drawing her brows together, Liz meticulously re-examined the child. Her thoughtful expression clouded. "Since she was in that field for a couple of days, I'm surprised there's not a tiny sore or insect bite on her." Liz put the baby on Andrew's lap and then wound the huge robe around the infant. Leaning over Andrew, she picked up the bundle. The child had fallen asleep.

Andrew pushed Liz's backpack out of the way. "What are you going to do with her?"

Liz peered into Andrew's eyes. "Do you want to keep her?"

What on earth was Liz thinking? He had no means of taking care of an abandoned baby. The child didn't belong to Liz, either. Who did she belong to?

She smiled. "She's technically yours since you rescued her."

Andrew shook his head. "You heard her cry and raced toward her. If you hadn't done that, I'd have never run in after you. What are you going to do with her?"

"I'm going to take care of her. She's at risk for pneumonia, so I'll give her antibiotics and take her to the hospital for an inoculation against tetanus." She stroked the baby's cheek. "People have given me babies they didn't want or believed were cursed."

"What happened to them?"

"I nursed them back to health and found good homes for them. Thank God we saw her when we did." She put the baby on her shoulder. "We need to stand outside behind your truck and let anyone who is watching see that I have accepted this baby. If someone sees the child wrapped in my robe, it will indicate I'm willing to take responsibility for her. Remember when the mother of baby Moses put him in a basket in the river? His sister Miriam followed the basket to see what would happen to her brother. Maybe a relative is watching only to see what happens." Liz took a deep breath. "Has the giant hog left, yet?"

He looked out the window. "Yes, he's gone."

"The leader of the pack thought I was attacking his family, which is why he came after us. I don't think they'll hurt us." She reached out and patted his shoulder. "Don't worry. We'll be fine."

He wished he felt as calm as Liz looked. Why did she want to go outside and announce to the world that she'd found this baby? The herd of hogs might get riled again and come after them. After glancing in every direction, he eased the door open. He didn't like going out there again, but the beasts still grazed in the field and acted like they wanted nothing to do with humans. After stepping down, he walked around to the driver's side to take the baby from Liz so she could get out. Then he handed the child back to her.

"How long are we waiting here?"

"Not too long. The baby's been here a few days so the family might assume she's already dead." Liz took a deep breath. "If someone is determined to kill the baby and we rescued her, they might try to murder us."

His heart plummeted to the pit of his stomach.

They were about to be slaughtered again.

CHAPTER FIVE

Andrew wiped the sweat from his brow with the back of his hand. "Who may want to kill us?"

"Someone wants the baby dead. If it's a father or brother, he may try to take us out of the way to destroy her."

"Why are we waiting around for that?"

"We also need to stay out here in case the mother has changed her mind or a member of the family wants the baby back." Liz adjusted the purple robe to show off the charcoal-skinned child. "If we've interfered with someone using this newborn as a sacrifice, the person might hurt us."

"Are we going to stand out here and wait for a guy to kill us?" Andrew reached into his pocket, checking to see if he had his knife, but a little blade wouldn't save them. Andrew only hoped they'd survive this peril.

Her green eyes twinkled. "If a bad guy wants the baby for a sacrifice, we'll take the child and run. We can fight, but Jesus doesn't approve of that."

Andrew pulled a stray blade of grass out of her hair. "So you never intended to resist that lunatic. If he lowered the blade. . ."

"I'd have gone to Heaven."

For a few seconds he was lost in the depth of her emerald eyes. He admired her bravery but didn't like her impulsive behavior. Taking out his knife, he opened it and glanced at her. She scowled at him so he slid it back in his pocket. Maybe whoever watched them had caught a glimpse of his weapon. Liz might not fight, but he wouldn't stand by and watch her and the baby be slaughtered.

If he couldn't protect Liz with his knife, he'd use his fists. He scanned the horizon, the field of wild grasses, and the herd of hogs. No one was there.

"What do you do in the bush villages?"

"I establish clinics, treat patients, and train health workers." She shoved her hair behind her ears again. "Tell me about your work."

"I fly to villages to deliver supplies for HOW." He glanced at the field. "I enjoy it."

If he flew his plane like Liz dashed into danger, he'd be dead. Andrew had always been cautious.

The clusters of elephant grass were taller than she was. So the wind had blown the dry stems all over her. Stalks of grass stuck out of her hair, near her scalp. He, too, was covered with brown pods, leaves, and shoots.

"My work is satisfying with a new adventure each day." She moved the baby to her other arm.

"Do you think facing a lunatic with a three-foot long knife is an adventure?"

"Yes." She grinned. "But I was praying the whole time."

"So was I, but I'm not the type who seeks near-death experiences. A little excitement now and then makes life interesting, though."

Seeing her cool manner, he relaxed. "Sometimes I get tired of traveling and would like to settle down in one place."

His eyes lingered on her long curls as he plucked dry blades from her hair. His hand grazed her cheek. Her skin felt soft and delicate against his fingers. He needed to stop or he'd be doing more than pulling little sticks from her hair.

"You don't have to stay with me. After all, I brought you into this mess." Liz smiled up at him.

"I guess you did." He chuckled.

There was no way he'd leave her all alone, at the end of a road with an abandoned child, a herd of bush hogs, and the possibility of being slaughtered.

He appreciated her determination. "Thanks for your permission to leave, but I'll stick around to see what happens. Besides, I like the view." He caught another glimpse of her delicate features.

"What view? There's nothing here but a barred steel gate, that field, and those pigs." She didn't look up. "What should we name the infant?"

Andrew laughed again. Did she think they were planning to adopt the child? She had been in the sun far too long. She talked about getting killed one minute and naming the baby the next.

Life would be exciting with her. She was reckless but thoughtful at the same time, an enigma he wanted to figure out.

"What name are you talking about?"

"I hate to keep calling her baby. Is it okay with you if I call her Mercy? Or do you want to name her?"

Andrew searched the field and deserted road for movement. Maybe she didn't believe they were about to be murdered, and it was another one of her jokes. No, the set of her shoulders and stiff posture indicated she was serious, but she teased far too much. Her emerald eyes twinkled which had to be a sign she was joking.

"Do you want me to hold the baby for a while?"

"No, it's best I keep her. Women are less threatening than men. No one would be afraid of me because I'm a little, helpless woman."

He laughed loudly.

The sleeping child jerked in Liz's arms. "Shh. Shhh." She whispered and rocked the infant. "You'll wake the baby."

"I don't think you're as weak as you imply. I understand what you're saying. Men are in charge here."

"That's right." Her eyes grew large as if she had an idea. "This infant may be the child of a mentally deranged woman. Have you seen the people called 'crazies' on the streets?"

"Yes, I've seen them. Aren't there any mental hospitals?"

"There's a government-run facility. The few mentally-ill people I've met are taken care of by their families in their homes. The out-of-control ones roam the alleys." She sighed. "Some street women are raped, deliver on the side of the road, and abandon the infants. Or a family member assumes the child is crazy because the mother is and so abandons the infant or sells it."

"Will this baby have any chance of being normal?"

"It depends on the physical and mental health of both parents."

A bush moved not far from them. Andrew took a few steps forward and stared at the shrubs. He relaxed when a baby hog darted out of the thick grasses. It must have wandered away from the herd.

"What about the name? Do you like Mercy?"

"That's fine. She's a little Mercy. How long are we staying here?"

"Thirty minutes will give whoever it is enough time to do whatever they want with us." She glanced at her watch. "It looks like we've been here more than thirty minutes, so we can go."

"Where are we going?"

"I don't know about you, but if your offer for lunch still stands, I'm starved."

How can she think of food at a time like this? They should take the baby to the hospital or buy her a bottle. He glanced at the sleeping infant. Maybe the child didn't need anything at the moment, and Liz needed a meal.

They went to the passenger side of the truck. Andrew opened the door and helped Liz climb up into the seat. Her dress rose higher, and he took a long appreciative look.

After climbing into the driver's seat, Andrew turned the truck around. A couple of young men waited at the fork in the road.

Liz touched Andrew's hand. "Let's stop and ask them about the restaurant."

After getting the right directions, he drove toward 'The Falls.' Five minutes later, he pulled up and parked in front of a gigantic mud hut with huge, open windows. "Wait there. I'll come around to you."

When he opened her door, he looked at Mercy. "What about her?"

"She comes with me."

He knew that. "May I carry her for you?"

She smiled and handed the baby to him. Taking her hand, he helped Liz down the steps. He could get used to carrying an infant around, especially if it meant spending more time with Liz.

That was the thought of an impulsive man, and he wasn't. So what was he thinking?

CHAPTER SIX

When Liz saw the front of the massive thatched hut, she was reassured it was a casual place to eat. It was also far enough out of the city she wouldn't run into anyone she knew.

Walking through the open doorway, she glanced at the brocaded tablecloths trimmed with stamped elephants. White dinner plates with matching cups, saucers, and silverware completed the elegant settings.

The waterfall was magnificent as water tumbled off a cliff and pounded the rocks. Blue and black birds with orange beaks, probably kingfishers, perched on branches of nearby trees. Monkeys chattered and jumped from branch to branch on the opposite side of the river.

A glance down at her skirt confirmed she was underdressed, but she'd have to make the best of it. Thank God that it was after the lunch hour and there were no other customers, to see her unkempt appearance.

A waitress led them to a table. After handing them menus, she curtsied. "May I get you something to drink?"

"What would you like?" Andrew asked

"Bottled water, please."

Andrew turned to the waitress. "Bring a large bottle for two."

Liz put the baby on her lap so she could open the menu. When the server returned with their drinks, Liz ordered the roasted chicken with noodles.

After the waitress wrote it down along with Andrew's order of peppered steak, she left.

Liz lifted Mercy. "Would you mind holding the baby for a few minutes so I can go to the restroom?"

Andrew stood, took the child, and pulled out Liz's chair.

She swung her backpack over her shoulder and made her way to the restroom. A glimpse at her refection in the mirror caused her to cringe. Scowling at her filthy appearance, she ran a finger lightly over the dirt that dotted her cheeks and circled her neck. She needed a bath.

Taking out her bar of scented soap, she breathed in the refreshing fragrance, much better than the musty smell of taxi cushions, baby's urine, poop from the field and those disgusting hogs. She scrubbed her face, neck, hands, and arms.

She unbuttoned her smelly blouse and stuffed it into a plastic bag and then washed her hands again. There was no point in changing her dirty skirt since she needed to hold an infant, who wasn't wearing a diaper, on her lap. After slipping into a clean blouse, she tucked the bottom of it into her filthy skirt.

Combing her hair, she let the thick curls fall around her face. There had been a slight breeze near the table, so maybe her neck wouldn't feel so hot with her hair down. She hoped the cross ventilation and overhead fans in the restaurant would keep her cool.

After brushing a little black mascara on her eyelashes, she applied beige foundation. She took another look in the mirror before tossing her cosmetics into her bag. Then she returned to the table.

With the baby in his arms, Andrew stood. Liz took Mercy from him and sat down. He pushed Liz's chair under the table. "You look lovely. I'd like to go and wash up before our food arrives."

As she waited for Andrew to return from the restroom, Liz fed more water to the baby. She wanted to make certain the water digested before starting the baby on milk. Liz checked the baby's heart and respirations again. The infant had only been slightly dehydrated, which surprised Liz. Perhaps an animal's urine soaking into the rag had kept moisture close to the child's body and prevented her from losing too much fluid.

Liz would never forget the way Andrew had lifted little Mercy out of danger and pulled Liz to safety away from the wild herd. She smiled at the thought of Andrew leaping into the truck and landing on top of her. Her face had been inches from his. For one insanely romantic moment she couldn't breathe. She'd been close enough for a kiss. Thank God that the baby had wailed and brought her back to reality.

By the time Andrew returned, the server was bringing their meals. Liz put her hand on the table. "Would you like to pray?"

He took her hand. "Lord, I thank you for meeting Liz again. Thank you for this food and for taking care of us. Bless little Mercy, in Jesus name. Amen."

"It smells and looks delicious." Liz picked up her fork and swallowed a bite. "This fowl in cream sauce and noodles is fabulous. How is your steak?"

Andrew cut a small piece of meat and chewed. "It's a little tough, but it's flavored well."

Liz caught a whiff of the pungent odor of the housecoat that still covered the baby. "It smells like Mercy's urinary tract is functioning, which means she can tolerate milk later."

After Liz swallowed the last bite of food on her plate, she poured more water and gave Mercy some by spoon

"Since our first meeting in the cockpit, I've wanted to see you again." Andrew sliced a bite of meat. "God answered my prayer."

"I'm happy we ran into each other."

"It sounds more like you run into trouble." Andrew took a sip of water. "My contract is over, but I'm trying to renew it for another year here."

Her chin dipped to her chest. What if he wasn't reassigned to Tamago?

"Are you engaged or dating anyone?"

"No, I'm not. Since I arrived, I haven't seen many eligible bachelors."

"If I get transferred back, may I bring you here again?"

Nodding, she smiled. "Thanks for lunch and saving the baby and me."

"You're welcome. I look forward to many more interesting dates with you." Andrew poured more water into the glasses.

She wanted to see him again, but suppose he wasn't sent back to Tamago?

***

Andrew was mesmerized by the assorted expressions that flickered across Liz's exquisite face. "If I can return, I'll need to live in the apartment they provide up north at the headquarters."

"That's far from where I live."

"You let me worry about that. I have a truck. I fly a plane throughout the country. My colleagues operate helicopters dropping insecticides into rivers, streams, and ponds. I can come to you." Andrew stared for a moment at her emerald eyes.

Liz lifted the baby to her shoulder. "I've enjoyed chatting with you and look forward to doing it again, but I need to excuse myself to get the baby settled in and prepare for the lecture this evening."

Andrew stood and reached for the bill. After paying, he grabbed Liz's backpack and walked her outside.

He noticed two grungy-looking men, with unusual tribal tattoos on their faces, leaning against his truck. Andrew whispered. "Wait here."

"It'll be safer if I stay with you." Liz kept pace with him.

The larger of the two fellows stepped forward, "Good afternoon master, I come about the baby."

Liz tilted her head. "What about the baby?"

"She belong to us."

"Who are you?" Andrew asked.

"We uncle. Our sister get brain sickness. She not normal. She have baby and leave. We want baby."

Why would scruffy men smelling of alcohol want a baby? Why hadn't they come when Liz and he waited by the field?

Andrew leaned closer to Liz and whispered. "What do you think?"

She handed him the baby and stepped closer to the men.

Andrew prayed. *Please Lord don't let her do anything foolish.* He suppressed the urge to pull her close to him, but instead moved next to her.

Liz shot the grungy men a fierce expression. "What proof do you have that this is your sister's baby?"

"We no understand proof."

"Where is your sister?"

They shrugged.

"If she delivered a baby a few days ago, she will have milk for the child." Liz patted her chest. "Where does she live?"

The big guy snarled, "We don't know."

30

"Here in Africa families are close. Everyone knows where everyone else lives. Tell me where she is, and we will take the baby to her. A mother should have her child."

"Give us money and we go away."

Liz shook her head. "Money for what?" She shrugged.

"For baby."

"Selling babies is against the law." Liz put her hands on her hips and glared at them. "Let's go to the police station. Why did you leave your sister's baby in a field with wild hogs?"

"No. No. No police. Give us money and we leave you."

The men took another step closer to her. Andrew had had enough. He stepped in front of her. "We're going now." He took a couple more steps and opened the truck door for Liz. When she was seated, he handed her the baby.

Andrew climbed into the driver's seat and started the engine. "Should we take the baby to the police?"

"The child protection service doesn't function well in this country." She let the air out of her pursed lips.

"What do you think about those rogues?" He turned into the road.

The two men shook their fists at Andrew.

"They must have seen us rescue the baby. Maybe they asked the same young men we did for directions and followed us to the restaurant." Liz shoved her hair behind her ears. "They probably thought we were rich white people, so they asked us for money."

"I'm concerned they'll find you, demand money, or hurt you."

"I don't think they'd find me. If they were telling the truth, they would have told us where the baby's mother is, which means they only wanted money. Don't worry. I'll be fine."

But Andrew didn't think she would be.

CHAPTER SEVEN

With the baby in her arms, Liz leaned back in the cushioned seat and asked. "Do you know where the mission guesthouse is located?"

"Yes." Andrew downshifted. "It's behind the large evangelical church in the center of the city."

"On the way would you mind stopping at a small shop, so I can buy canned milk for the baby?"

"I'd be glad to."

She reached the top of her head and sighed loudly. She ran her fingers through her hair to make certain her sunglasses weren't tangled in it. If her hair had been neatly clasped behind her head with the barrette, it would have held the sunglasses in place.

"I must have dropped my sunglasses in that field."

He parked the truck a few minutes later in front of a boutique and turned to Liz. "The baby's sleeping, so I'll run inside. Is there a special milk you want?"

She laughed, "There's only one brand of canned milk. Let me find my coin purse."

"Don't disturb little Mercy. I'll buy it." He left.

Five minutes later he returned with a large sack which he handed to her.

She peeked inside. "Ten cans is a lot of milk. Why are there four pairs of sunglasses?"

"You might need them."

"Did you buy out the store?"

"I bought all the milk and sunglasses they had. I wanted to make certain you had a good supply." He laughed.

He pulled into traffic and drove toward the guesthouse. After parking in front of it, he jumped out and escorted Liz to the door. "Goodbye. I'll see you soon."

After watching him get into his truck, she waved.

Then she stepped inside and went to the check-in desk. After collecting the key, she walked down a long hall to her room. As she was putting Mercy into the crib, someone knocked.

Liz crossed the room to open the door and was surprised to see two young ladies.

"Good afternoon, Sister Liz." The taller one lifted the bag from her head and set the sack on the floor. "Dr. Luke sent us to help you in the clinics."

"Come in." Liz held the door open for them. "What are your names?"

The taller one pointed to herself. "My name is Tamara, and this is Henry."

"Where are you from?" Liz cocked an eyebrow at the speaker.

Tamara removed her headscarf and wiped the sweat from her face. "I am from Edu, in the south on the ocean."

Henry stood ramrod straight with a stuffed cloth sack balanced on her head. Then she lifted the rucksack and set it on the floor. "I'm from Murooni. It's in the east." She stared straight at Liz's hair. "You look like a wild woman, and it's not proper."

Tamara's eyes widened and she raised her voice. "Henry, we are here to help Sister Liz, not judge."

For a brief moment Liz was at a loss for words. Then she smiled. "Thank you for coming. I truly need your help."

Henry's frown deepened. "Take a bath first."

"That's a good idea." Knowing the girls would keep an eye on the baby, Liz reached for her bag and went into the bathroom.

After scrubbing off the dirt from the field, she shampooed her hair. Liz closed her eyes and her mind swam with images of Andrew. Liz had to get him out of her mind to prepare for the lecture. The student nurses were a blessing, but she had never met anyone like Henry, and why did she have a man's name?

As Liz dressed, Mercy cried. A moment later, the wailing stopped, so Liz finished getting ready. When she opened the door, the baby was gone, then she noticed the infant tied to Tamara's back.

Liz sat down and opened a can of evaporated milk. After diluting it with water, she said. "I need to feed the baby." Taking the child from Tamara, Liz picked up a spoon and fed little Mercy.

Henry stared at the baby. "The child is black like us, so she can't be yours. Whose baby is it?"

"This afternoon, I found this child in a field. She'd been abandoned and left to die there."

Henry's eyes widened. "So that's why you looked like a crazy woman with dirt in your hair."

"Yes, and I'm sorry for offending you. I lost my hairclip which kept my hair neat and proper."

"Don't worry." Tamara went to her bag, "I have lots of fasteners and bands because my sister is a hairdresser."

Henry stared at Liz as she fed the baby. "The child is intelligent. I've never seen a tiny infant sitting up like a man and eating from a spoon."

"Doctors say spoons are better than bottles." Liz turned to the girls. "Why do you think this baby was left in a field to die?"

Tamara lined up barrettes, bobby pins, and yellow ribbon on the table. "If a baby is born with her feet coming out first, superstitious people believe the baby must die."

"There are pagans who sacrifice babies to idols." Henry scowled. "If a girl becomes pregnant and wants to continue her education, she may throw the baby away."

When Liz was finished feeding Mercy, Liz carried the baby into the bathroom and filled the sink with tap water. Both girls frowned and shook their heads.

Henry put her hands on her hips. "Let me boil some hot water to bathe her the proper way."

"No, thank you. Her skin is delicate and I don't want to hurt her."

When Mercy was clean, Liz wrapped her in a towel and handed her to Tamara. Then Liz picked up her manicure scissors and cut one of her cotton skirts into diapers. Both girls glared at Liz as she pulled two safety pins from her backpack to fasten the bright-green cloth on the child's bottom. Then Liz wrapped the baby in a denim skirt and mumbled, "I'll look for baby clothes later."

"Baby clothes?" Henry crossed her arms. "You go to lots of trouble for a baby. Are you trying to turn her into an American?"

Liz laughed. "No. I'm trying to manage with what I have."

Henry took the child and held her while Tamara opened her bag. She handed Liz a lightweight, foot-square package. "Dr. Luke wanted me to give this to you."

When Liz unwrapped it, she found pieces to a baby weighing scale. She pulled out the written sheets and began reading them out loud. "Dear Sister Liz, This is a newly invented scale, special for the rural areas. It is portable and intended to be carried to villages and tied to the branch of a tree at eye level. Enclosed are directions to assemble the spring with the adjusters on the board. The pictures are self-explanatory." Liz sighed. "Since you see so many children less than five years of age each month, I recommended to the institute of tropical disease that you test the scale. The European doctor who invented it needs a full report including advantages and disadvantages. He suggested using a mother's wrapper to weigh the baby, but he's never been to Africa. A woman's wrapper might not be the best solution. I trust you will come up with an improved means to encase the infants for weighing and will carry out his test. I am sending you these two, hard-working nursing students, who are waiting to take their final examinations in three months. They can assist you in any way you need. Yours, Dr. Luke."

Liz grinned. "We'll need to wait until we get home before we put this scale together and test it."

Then she looked in the package again and pulled out a folded paper plastered over with scotch tape. On it was written, "Private and personal." She stuffed it in her backpack to read later when she was alone.

Liz turned to Tamara, "Did you take your name from the Bible after you became a Christian?"

"Yes, on the day I was baptized the pastor said 'Tamara' would be a good name for me."

Liz asked, "How did you get a name like Henry?"

"I am named after my mother whose name is Henrietta, but people in my family never pronounced all those syllables. So they call me Henry."

"What do people call your mother?"

"Everyone calls her Mrs. Bellolare."

Liz pressed her lips together trying not to laugh. "I need you girls to help me look presentable tonight."

Henry frowned. "You should be proper all the time, not only on one night."

Liz bit her lip. "I only meant I have to look extra proper this evening because I'm teaching university students." She turned to Tamara. "Can you arrange my hair into a nice chignon that would be decent for a lady?"

Tamara reached for the comb. Henry scowled, "I've never seen such stubborn hair."

"Don't worry, Sister Liz, I can tame wild hair." In a few minutes Tamara had styled the hair into a dignified twist.

Liz felt the back of her head. "We need more bobby pins. It's hard to keep my stubborn hair in place."

After Tamara poked in more pins, she gave Liz a hand mirror. "Do you like it?"

"It's beautiful." Liz smiled. "Thank you."

Then she went to the large mirror in the bathroom and applied smoky gray eye liner, black mascara, blush, and maroon lipstick.

"Why are you wearing cosmetics?" Henry's mouth fell open.

"Many city girls use make-up, especially university students. Is it wrong?"

"You look like a harlot." Henry's forehead wrinkled.

"I don't think so." Tamara smiled. "You look elegant."

"Thank you." Liz slipped into a two-piece cranberry business suit and added a necklace and matching earrings.

"Those are expensive. Are they the five dollar ones?"

"Yes." Liz giggled, but then she asked, "Do you girls have plans for this evening?"

"Our assignment is to work with you and help any way we can." Tamara put the rest of the hair fasteners away. "We planned to stay with you tonight, so we can watch the baby."

After explaining Mercy's milk preparation and feeding with a spoon, Liz picked up her backpack and briefcase.

Before stepping out of the door, she grinned at them. "Thank you for coming. You've already helped me lots."

Henry rocked the baby. "Sister Liz, when you don't look like a demented woman, you seem quite normal."

Liz walked to the curb to hire a taxi. Glancing down at her expensive outfit, she wished she had met Andrew when she'd been dressed nicely.

CHAPTER EIGHT

Liz strolled out of the guesthouse and waited for a city cab. Taking out the letter addressed to her, she frowned at the scotch tape covering the front and back of it. She'd need a knife to slice open the edges or the writing would be ruined.

After stuffing it back in her bag, she stopped a taxi going to the university auditorium. When she arrived at the hall, the school president accompanied her to the platform. As she stood next to him, she smiled at over a thousand students that filled the assembly.

He beamed. "I am proud to introduce Miss Elizabeth Connor. She is a nationally registered nurse from the United States of America."

Liz shook hands with the university leader. After he left the stage, she took out her notes and began her lecture. "Many illnesses are preventable."

At the end of her talk she had a question-and-answer period with the students. Then Liz stacked her papers and stuffed them into her briefcase, which she carried, along with her backpack.

She went outside and headed toward the road to hire a taxi. Her low heels clicked on the driveway until a pebble landed in her shoe. She stopped and set her briefcase on the ground. Lifting her right leg, she balanced on the other one. Liz pulled off the shoe to take out the stone. To keep her equilibrium, she extended her free arm. She hopped a couple of times on the uneven path and nearly lost her balance to slip her shoe back on.

A hand grabbed her elbow. She froze. Her breath caught in her throat. It was a taboo for a man to touch a woman. Her limbs shook as she slowly turned.

Her eyes flew open wider. "Andrew?"

"Let me help." Maintaining one hand on her arm, Andrew lifted her briefcase with his free hand.

"What a surprise." Liz raised her eyebrows. "Are you following me?"

"Yes." His hand tightened and steadied her.

"Why?" She staggered getting her shoe back on her foot.

"After I left you, I returned to headquarters and checked the schedule. I was supposed to be on call tonight, but it was cancelled. I wanted to see you again and hear your lecture, so I came."

"Did you enjoy it?"

"Yes. By the way, you look gorgeous this evening."

Smiling at him, Liz took a tentative step, but her backpack slipped off her shoulder. Andrew grabbed the bag. "I wasn't sure if I was welcome after seeing the progressive young people, so I hid in the back behind the curtain."

"Of course you were welcome." She brushed a few tendril curls back that escaped her pinned hair.

"You're a fascinating speaker. I enjoyed that inspirational talk."

"Thank you." Liz reached out for her backpack.

"I'll carry it for you. How is Mercy?"

"She's a sweet and agreeable child."

"Where is she?"

"Dr. Luke sends new graduates for a practical nursing experience with me. Two arrived this afternoon, and they're caring for Mercy."

"That's wonderful, especially since I have an ulterior motive." Andrew swung her bag over his shoulder.

"It sounds sinister, Mr. Thomas."

"I have your interests in mind." He stopped at the curb. "I hoped if I dropped by this evening, you might accompany me to supper. I enjoyed our lunch."

Her heart beat faster. She liked him and wanted to spend time with him.

His formal speech prompted her to ask, "Have you lived in London?"

"Yes, I have. I had an assignment flying officials from former British colonies there. Certain dignitaries frown on American slang. Others found our clichés difficult to understand."

She raised her hand to stifle a yawn. "Please excuse me. I'm tired."

Andrew sighed with disappointment. "I can see you're exhausted. Rescuing mothers and babies in trouble and teaching a stadium full of students can be tiring."

She glanced at her watch. "It's now ten o'clock. I don't stay up this late, nor do I eat at this hour. I'm not very good company at night. I've been talking nonstop for the last three hours, and my throat is slightly raw." She bent down and removed another pebble from her shoe. "The guesthouse where I'm staying serves breakfast at seven in the morning."

"What did you say?" Andrew tilted his head to the side. "I didn't quite understand."

"I'm sorry. Sometimes my brain leaves my head when I'm tired. Can you return tomorrow morning so we can have breakfast together? If you like, I can put your name on the sign-in sheet at the guesthouse."

Andrew's forehead wrinkled.

"Is something wrong?" She arched an eyebrow. "Did my brain leave my head again? Sometimes I say crazy things when I'm exhausted."

He roared with laughter. "You deserve a better breakfast than an institutionalized one at a guesthouse."

"Better? They serve toast and peanut butter. How much better can that get?" Liz giggled.

"Lots better. The best hotel in this city has a breakfast buffet which includes eggs, cereals, and fruits. May I take you there?"

"I'd like that, but what about church? Tomorrow is Sunday and I'm committed to attending the service at the headquarters. It starts at nine."

"That's fine. I can pick you up at six-thirty. We can go to the buffet and after breakfast drive straight to the service at nine. Does that meet your approval, Miss Connor?" Andrew bowed.

"Yes." She reached out for her briefcase and bag. "I'll see you tomorrow morning at six-thirty at the guesthouse."

"It's late. I'll drive you back to your room this evening. Or did you already reserve one of those bush taxis?"

"I would appreciate the ride." She curtsied African-style, which was a slight bob of the head with a shallow knee bend. It would be convenient not having to flag down a taxi. Most likely there were few vehicles available after the students hired their rides.

As Andrew opened the passenger door for Liz, a HOW vehicle drove up to them. A short bald driver jumped out of it and ran to Andrew. "Excuse me, Mr. Thomas. You left word with the supervisor that you could be reached here. I brought an important letter." He handed it to Andrew.

Going to the security light, Andrew tore the envelope open and scanned the contents. Then he stuffed the letter in his shirt pocket. "Liz, I need to evacuate an injured man immediately to England. The doctor is preparing him for an emergency flight." Andrew turned to the driver who'd delivered the message. "Please tell Mr. Sloan I will be there in thirty minutes. Thank you."

"What's wrong with the patient?" Liz asked.

"He has a complex leg fracture. If I don't fly him to England soon he may lose his leg."

"Perhaps, it's best to go right now. I can take a taxi." Liz reached out for her briefcase.

"I'll drop you off at the guesthouse because it's on the way to the clinic." Andrew helped Liz into the seat. "I'm sorry I have to cancel our plans for tomorrow."

"I understand. Nurses deal with emergencies all the time."

Andrew gave her the backpack and briefcase. He pulled the seatbelt out for her and handed her the buckle.

Liz fastened it and leaned back in the deluxe cushioned seat. She closed her eyes for a minute.

The next thing she knew, she heard her name being called.

"Liz." Andrew gently touched her arm. "We're at the guesthouse."

Her eyelids fluttered open. The truck was stopped in front of the mission guesthouse. She turned to Andrew and gasped as a flicker of surprise crossed her face. "I'm so sorry. I must have dozed off. That's so rude of me. Please forgive me."

He laughed. "There's nothing to forgive. You've been up since the crack of dawn."

She opened her door as he jumped out from the driver's side and ran around to hers. "Liz, I want to see you again. I'll be contacting you after I return."

"I look forward to it. It's best to call me Sister Liz in front of the Africans. People address single persons here as brother and sister."

Andrew escorted her down the sidewalk. The night guard raced ahead of them to unlock the guesthouse door. As she stood under the outside light, Liz held out her hand to shake Andrew's.

He reached for her hand and held it in both of his. "You're a lovely lady. Lord willing, I'll see you again."

"I shall look forward to it, Brother Andrew."

"Good night. Sleep well, Sister Liz."

Liz turned toward his truck and followed him with her stare. She lifted her hand to wave as he opened his door.

Would she ever see him again?

CHAPTER NINE

After a seven-hour flight to England with a brief refueling in Morocco, Andrew landed the aircraft. He steered the plane to the designated gate and shut off the engine.

All he ever wanted to do since he was a small boy was fly planes, and since he worked fulltime for a nonprofit organization as a pilot, he had his dream.

He grabbed his checklist to secure the aircraft but couldn't concentrate on his duties. The detailed tasks made him think of Liz's impulsiveness. Had she ever prepared a list and followed through, step by step?

It didn't matter. He was attracted to her, in spite of her spontaneity. Maybe God was sending him a risk-taking woman to complement his cautious nature. He'd only been away from her for a few hours but already missed her beguiling grins, raised eyebrows, and terrifying scowls.

He closed his eyes and thought about their last moments together. She had looked adorable as she slept in his truck in the moonlight. He didn't want to wake her.

Shaking his head, he went back to the job of securing the plane. After he checked off the tasks in the book, he opened the door of the cockpit, hopped out, and stretched his legs. Andrew glanced around the small airport and shivered. Cold shot through him like an arrow. He reached inside and picked up his leather jacket from the seat. He'd be glad to get back to Africa because he didn't like the damp, frosty weather of England.

After he zipped up his jacket, he opened the side door of the plane. A male nurse adjusted an IV bag for the patient with the broken leg.

Andrew asked, "How's he doing?"

"Fine, sir. The pain medications put him to sleep."

Andrew turned up his collar. "It's cold out here."

"It was a great flight, even landing for fuel in northern Africa and the take-off. We usually bounce around a lot, but either you're an experienced pilot, or there wasn't any turbulence."

"I've had lots of flying hours, but it was calm for which I thank God."

The medical worker pointed toward the end of the runway. "The ambulance is coming."

Andrew leaped into the doorway of the aircraft. "Let me give you a hand to get the patient out."

The nurse spread two more blankets over the injured man. Andrew and the nurse lifted the stretcher and set it on the ground as the ambulance parked. The paramedics jumped out and took care of the patient.

Andrew had forgotten the nurse's name. Embassies discouraged foreigners from wearing name tags in potentially unstable countries. It was required in England, though, and the young man took out a tag and pinned it to his shirt pocket.

Andrew glanced at the nametag. "Dan, it's been a pleasure working with you." He reached out to shake his hand. "Will you be coming back with me, or will you wait here and go directly to your next assignment?"

"I have to check in with the boss. Can I call you later?"

"Sure. I'm staying at the Hilton by the airport." Andrew handed him his card.

He loved to serve his God, help people, and save lives. Liz had the same goals, except she rescued mothers and babies. Liz and Andrew's lives and work were ministries.

Andrew had been giving his paycheck to the church headquarters each month to be divided among several village congregations. Few people knew Andrew didn't need a paying job but worked for the pure enjoyment of it.

After collecting his overnight bag, he locked the aircraft. Then he ran his hand along the curves of the shiny fuselage. His fingers tingled as they touched the angles of the plane. Grinning, he tapped his fingertips lightly on the gleaming surface.

God was good and had given Andrew so much. The Lord had sent him a Christian woman. He didn't like the way she dashed into trouble all the time, but he admired her courage and vivacity. He'd have a hard time keeping her out of danger, and did he even want the job? Then he laughed.

As he blew on his cold hands, he remembered how Liz's slender, tapered fingers and warm palm had fit into his large hands perfectly. Liz might be the woman he'd been searching for, but they needed time to get to know each other better.

If he wasn't able to fly for HOW, what would he do? He'd already lost his parent's approval by working in Africa. Going home and running the family lumber business would delight his parents, but it would be the last job Andrew would ever do.

He walked into the terminal, shook hands with the airport officials, and handed them his passport and documents. After signing the necessary papers for the aircraft, he headed to the street exit.

Andrew turned to another pilot. "I'd forgotten how cold it was here."

The man laughed. "It's not cold yet."

With his overnight bag slung over a shoulder, Andrew crossed his arms and rubbed them.

He shuddered as he thought of his parents. They wouldn't approve of Liz. If his dad and mom were willing to get to know her, they'd love her like he did. His heart skipped a beat. Did he really love her? He'd never felt that way about any other woman.

His father would appreciate Liz's beautiful long curls and sparkling green eyes, but his dad would never understand Liz's crazy impulsiveness and sense of humor.

His mother never wanted him to date anyone outside her social circle. She arranged local heiresses and socialites for him to meet. His mom would never accept Liz's strange knack for dropping and losing her belongings. Neither would his mother understand anyone getting dirty for anything, or the need to carry out a job in old clothes.

Liz was fetching in filthy clothes with soot on her face. She had looked endearing in a frayed cotton blouse and dusty skirt. When she had raced across the field to rescue the baby, with her hair flying around her, she resembled a goddess. Later that night, dressed in the burgundy outfit and standing on the podium, she, like a queen, held the attention of a stadium full of students. She was a woman worth pursuing and he was going after her.

He shivered as he walked to the shuttle bus stop.

If his parents disapproved of Liz, he would be hurt but wouldn't give her up, if God meant them to be together. They could disown him, but he could manage well financially to support Liz. He had made wise investments over the years.

Shuddering, he pulled his gloves out of his pocket and tugged them on.

The shuttle bus to the hotel stopped. The door opened, and he climbed up and took a seat.

Sometimes he needed to travel for days at a time with no idea of how long he'd be gone. Would he be a good husband if he was away from home for a week or more? Liz was strong and independent. She made decisions and got jobs done. He closed his eyes and saw her with a little boy and a girl. She'd make a good mother.

The bus stopped in front of the hotel. He went inside and headed to the reception desk. Andrew collected his key and climbed the stairs to his room.

After he was inside, he locked the door behind him. He dropped to his knees and bowed his head. When he closed his eyes, he prayed. "Lord, I thank you. You've given me a job I love and sent a fascinating woman into my life. Protect her. Keep her safe until we meet again."

He had asked the leaders of HOW to let him serve another tour in Tamago. If he was granted the request, he would figure out a way to date her as she deserved. He prayed that one day she would feel the same about him as he did for her.

Andrew's life was nearly perfect since he found Liz again. Nothing could go wrong now.

***

After a seven-hour taxi ride Liz, Tamara and Henry arrived at Liz's house. "I have a small home. There is only one bedroom with a single bed. You girls can sleep on the large mattress in the sitting room. I hope you'll enjoy staying here and working with me."

Henry looked around the room. "Where is your broom?"

Asking for a cleaning utensil instead of a meal indicated she was prepared to work.

The baby needed to be fed first. Since there were no cans of tinned milk in the village and soybean milk was better for an infant, Liz asked, "Do you know how to make soybean milk?"

Both of them shook their heads.

"I'll show you." Liz went to the kitchen cupboard, unrolled a sack and poured soybeans into a cup. "We'll soak these in water until they are soft. After that we'll crush them on the grinding stone. Then we'll add water and boil the liquid before straining it." Liz asked, "What would you girls like for supper?"

Henry furrowed her brows. "We are not used to white man's food."

Liz's lips twitched. "What do you want to eat?"

"Can I have a bowl of rice and tomato sauce?" Henry asked.

"Cook whatever you like. If I don't have the ingredients, you can go to the market and buy them."

Liz opened her bag. "I need to assemble the baby scale, so we can take it to work with us tomorrow."

Then she remembered the scotch taped letter, still in her backpack. She went to the kitchen and collected a paring knife and slowly slit open the edges of the note. As she unfolded the paper and read, she shook her head. Why did the nursing school send her a troublesome student like Henry? Liz put the letter back in her bag. She'd deal with Henry's unusual situation later.

To take her mind off the problem, she put together the baby weighing scale.

Going outside, she tied it to a branch and then called. "Come look at this scale."

When the girls came, Liz asked, "Do you see a problem using a mother's wrapper for weighing infants?"

Henry walked up to the scale and touched the ring at the bottom of it. "The hole is too small. A mother's skirt will never go through it."

"I'd like to see for myself." Liz looked from one girl to the other. "Do you have a wrap-around skirt I can borrow?"

Tamara left and returned with a cloth and flicked it open. Liz threaded a corner of the skirt through the lower ring and tied the fabric in a knot. "Let's weigh Mercy."

Henry untied the baby from her back. "Why is she wearing plastic on her bottom?"

"So we won't get urine and poop on us."

"Don't you think it's ridiculous to care about that?"

Liz gasped. Tamara's jaw fell open. Henry stepped back and looked down at the ground. "Forgive me for making you angry. I am sorry. I will try hard to get used to white people's ways."

"I'm not angry. I like it when people ask questions, it proves they are listening and thinking of possibilities."

Henry patted the baby's bottom. "Where did you get this plastic?"

"I had a rain coat, which was too hot. So I cut it in pieces."

"Do you Americans wear a special coat when it rains?"

Liz snapped her mouth shut, but the giggles erupted in her throat. Her lips lifted.

Tamara ran her fingers over the plastic that covered Mercy's diaper. "You white people are intelligent to invent a rubber coat to wear in the rain."

Liz smiled. "Let's put her in the scale to see what happens."

Henry scowled. "Nothing will happen, but it will with babies who don't wear plastic on their bottoms. When a baby urinates on the skirt, it will be soiled for others. No mother wants to give up her outer skirt to weigh the baby."

"You're right. That's very perceptive."

Holding Mercy, Henry asked, "What is "ceptive?"

"It means observant or understanding." Liz pulled the skirt tied to the scale down until the pointer stopped at fifteen pounds to test it. "Mercy is less than ten pounds, probably six, so I know this knot will hold."

Tamara and Liz each pulled an edge of the skirt toward them so Henry could put Mercy in what looked like a hammock.

Liz frowned. "It shouldn't take three women to weigh one baby. It's too much manpower for a little job."

"There aren't any men here." Henry glanced around the backyard. "What man are you talking about?"

"It's an expression. If you like, I can say that it takes too much female power to weigh one little baby. So how can we weigh a baby without all this work?"

Henry lifted Mercy out of the cloth. "Do you call this work in your country?"

"We weighed a baby." Liz slowly let a little air out of her pursed lips. "It's a job, so it's work."

Liz had never had an assistant like Henry. Student nurses who had worked with Liz never asked anything or spoke unless they were spoken to.

Turning back to the scale, Liz asked. "Can you envision a pair of little boy's shorts instead of the cloth for weighing babies?"

"What's envision mean?" Henry raised her eyebrows.

"It means you close your eyes and try to picture it in your head."

Both Tamara and Henry closed their eyes. A moment later, Henry's eyelids fluttered open. "How do you attach the pants to this little ring?"

"With two short pieces of rope fastened to two loops in the waistband of the trousers. If we had an extra pair of pants, we could use them while the mother washed the one her child soiled." Liz checked Mercy's diaper. "I appreciate you girls helping me brainstorm."

"What's a brainstorm? It sounds like a sickness, a storm in the brain."

"It means we put the ideas from our minds together to figure out the best solution to this problem. Tamara, can you go to the market now before it closes, buy the ingredients to prepare your supper, and two pairs of trousers for a small boy?"

"What size pants do you want?" Tamara asked.

"The size a four-year-old wears."

Liz gave Tamara money, and she left.

Henry tied Mercy to her back and swept the floor while Liz made an inventory of medications.

When Tamara returned, she handed Liz the leftover change and a small bag.

Liz took out two pairs of shorts and held them up. "These trousers look like they'll work well."

During supper, Tamara and Henry were silent. Then Liz remembered local people didn't talk while eating a meal. After the dishes were washed and the kitchen cleaned, they went outside and tested the boy's shorts. They worked perfectly.

Going back in the house, Liz brought out the tins of medication and explained the preparation of dosages. They worked at the table to count pills for the treatments.

"Everyone in the village knows we sell 20 aspirin or 20 Tylenol for a hundred francs. All the patients count their tablets. So if you girls do not get the number correct and there are only 19 tablets in the envelope, someone will get upset. Please don't talk while you are counting."

Liz enjoyed the silence. Henry's lips moved, most likely counting, but no words came out.

When they'd finished packing the dosages, Henry wiped the table. "It seems to me that it is dangerous to tell the people all your secrets."

"What secret are you talking about?" Liz asked.

"People should never know how many pills are in their treatment."

"If I tell them the number of pills, it keeps everyone honest, including us." Liz put the containers of medication away in the carton. "The people should know how many tablets they are buying."

Henry raised her eyebrows. "No one at the hospital or clinic informs the patients how many tablets they receive for a price. Each of the medical workers gives a different number. No one posts the numbers like you do, and no one writes the name of the medicine on the envelope. It seems to me that you are too honest of a human being."

"I never heard of anyone being too honest." Liz's gaze clouded. "Is there such a thing?"

Tamara shook her head. "There is no such thing as being too honest. God wants us to be perfectly truthful."

Henry shook her head. "I don't know how you will be successful if you tell everyone all your secrets."

"I'm not interested in success. I only want to treat sick people."

Liz would keep telling her patients the names of their sicknesses, their medications, and the number they should have.

How could it possibly be wrong?

CHAPTER TEN

The next morning after Liz prepared tea, she asked, "What do you girls like to eat for breakfast?"

"Do you have corn meal mush?" Henry cocked an eyebrow.

"No, but I can buy it."

"I have some in my bag." Tamara left and returned with it. She took it out and started cooking.

After breakfast, Liz, Tamara, and Henry hiked to the taxi station. They slid into the last three seats inside a mini-van.

Liz never liked the tight squeeze, but local travelers made no objections to forced intimacies with strangers in public transportation. Liz gripped the doorframe to maintain her balance on a few inches of bench.

She was a half a foot taller than Henry, but Liz felt large sitting next to the girl. Liz felt small next to Tamara, who was built like Lady Goliath and a half a foot taller than Liz. Standing next to each other, Henry and Tamara looked like a dwarf and a giant.

The springs poked out of the seat cushion forcing Henry to lean forward to protect the baby on her back, but still Henry looked comfortable scrunched between Liz and Tamara. Men and women fit together in the taxi like pieces of a puzzle.

The vehicle stopped in the center of Jeetiwa.

Liz, Henry, and Tamara walked to the church and opened the basket to set up the medications. Henry registered the sick. Tamara weighed the patients, took blood pressures, and recorded the vital signs.

The first patient brought her sick child.

Liz examined the tiny infant. "How did your baby get third-degree burns all over its body?"

The mother shrugged, "No one burned my child."

"If he is not burned, why are you bringing him?"

"His body is too hot."

"He has infected burns." Liz's sighed. "It looks like someone poured hot water on him, and it burned him."

The mother snapped, "We have bathed our children in boiling water for years."

Liz shuddered. Bathing babies in hot water was a widespread custom, but how could mothers pour hot water on helpless babies and not associate it with burns? Liz slumped back against a tree and her frown deepened. "After the skin was burned, it formed blisters which broke open. Germs went into his body to make him sick and give him a fever."

The mother shrugged. "I don't understand."

Liz pointed to a cut on her finger. "If I break the skin on my hand so blood comes out, then the dirt and sickness can go inside the opening and make me sick."

"We want the birth skin to come off so the child will get his new skin for life." The baby cried and the mother started nursing him.

"What is wrong with the skin the baby was born with?" Liz rubbed her brows to ward off a headache. She suddenly understood why half the infants never reached adulthood.

"That skin is from the woman's dirty blood inside of her. It is soiled and must come off."

Liz pointed to the pus-filled burns on the baby's skin. "What do you call these?"

"They are necessary to get the bad skin off." The mother scowled.

"Your baby has a serious infection." Liz glared at the mother. "The bath water was hot enough to burn the child."

Looking away from the people, she closed her eyes and let out a long, deep sigh. She had to convince them of the correct way to care for their children.

Liz tied the scale to a tree branch at eye-level. "Bring Mercy here, I want to weigh her."

Henry untied the baby from her back and lowered the infant into the boy's pants. She slipped each of the baby's feet into the trouser legs and leaned the infant back in the crotch of the dangling shorts.

The pointer of the scale stopped at 3 kilograms. Liz exclaimed. "That's at least six pounds."

Liz turned to Henry and Tamara. "Did you pour hot water on this baby to remove her skin?"

Tamara shook her head. "You told us not to, and we want to obey you."

"Why do you think she is fat and healthy?"

"We are taking good care of her and feeding her the best food." Henry lifted the baby out of the dangling trousers.

Liz put the infant with infected burns into the pants. "He weighs 2 kilograms and looks like a month old." She plotted the weight on the graph of the health card and then sold an antibiotic to the mother for the child.

As Liz waited for the next patient she glanced around the village. A man was shaving the head of a newborn infant. Liz went to him. "Why are you removing all of the baby's hair? Does he have an infectious disease like head lice?"

The man didn't answer, but Tamara, who had followed Liz, asked. "What's a lice?"

"It's a tiny insect that lives in the hair and causes sickness. Many people shave the person's head to get rid of the lice."

"This baby was just born." Tamara scowled. "He doesn't have a sickness."

"Why is the man shaving the baby's head?"

Henry rolled her eyes. "It's necessary to prevent the child from dying."

Liz laughed out loud and couldn't stop laughing. She'd heard just about everything. "How does it stop the child from dying?"

"The baby's hair is evil and came from the place of bad spirits. After a child is born, the parents destroy the hair by fire so it goes back to where it came. If they do not do this, Heaven or the place of evil spirits will extend its hand." Henry stretched her arm out and pulled it back. "It grabs the baby by the hair and yanks the child back to where he came from."

Liz's lips twitched. The superstition sounded amusing, but she had vowed not to say anything unless a tradition was dangerous. Shaving a baby's head wasn't harmful, so she went back to the treatment table.

Henry wasn't finished. "If the infant's hair is removed, the hand of death will not be able to snatch the baby away."

Liz frowned. "I've seen children with shaved heads die."

"Maybe another sickness took him, but not the evil spirits." Henry tied Mercy to her back. "You were smart to call this baby Mercy because it means pity. She still has all her hair, so everyone who looks at this child will feel sorry for her."

"Mercy also means forgiveness and compassion. Mercy should remind people that God forgives and is compassionate."

Liz picked up the card for the next patient.

Tamara handed a feverish child to Liz. The infant urinated all over her, but she was accustomed to babies pooping and peeing on her. She put the child face down on her lap to insert a suppository.

By the end of the day several other children had used her dress as a diaper.

Liz leaned back. "We're finished for the day."

Henry frowned. "You should not be seen in public the way you look and smell."

"It's not polite to travel in stinky clothes." Tamara tied Mercy to her back. "You should let a mother wash your dress before we find a taxi to take us home."

"If we wait for a mother to wash my clothes, it'll be late and we might not get any vehicle home. Let's leave."

"Your appearance is embarrassing." Henry glared.

"I'm sorry." Liz pressed her lips together. "I'm not taking time to wash clothes and miss a taxi to go home."

***

When the taxi stopped at the junction to Liz's house, she followed Tamara down the narrow trail. Tamara took long quick strides, so Liz glanced back to see if Henry was keeping up. Even with the baby on her back she wasn't far behind.

Turning forward, Liz gasped at the eight-foot long mamba. It reared its ugly black head and opened its inky mouth, only inches from Tamara's feet. Liz stretched out her arms to stop Henry from moving forward. Then Liz leaped and tried to shove Tamara out of the way, but the serpent bit Tamara on the ankle, and she fell. Africa's most deadly serpent slithered away into the bushes

Liz lost her balance and tumbled to the ground with Tamara. Liz broke out in a sweat, and her heart beat faster. The snake delivered enough venom to kill a dozen men within an hour.

CHAPTER ELEVEN

Liz's hands shook as she examined Tamara's foot. The deep fang bite was fatal. Shivers ran up and down Liz's back.

Tamara writhed in pain. She shrieked and sobbed as tears ran down her face. A moment later, the girl's movements slowed down.

Liz swallowed her own screams as she lifted Tamara's head and shoulders onto her lap.

Henry shrieked. "That was the ten-step snake!"

"Tamara's leg has already swelled." Liz gulped down a sob. "Her nasal and lung passages are collapsing." No one ever recovered from a mamba bite, but she prayed. "Please Lord, we need a miracle. Touch Tamara. In Jesus name, heal her. The Bible says we can pick up deadly snakes with our hands and when we drink poison, it will not hurt us."

Tamara gasped loudly and struggled to take in air. She panted and gulped several times to catch her breath. Respiratory paralysis seized the muscles in Tamara's throat and chest.

Liz yelled to Henry. "Run and bring the pastor."

Tamara choked on her saliva and frothed at the mouth. Huffing and puffing, she heaved. A few seconds later, Tamara stopped moving and then she no longer breathed.

Liz clutched Tamara's head and shoulders closer to her. Tears ran down Liz's face. With trembling hands, Liz stroked the girl's cheeks. Liz loved Tamara like a sister even though she'd only been with Liz, as an assistant for a few days.

Henry returned with the pastor and several deacons. One of the men examined the bite and put his head to Tamara's chest. He shook his head. "She's dead. We'll carry her to the church."

The pastor and a deacon lifted Tamara and put her on the third man's back.

Liz shivered in the warm air. "I can't believe she's dead."

"Some dangerous snakes have powerful venom to kill a victim in less than a minute." Pastor Ebenezer frowned. "Come later to the church and we'll make arrangements for the burial."

After the men left, Liz walked back to the house with Henry, who talked on and on. "How could this terrible thing happen to Tamara? She wanted to serve the Lord."

"What's a ten-step snake?" Liz stopped at the front door and unlocked it.

"A victim can only take ten steps before dropping dead. The venom is lethal."

Inside the house, Henry untied the sleeping baby and put her on the bed. Then Henry paced back and forth and wailed. Tears raced down her face as she sobbed loudly. "Why did this happen? It's hard for me to accept why good Christians suffer and die." Henry sobbed, "There are pastors who believe people can became so pure on this earth, that the evil world rejects them. They become perfect and can no longer live in this sinful, old earth, so the Lord takes them to Heaven." She asked. "Do you think Tamara was too good to live here with the rest of us?"

Liz brushed a tear off her cheek. "Maybe there's truth in that. It's often the good people who sacrifice their lives to save others. The greatest love is giving your life for another."

"Maybe Tamara sacrificed her life for us." Henry sat next to Liz. "She went first and the snake bit her so it didn't bite us. She laid her life down for us."

"You may be right." Liz sniffed.

"When I hear of criminals or sorcerers dying, I'm not sad." Henry scrunched up her face.

Liz put her hand on top of Henry's "It's hard to have compassion for evil people, but Christ died for them, too. We must pray and hope they will repent."

Henry snarled, "Most of them deserve to go to Hell and that's where they should go."

"All of us deserve to go to Hell because we have all sinned. God showed us his love and mercy and sent His Son to die for us. We must turn our back on our sins."

Liz asked, "Do you know where Tamara's family lives?"

"No, I've never traveled to that village."

Liz opened her backpack and handed Henry some money. "Can you please go to the city and find Dr. Luke. Tell him what happened and ask him to inform Tamara's family."

Henry put the coins in a small purse and then changed her clothes. She stuffed a bottle of water, bread, and a headscarf into a bag. "I plan to be back tonight."

"Yes, you should be unless there's a problem or you're unable to get a taxi home."

Several hours after Henry left, someone knocked on the door. Liz opened it to a tiny man wearing dirty clothes. It looked like he'd dropped everything or left his farm to come straight to Liz's house, so he had to be a relative of Tamara.

Tears filled Liz's eyes. "I'm so sorry."

The smelly man glared. "About what?"

"Her death."

"Who died?"

"Tamara, aren't you a member of her family?"

"No, I've come about my daughter, Henrietta Salugouta Bellolare."

Crossing her arms, Liz rubbed them to suppress a chill. Was the obnoxious and filthy man Henry's father? His hard, beady eyes stared at her. "That's a long name, is that what you call her?" She gulped in air to calm her racing heart.

"No, we call her Henry."

Darkness shot from his eyes. Liz shivered. Then she forced her limbs to relax. "Do you have a letter for her?"

"No." The man glared.

"Why are you looking for her?"

"It is family business, madam."

His vague responses and guarded behavior aroused Liz's suspicions. She'd always protected her girls against undesirable men, abusive fathers, and unsuitable callers. She couldn't save Tamara, but she might be able to save Henry.

Liz drew her mouth into a straight line and bit her lip to avoid wrinkling her nose. When someone traveled or came for a social call, the guest always took a bath and put on his best clean clothes for the visit, but this man didn't. "Henry left on a trip." Liz averted her eyes from his soiled appearance. "Can I give her a message or a letter when she returns?"

He scowled. "I can come back."

Keeping her mouth closed, she debated a response. Henry had never mentioned her father.

Liz maintained an impassive expression. "There's been a death in our home. It's not a good time for a social visit. If you have come on an urgent matter, I will be glad to tell Henry."

"What time will she return?"

"I don't know when she'll come back."

His cruel eyes and dark stare sent tremors down Liz's spine. She had a feeling he'd been watching the house and knew Henry wasn't there. Liz was thankful for the chaperon law, which forbid her from inviting him into her house alone.

The man nodded and turned away. After he departed, Liz breathed easier, but he'd be back.

Liz fed Mercy and put her to bed. Liz had taken aspirins for her pounding headache. Her stomach pain and backache had grown worse throughout the day and her skin felt hot. She recognized the symptoms.

Cerebral malaria was fatal, and she needed a treatment. Liz should take the pills for it and go to bed, but she should also wait up for Henry's return. She couldn't do both.

Peering out the window, Liz looked toward the bushes. What if that awful man who claimed to be Henry's father was waiting out there to hurt Henry? If Liz fell asleep, she might not hear Henry's return or her scream if she tried to get away from the disagreeable stranger.

She waited as long as she could but at last took out the malarial cure. Her hands shook, and she dropped the pills. Was she reliving the attack of the snake? Or was she afraid of the danger Henry was in? When she picked the tablets up, she popped them into her mouth. After swallowing the pills, Liz collapsed on the bed.

Lord, please keep Henry safe.

CHAPTER TWELVE

Someone pounded on the door. Liz's eyelids fluttered open and shut. A baby was crying. She sat up in bed and looked around the room. Little Mercy had to be hungry. Liz's headache was gone and so was the fever, but the dizziness was worse. As she got out of bed, she grabbed the dresser to keep her balance.

When the world stopped turning, she picked up the crying infant.

The beating on the door started up again. Someone yelled. "Sister Liz, Sister Liz."

"I'm coming."

When Liz reached the door, she opened it. She blinked several times until she had focused on Henry. "I'm glad you're back."

Henry set her bag on the floor. "What is wrong?" She reached out and took the child from Liz. "You look terrible, just awful. Are you sick?"

"I have malaria fever."

"Go and rest. I will take care of the baby." Henry tied Mercy to her back. "I found Dr. Luke at his clinic. He will go to Tamara's family and tell them."

"I need a cup of tea." Liz shuffled to the kitchen. "This poor baby hasn't been fed since last night. I took a treatment, and it must have knocked me out."

"Medicine can't knock you out. Did someone hit you?"

Liz groaned inwardly. She was too groggy to deal with Henry, but she had to give an answer. "The medicine was so strong it made me sleep through the night. I didn't hear Mercy crying."

Liz set the teakettle on the flame while she prepared a couple slices of dry toast. When the water boiled, she poured two cups. Putting tea bags in both, she slid a steaming mug along with the sugar bowl, toward Henry.

By the time Liz had finished sipping on the hot liquid and munching on the bread, her dizziness had passed. She needed the second dose of medication, which was half the strength of the initial one and didn't cause as many side effects. So she left to get the pills. When she returned, she swallowed them with another piece of toast and cup of tea.

Liz felt better. "Tell me about your trip."

"I took the taxi to see Dr. Luke, but there were no returning vehicles last evening, so I stayed with his family and left early this morning." Henry prepared Mercy's milk.

Opening the Bible, Liz read a Psalm to Henry as she fed the baby.

After Henry had put Mercy to bed, Liz poured each of them more tea. "Yesterday, you had a visitor who claimed to be your father."

Henry covered her mouth and collapsed to the floor and lowered her head. "No! No! No!" she wailed.

Why did Henry have to dramatize everything? Liz wasn't strong enough to deal with the girl's theatrics.

"How did he find me? Do you know I am 25 years old?"

What did Henry's age have to do with her father's visit? Sometimes the girl made no sense.

With shaking hands, Henry covered her face. "My father thinks he owns me."

Liz helped the girl stand and led her to the couch. "Perhaps your father came on family business."

Tears ran like a waterfall down Henry's face. "Yes, the business of my wedding."

"What wedding?" Liz asked, "Do you have a fiancé?"

"My father has no right."

No right to do what? If Liz hadn't been feeling so badly, she might have been more patient with Henry. "I don't understand." Liz put her arm around Henry's shoulders and gave the girl her full attention. "Start at the beginning and tell me everything."

Liz wasn't sure she was alert enough to hear it all from the hysterical girl. She hoped Henry would tell most of the story before the medicine took effect, and Liz fell asleep.

"When I was twelve I believed on Jesus. I witnessed to my family. Father was angry and told me to abandon Jesus. I could never do that because Jesus did more for me than my father's god ever did."

Liz asked, "What did your father do?"

"He threw me out of the house and locked the door, so I went to my aunt's home. She ordered me to abandon Christ and beg my father's forgiveness." Henry sniffed. "She let me spend the night, but she didn't allow me to stay longer because it might have made my father angry enough to hurt her."

Holding her breath, Liz wasn't sure she wanted to hear how a twelve-year-old survived. Had Henry been a beggar on the streets? Or had she turned to stealing or prostitution? Henry hadn't abandoned Christ, so she must have found another way.

"I went to the church where I had been saved and talked to the pastor. He and his wife came with me to my father's house, but he refused to speak to them. My father never let me back into the house. " Henry sighed. "The pastor had to take care of eight children and his old mother, so he couldn't provide for me, too. He introduced me to members in the church. I stayed with different families, took care of the children, cooked, cleaned, and did the marketing."

"Thank God you had a roof over your head and food to eat."

Henry nodded. "Six years later, a missionary visited our church. She was looking for a nanny to take care of her children. I was recommended."

"How did that work out for you?"

"I loved it very much. The missionary paid me lots of money so I saved for nursing school."

"Didn't you have to finish high school first?"

"Yes, the missionary tutored me with the classes, so I passed all the tests. Then I went to nursing school and came here when I was finished."

"When was the last time you saw your father?"

"Back when I was twelve years old and he threw me out of the house for believing in Jesus."

Henry was a strong and courageous young lady to have obtained a nursing degree in a developing country without anyone's help.

"Are you saying you've had no communication with your father for thirteen years and now he has come here for you?"

"That's what I've been saying all this time." Henry wiped her eyes. "He must have arranged a terrible marriage for me."

Liz's heart clenched. "How can he do this when he hasn't seen or spoken to you for over a decade?"

"Fathers can do whatever they want. My aunt kept him informed of what I did and where I went. If she didn't tell my father, he threatened to hurt her." Henry started crying again. "And now working for you is my curse."

"How did I curse you?"

Henry twisted the rag she used as a handkerchief and blew her nose. "My aunt must have told my father that a rich white lady employed me which was how my father found out I was here." Henry sobbed loudly. "I don't want to leave. I love working for you and living in your house."

"You can keep working here."

"My father is wicked. He'll kidnap me and force me to marry his choice." Henry wailed. "A higher education makes a daughter more valuable. Now my father will get more money for me as a wife. Most parents help their children go to school so the bride price gives them back the funds they invested in the child. My father didn't put me through school, and now he is selling me to collect the money and it's not right."

Liz suppressed her shudder. "There is nothing to fear. The Lord will protect us."

"You don't know my father. He consorts with witches and wizards and hires them to put curses on people." Henry shook so badly even her lips trembled. "When he sets his mind to do evil, he does it."

"The Bible says that greater is He that is in you, than he that is in the world."

"Can you show me where it says that?"

Liz brought her Bible, flipped through the pages, and opened it to I John 4:4. "When God lives in us, His power is greater than any other force in the world. So let's pray." Closing her eyes, Liz bowed her head.

After praying, Henry said, "Amen."

If her father was so malicious that he hired sorcerers to put curses on his own daughter, there was no limit to what he might do. When

Henry refused to marry the intended groom, would her father try to hurt them?

CHAPTER THIRTEEN

Liz had just finished feeding Mercy when Henry came into the house and announced, "Sister Liz, the pastor has brought an important visitor for you."

It sounded like a town crier proclaiming the prince was on his way. Liz was surprised to see Pastor Ebenezer and Andrew. She wiped her sweaty hands on her skirt before shaking theirs.

Dressed in jeans and a blue polo shirt, Andrew followed the pastor into the living room.

Andrew grinned, "I'm glad I found you at home."

Liz turned to Henry. "This is Mr. Andrew Thomas. I met him in the city." She pointed toward the couch. "Please sit down."

"What would you like to drink? We have water, tea or coffee."

The pastor remained standing. "I can't stay. I have a meeting at the church. Please excuse me, Sister Liz." He left.

Henry stood at attention as if she was on duty, and maybe so, as a chaperon.

"What would you like to drink?"

"Coffee, please." Andrew looked at the baby in Liz's arms. "How is Mercy?"

"She's an adorable child. Abandoned babies aren't as demanding as other infants.

"Why is that?"

"Most of them received no human touch and went without food for periods of time. They cried when they were thirsty, hungry, or cold. No one came, so they stopped bawling and learned to be content."

Henry carried a tray with a carafe of hot water, instant coffee, teabags, cups, sugar, and milk. She set everything on the end table. Then she stood next to Liz as if waiting for more orders.

"Thank you, Henry. Would you like to sit and join us?"

"No, I have work to do."

Liz handed Andrew a cup of coffee. "How did you find me?"

71

"It was easy. You're the only white lady living in this state. Everyone knows you. I went to the church and was given an escort."

Liz picked up her cup of tea. "How was the trip to England?"

"My boss asked me to stop in Norgia to collect water samples. They weren't ready so I had to wait a few days. That's why it took me so long."

"Do you transport all seriously injured workers to England?"

"Yes." Andrew sipped his coffee. "When HOW was established, the West African area was unstable politically, so the British-based organization guaranteed health insurance only if workers were transported to a designated medical facility in England."

"That makes sense." Liz set her empty cup on the table. "What time do you have to be back?"

"I need to be in the city by nine this evening. I hired a private car for today. I had to turn in my truck before I could leave for the States."

"That means you can stay for lunch. Do you like spaghetti with tomato sauce?"

"Yes, I do."

"It's nearly ready. Would you like to wash up in the bathroom?"

"Yes, please." Andrew stood.

"It's a rather primitive flush toilet and shower." Liz led the way. "The original house had a pit latrine. After I arrived the local church built this for me." She took a clean towel from a shelf and handed it to him. "After you finish, come to the kitchen."

When Andrew joined the ladies, he asked, "Can I help with anything?"

"No thank you." Liz put plates and napkins on the table. "Brother Andrew, sit down and visit with us."

He sat at the table. "If I came for an overnight visit, where could I stay here in the village?"

"There aren't any hotels or guesthouses. If a Christian is stranded in the village, the pastor and his family will put him up." Liz poured water in the glasses. "What's the first thing you'll do when you reach the States, Brother Andrew?"

"Go swimming at my parents' home. It's not safe to swim here because of the open sewers and diseases in the rivers."

"River blindness is the worst one." Liz shook her head.

"Our pilots drop chemicals into the rivers to kill the pests, but the waters continually become re-contaminated."

Liz asked, "Henry, why do you think the people pollute the rivers after they've been treated?"

"Most of our people do not like change." Henry set a platter of sliced bread on the table. "Many villages do not have wells, so people must use the river water. The villagers are habituated to drinking that water and use it for bathing, washing clothes, and dishes."

Liz was the last person to sit down. Andrew put his hand on the table and moved it toward Liz to pray.

Shaking her head, Liz kept her hands in her lap. "Would you ask the blessing, Brother Andrew?"

Thank God that Andrew had taken his hand off the table. She and Andrew must have no physical contact with each other, especially in front of the chaperon.

After the prayer, Liz passed the spaghetti and the sauce to Andrew. "Have you thought about digging a well in the village before cleaning up the contaminated river?"

"That's a good idea, but the organization isn't budgeted for projects like that." Andrew wound his spaghetti onto his fork. "How do the people feel about wells? Is that too big of a change?"

Henry bowed her head and then looked left and then right.

Liz smiled. "Brother Andrew asked you a question. I know it is rude to speak directly to men, but in my culture it would be impolite if you didn't answer him."

Henry looked at Liz. "Our people would have a hard time getting used to well water. It tastes different from river water. There are people who have traveled to the city and drank other kinds of water who might get used to it, but an ordinary person cannot adjust to the flavor of well water."

Andrew took a piece of bread. "Maintaining water that's not contaminated is harder than I imagined."

Henry stared at Liz and Andrew as they wound spaghetti on their forks. Henry stuffed a soup-spoon full of rice and sauce into her mouth. "It looks like you white people even have special ways to eat spaghetti."

Liz was surprised at Henry. Speaking while she ate was contrary to the local culture. Liz swallowed her grin and finished chewing. "Not all Americans twirl their spaghetti on a fork."

Henry frowned. "Isn't winding spaghetti a waste of time? You are only going to put it in your mouth."

"No, it makes the bites easier to eat." Liz popped another forkful of spaghetti into her mouth. "Many people cut it up on their plates. My mother taught me this way." Liz passed Andrew the spaghetti platter and sauce.

Andrew took another helping and gave the bowl back to her. "I'll be in the city this weekend to assist new workers. Will you come for supplies?"

She wanted to spend more time with Andrew but mustn't give Henry the impression she was going to meet him.

Liz shrugged. "I'm not sure. I need to check my calendar and the level of provisions."

Henry raised her eyebrows. "If you go to the city this weekend can I come?"

"Let's pray about it. If I need medications, perhaps we can travel together so I can show you where I purchase the supplies."

Henry picked up the bowl of rice and offered it to Liz and Andrew. Both shook their heads, and Liz grinned. "You may finish it."

Using slices of bread, Henry wiped all the remaining bowls clean. There were few leftovers in Liz's house, and none of the student nurses who stayed with Liz ever watched her waistline.

Shrieks interrupted them. Dropping her fork, Liz jumped up from the table and ran to the front door. Several men and women stood behind a child with a blood-soaked headscarf wrapped around his wrist.

Liz knew the family and walked to the father. "What happened?"

The father held the child's hand. "You know that my son's brain is not normal. He used a stick to take an empty tuna fish can out of your trash pit. When he reached inside the can to get the oil he slit his wrist."

Liz gasped.

The father pushed the little boy closer to Liz. The man untied the cloth around his child's wrist. Blood spurted to the ground.

Liz reached for the boy's arm and applied pressure. "Henry, bring a chair and the medical basket, please."

Andrew moved closer to Liz. "How can I help?"

"Go into the bathroom, fill the bucket with water and bring it and the bar of soap." Liz lifted her hand to examine the wound.

"Don't you need hot water?" Andrew asked.

"I don't have a water heater." Liz shrugged. "It doesn't matter at this point. The child is filthy. I'll clean and dress the wound and give antibiotics."

After Andrew left, Henry returned and arranged bandages and strips of tape on top of the chair.

Andrew brought the bucket and soap.

"What now?" Andrew asked.

Liz tossed a plastic cup into the pail. "When I nod at you, pour water over my hands."

She pressed a clean, cotton dressing to the child's wrist and said to the father. "Hold this tightly on the wound."

Then she picked up the bar of soap and nodded at Andrew. She scrubbed her hands with soap and water. After washing and rinsing the boy's wound, Liz let it bleed for several seconds.

"What are you doing?" Andrew asked. "It looks like the child has already lost enough blood."

"I'm letting the blood flush germs out of the wound." Turning to Andrew, she said. "Press this cotton dressing on the gash while I cut out butterfly sutures." Liz picked up the scissors. "Henry, put antibiotic cream on another small dressing and then tear off a meter long strip of rolled bandage."

After Liz closed the wound with the tapes, she covered it with several dressings and then wrapped the bandage around the child's wrist. She ripped the cotton cloth lengthwise down the middle, tied a knot, flipped one side to the back, and brought both ends together and tied them.

"All finished." Liz smiled at the child and then looked at the parents. "You need to take your son to the hospital to get a tetanus injection."

"Sister Liz, thank you." The mother lifted the corner of her wrap-around skirt and wiped the tears from her little boy's face. The child gave Liz a big toothless grin.

"I know your son isn't like other children, but can you teach him not to play with dangerous cans?" Liz nodded at Andrew, who poured more water over her hands. She scrubbed them again with soap and water.

After the family left, Liz, Andrew, and Henry packed up the supplies and carried them into the house.

"I feel responsible. The poor child doesn't know the danger of a sharp, open can. All the people in the village eat dried fish. I'm the only one who eats tuna fish and cooks from tins."

Andrew shook his head. "What could you have done to prevent this?"

"I'm buying a plastic bucket with a lid to keep the sharp tins. When it's full, I'll dig a hole and bury the cans. If I hadn't been here, that poor boy might have bled to death." Liz led the way to the kitchen. She set the teakettle on to boil water, while Henry started washing the dishes. "I have peanut butter cookies to go with our coffee."

Andrew cleared his throat. "Sister Liz, I'd like to see your trash pit before I leave today."

She stood and turned to Henry. "I'm going to show Brother Andrew the garbage pit where that little boy cut himself. I won't be gone long. Fill the thermos with boiled water so we can have coffee when we return."

Liz hesitated for a moment. A chaperon shouldn't be necessary, since the garbage pit was located in a public place next to a well-traveled path to the village.

At least she hoped not.

CHAPTER FOURTEEN

Andrew didn't know the way, so he followed Liz on the narrow footpath. She'd amazed him again by calmly stopping the bleeding and giving orders as if she were a general preparing to go to battle.

His heart lurched as he remembered a large AIDS outbreak not far from her home. "Aren't nurses supposed to wear gloves?"

"Yes, we are." Liz laughed. "Look around. See any places I can buy them?"

"Don't they have any in the city pharmacy?"

"They ran out when AIDS started, so I wash my hands extra-long and twice as much. I'm not worried."

But Andrew was concerned. She took far too many risks with her life and her health.

After walking five minutes, she stopped. "People are coming. I want them to pass us, or they might follow us to the trash pit."

"Why would they do that?"

"People will be curious as to why we're out here alone. Single people are never allowed to be by themselves here. We should have a chaperon. I'm not sure we can ever go on an American-style date."

"Are you teasing me?"

"I'm serious." Her eyes didn't twinkle and she wore her no nonsense expression. "I respect the local culture and try to set a good example."

He sighed. "I'm nearly forty and have dated lots of women. I'm sure you've dated."

"Yes, in the States, but this is Africa. Don't worry, Brother Andrew, we'll find a way, even if we must meet at the garbage pit."

He was getting used to her jokes and even liked them. "I want to spend more time with you to get to know you." Andrew lowered his voice and winked.

"Brother Andrew, it's not acceptable to wink at me in public."

He glanced down the trail. "We're alone."

"People are watching us and others are coming." Liz whispered, "Behave yourself."

His heart skipped a beat at the thought of getting alone with her one day. As he walked around a bend, he wrinkled his nose. The rancid stench meant the garbage pit was close.

Three boys were stretched out on the ground. Their arms dangled down into the smelly hole. They turned their heads toward Liz, who yelled. "What are you doing?"

Her sudden shout startled Andrew.

Liz screamed again. "What are you doing?"

The boys jumped up and ran into the bushes.

She jogged toward the pit, and Andrew ran after her. Was she dashing into danger again or only worried a child was down in the hole getting cut on another tuna fish can?

When she reached the edge of the giant dump, she wrapped her full skirt around her legs and dropped to her knees. She peered down into the cavity and groaned, "Oh no. I forgot that Henry used canned tomato paste for sauces. It's easier and quicker than grinding fresh tomatoes on a big stone. There must be fifty dangerous cans inside this dump." She reached down into the stinky pit and began to lift the tins out of it.

Andrew moaned. Why did she have to be so impulsive? One of the sharp lids might slice her.

He bent down. "Leave the cans. Don't rummage through them." Andrew took her arm to help her to her feet.

With a harsh tone, she snarled, "Don't touch me."

He dropped his hands. "What?"

"Two boys are watching us."

"Where?" Andrew turned around. "No one's here."

Her frostiness and sharp response upset him. She'd been so warm and accommodating. Maybe he didn't want to get involved with a reckless female who snapped orders, but this was the first time he'd seen her harshness.

"The boys are over there in the bushes." She nodded and twisted her head in the general direction as she stood up by herself.

He turned to the shrubs and saw a flash of red shirt. Liz had been right. People were spying on them. Andrew stared at the thick grasses, willing the spies to leave. "

He turned back to Liz. "If you have a shovel, I'll cover these cans for you."

Liz nodded and turned away. She left him standing there as she ran toward the house. She had darted away so fast, Andrew looked around to see if anyone was after her. Why did she always run off like she was saving someone? The sharp edges of the cans could have hurt one of the children, but no one was being threatened at the moment.

Several minutes later she returned with the spade.

Andrew took the shovel and jumped down into the hole. He tossed dirt over the cans. "This won't take me long."

"Let's look on the bright side, this could become an interesting date for us." She teased. "From the moment we left the house, those two little boys have been following us."

"I'll try to be more careful, Sister Liz. You're the first lady I've been interested in since I've lived in Africa, so I didn't know all these rules."

After covering the old cans with dirt, he stomped them into the ground and shoveled more earth on them before leaping out of the pit. "Are those little fellows still watching us?"

"Yes. They've pulled the bushes aside to get a better look."

As Liz led the way back to the house, Andrew waved at several farmers with hoes returning from their fields. They passed a few boys carrying school books on the footpath, and after that they met a couple village women on their way to the market.

Andrew frowned. "It looks like more people are coming on the path."

"It wouldn't surprise me if they took this trail, instead of the short-cut, just to see us." Liz increased her pace. "I appreciate you trying to help me stand up, but it's a taboo here to hold hands with someone from the opposite sex unless you're married to that person. Even then, it's frowned on in public."

"If I held your hand in public, would it be a proposal?"

"No, it would be unacceptable, which was why I didn't take your hand at the dinner table and didn't let you help me up from the ground."

He'd never be able to keep up with the taboos she hurled his way. "I'll trust you to keep an eye on me and let me know if something is wrong."

"I'll have to do that. Otherwise, we might get into a lot of trouble." Her eyes sparkled.

She would keep running into hazardous situations without thinking through the consequences. And if he kept helping her out of danger, he might break taboos and get them into more trouble. How could they ever spend any quality time alone together?

When they reached the house, Liz took the spade. "If you want to wash up, you can use the bathroom."

When Andrew came into the kitchen, Liz handed him a cup of coffee. "Sit down."

Henry sat down with the baby in her arms and started feeding her by spoon.

"Mercy looks so much bigger than she did on the day we found her." Andrew bit into a cookie.

"I took her to the hospital for shots and gave her a dose of antibiotics. We feed her every four hours."

Andrew finished a couple cookies with his coffee. Everything he wanted to say might cause a problem with the chaperon, so he kept quiet. He glanced at this watch. "I need to be going."

Liz walked him to the door.

"Goodbye, Sister Liz." He lowered his voice for her ears alone. "I'd like to see you this weekend in the city, if you're able to come, even if you must bring Henry."

He winked and strolled toward his hired car. He was falling in love with her, and he could live with her headstrong ways. She was a good, sweet woman. Her impulsiveness might test his patience, but he'd rather have her with it, than not have her at all.

***

A couple days later Liz made an inventory of her supplies while Henry finished the household chores.

Liz lifted her head and smiled. "We need more Tylenol and chloroquine, so we'll go to the city this weekend to buy them. It's important you know where I purchase drugs so you can buy them if necessary. Besides, you can help with Mercy."

Henry stood still as if she was about to make an announcement. "I visited the trash pit."

Liz bit her lip. It sounded like Henry paid a social call on a garbage heap. "Why?"

"I had trash to get rid of." She set the empty bucket down. "I wanted to see how Brother Andrew fixed it."

"Why?" Liz put the medical basket away.

"Brother Andrew volunteered for the task of arranging it. He did a good job repairing the garbage dump." Henry wore a serious expression. "Brother Andrew is an important man. He is a pilot and a high official for HOW but humbled himself like an ordinary servant to organize garbage. It shows that he respects you and thinks well of you."

Liz choked. "It's not everyone who's willing to arrange garbage."

Henry kept standing. "Has he spoken to your father about you?"

Liz raised her eyebrows. "Who?"

"Has Brother Andrew Thomas asked your father for permission to court you?"

"It's complicated. We're in Africa and my parents are in Indiana."

"I didn't know your parents were Indians."

"They're not Indians. They live in Indiana, which is a state in America."

Henry shook her head. "With problems like that, courtship never works."

"In my country, a lady and gentleman get to know one another before we visit the parents."

Henry scowled. "That sounds upside down to me. Suppose you spent time getting to know each other and then your parents disapproved. You'd have wasted your life."

Liz choked. "It's not a waste."

"What do you call it?" Henry asked.

"If I got to know someone and then learned it wasn't God's will that we be together, maybe God was teaching me patience."

Was there a way her relationship with Andrew could demonstrate good Christian dating to the young people? Screams jolted Liz back to the present time.

Henry ran to the door and yelled. "Something bad has happened. People are weeping and wailing."

Liz followed Henry outside.

The pastor approached Liz. "The deacon's wife was bitten by a mamba and died."

Liz's heart plummeted to the pit of her stomach. The deacon and his wife had seven children under fifteen years of age. Her death was a tragedy.

She whispered. "We shall pray for the deacon and his children."

"Thank you. We are going through the village and announcing the burial will be in an hour."

After the group of mourners left, Liz and Henry went into the house.

Henry started weeping. "My father did this."

"Did what?"

"He sent the snakes to kill people."

"I don't think so."

"If it wasn't my evil father who sent the snakes, then it had to be this cursed baby who did it."

Liz ran to Mercy and picked her. "A newborn baby cannot be cursed. Mercy is not responsible for mambas biting people."

"You don't know anything about this child. She might have a witch doctor curse on her that could kill us."

Liz should have let Henry believe that her father sent the snakes instead of the innocent baby.

Henry glared at the baby.

Liz shivered and clutched Mercy closer to her chest. If Henry believed the baby was cursed, was Mercy safe in the house with Henry?

CHAPTER FIFTEEN

When they arrived in the city, Liz headed to the guesthouse to check into her room. After unpacking her clothes and toiletries, she picked up Mercy and went into the lounge to wait for Andrew.

Her breath caught. "I'm glad to see you." She sat down in the vacant chair next to Andrew.

"I've looked forward to seeing you again and glad you made it." He stuffed the book he was reading into his bag.

She nodded to the other people in the drawing room. "We found a fast taxi, so I sent Henry to buy street food and do the marketing."

"Can you join me for lunch?"

She nodded. "I'll leave a note for Henry."

He picked up her bag. They walked down the sidewalk and stopped at the main road. Liz bargained for the taxi fee, and they got in. "The Grand Hotel is a busy place with lots of chaperons."

During the ride, Liz told Andrew about Henry's terror of her father. Liz shook her head. "Henry claimed if her father didn't send the mamba, then little Mercy was cursed and sent the snake. So I've kept Mercy with me day and night. I've let Henry care for Mercy only under my supervision."

"Can you convince Henry that Mercy isn't cursed?" Andrew asked.

Liz shrugged. "I'm trying."

"If you think she'd hurt Mercy, why don't you ask Henry to leave?"

"I can't because it would seal poor Henry's fate and future. I'm under strict orders to keep her case confidential and I will." She sighed. "Besides, if I ask Henry to go, the doctors might not send any more student nurses. Sometimes I need their help when we have lots of patients."

Andrew frowned. "It sounds like it's hard no matter what you do."

"That sums it up. And now that you and I want to spend time together, you could never visit me in my home without a chaperon."

When the taxi stopped in front of the hotel a few minutes later, Andrew opened the door and took her backpack. He walked her to a table and held the chair for her.

Liz sat down and took the menu he handed her. When he was seated across from her, she asked. "Have you eaten their cheeseburgers?"

Andrew laughed. "I've tried, but they never seem to have any cheese."

"Let's ask if they have it today."

The waitress approached with two glasses and two sets of silverware. Andrew put the menu down and pointed toward Liz. "We would both like cheeseburgers with French Fries."

"We have no cheese and no minced meat today."

Picking up the menu again, Liz looked at the server. "I know it's late, but can you make breakfast food?"

"We make omelets all day."

"I'd like one with tea."

"Me, too, with coffee." Andrew took the menus and handed them to the waitress.

After the server brought their drinks and meals, Andrew reached out for Liz's hand. She put hers in his, and he prayed.

Andrew took a sip of coffee. "I received my new assignment and was pleased to learn HOW is stationing me in Tamago for another year. So I intend to see you every chance I have."

Her emerald eyes sparkled. "I'd like that."

"My boss insists I take the forced vacation before I start my reassignment, and I need to see my parents. They weren't pleased with me when I became a Christian, so I'm trying to keep the lines of communication open by spending time with them whenever I'm in the States."

"Aren't they believers?"

"No. They're members of a prestigious, old church and attend every Christmas, but they don't have a personal relationship with Jesus."

"I'll be praying for them." Liz glanced at her wristwatch and gulped down the last of her tea. "I'd like to hear more about them, but I need to check in with Henry."

"I've enjoyed lunch." Andrew stood. "Are you free tomorrow?"

"Yes, but Henry will be with us." Liz stood and reached for her backpack.

Andrew took it and carried it to the street to get a taxi.

When they returned to the guesthouse, Liz headed to her room and found Henry asleep.

Henry woke as Liz was feeding Mercy. Henry handed Liz the change from the marketing along with the receipts. "I bought everything on your list."

"Tomorrow morning I'll take you to the pharmaceutical warehouse and introduce you to the people in charge. We'll leave at nine. Is there anything you'd like to do this evening?"

"I want to attend the revival at the city church."

"Mercy can stay with me, so you can go whenever you like."

***

Sunday morning after church, Liz left the women's section and maneuvered her way through the crowd. Henry went with Liz as she headed to the front door. "I'm going to escort Brother Andrew to get a taxi for the airport. Go to the guesthouse and pack."

Liz smiled at Andrew and followed him down the trail. When it became wide enough, they walked side by side. Andrew reached for her hand. She shook her head and pointed down the path. "People are coming. We have to careful."

"Did you get in trouble the first day we met and were alone in the truck without a chaperon?"

"No, you and I were far enough away from the city no one from my village saw us. Thank God. I was so concerned about the baby that day and finding the restaurant I forgot about needing chaperons." Liz tightened the cloth that held Mercy to her back.

Andrew took his handkerchief out and wiped his sweaty face. "Once I gave the African director's wife a ride. The local guys chastised me for making a pass at her. I didn't pay too much attention at the time, but now I understand that I could have been in serious trouble."

"I'm glad you comprehend the problem."

"I'll miss you while I'm gone. Promise me you'll be here when I return. I'd be devastated if you disappeared again."

"This is the second year of my three year commitment. So I'll be here when you get back."

Andrew stopped at the road. "Do you see any taxis coming?"

She shook her head. "I broke a taboo last year and almost got escorted out of Tamago in disgrace. I vowed to never take another risk like that. We won't go anywhere alone in the truck again."

"Yes, ma'am," Andrew saluted.

A taxi stopped and she negotiated a price for Andrew. Liz reached out to shake his hand. "Have a safe journey and a good visit with your parents."

"Expect me back in two weeks."

"Look on the bright side. The sooner you leave, the sooner you can come back." Her eyes moistened.

"You always look on the bright side, don't you?"

"I try."

He climbed into the back seat of the cab. "I'll count the days until I get back."

"Me too." She dipped in a little curtsey.

Liz's heart thumped wildly as if something was wrong. A horrible feeling that she might never see Andrew again flashed through her mind. She shivered.

Andrew leaned out the window. "What's wrong?"

Her mouth went dry, so she shook her head.

"What's troubling you?" He asked.

"It's nothing. Please be careful."

As the taxi drove away, Liz couldn't shake the premonition something awful was about to happen.

CHAPTER SIXTEEN

The following morning when Liz went to her kitchen to put the teakettle on, she glanced out the window. Seeing Mr. Bellolare sitting under the mango tree, she called, "Henry, come here."

When Henry came, she peeked outside. "Where can I hide?"

"We shouldn't run from our troubles. If we do, those problems will come back later. Let's go and speak with your father."

"Please stay with me?"

"I promise." Liz tried to keep the mood light. "Let's get dressed, first."

"Good idea. That way if we have to run, we'll be ready."

Shaking her head, Liz giggled.

A few minutes later, they went outside. Liz walked up to the man and shook his hand. "Good morning, sir."

Henry brought a wooden bench and placed it as far from her father as was acceptable. After Henry curtsied, she sat next to Liz.

Mr. Bellolare looked at his daughter. "I must talk to you about urgent business alone."

"Sister Liz is staying with me."

He puffed out his chest. "I have taken care of you and provided everything for you."

Henry glared. "You threw me out of the house when I was twelve years old. I worked hard for thirteen years to become a nurse."

"From the time you were born, I carried you to the hospital when you were sick. I bought you food and clothes and sent you to school until you disobeyed me. You must respect and honor me." Darkness shot out of his eyes. "Your mother brought you into this world. We gave life to you, so you owe it to us to come back home to your religion and marry the man we have planned for you."

"I am an adult and have taken care of myself for many years." Henry rubbed her forearms. "You didn't pay for me to go to nursing school."

"I will always be in charge of you." He stood. "I'm leaving to bring the police so they can force you to your wedding. I need the money your fiancé has promised me for you."

His daughter growled. "I am not a cow or goat that you can take to the market and sell for a price."

Liz's jaw fell open. She'd never heard an African young lady speak to an older man with such blatant disrespect. Liz wasn't sure what to say because the girl was right.

Henry glowered at him. "You no longer have authority over me."

"Come home. If you do not agree to marry I will bring the authorities with me. They will not be gentle with you." He pointed both his index fingers at Liz. "This white lady can help."

Liz gasped. "How can I help?"

"My daughter is working for you. She is no longer helping me, so it is only right that you pay me something."

"What do you want?"

"Give me fifty thousand francs and I will allow Henry to stay here and work for you. She will not need to come and marry the man I have for her."

Liz narrowed her eyes and curled her lip. "Goodbye." Then she stood and crossed her arms.

"I'm not finished with you ladies. You will hear from me again and won't like what I have to say." He stomped away.

Henry shuddered from head to foot. Her teeth even chattered.

Liz wrapped her arm around Henry's shoulder as she watched Mr. Bellolare disappear down the trail. "Don't worry."

"You keep forgetting that my father is evil and can do horrible wickedness."

"Our God is bigger and can defeat your father's plans."

Henry shivered. "You haven't seen the evil deeds my father and his witch doctor friends have done."

**

After supper that evening, Pastor Ebenezer arrived for a visit. He brought three giant-sized women.

Seeing the oldest female, Liz blinked several times. It had to be Tamara's mother and sisters because Tamara had looked exactly like the visitors.

The pastor introduced the mother and two sisters.

Henry remained standing. "Would you like tea?"

"That would be nice." The pastor nodded. "These ladies had a long and tiring journey."

The gray-haired woman started crying. "I can't believe my sweet Tamara is dead. I had eight children, and now I have only these two daughters left. Why does God keep taking my youngsters away from me?"

The pastor sighed deeply. "No one knows why God takes people home with him."

Liz didn't understand why the Lord took Tamara. It was the first time a girl had died while working for Liz.

"How did she die?" Tamara's mother leaned forward.

"She was bitten by a ten-step snake and passed away a few minutes later." Liz sniffed.

"I am sorry for your loss." The pastor asked, "Would you like me to organize a funeral in the church for your dear daughter?"

"No, thank you." Tamara's mother frowned. "The pastor in our village will prepare a send-off for her. We came to see where you put her."

"We have no means to preserve a body from the heat so we buried her that evening. She is in the church cemetery. I'll show you after we leave." The pastor looked at the visitors.

Henry brought a large platter and set it on the coffee table.

Liz poured the tea and handed each visitor a cup. Turning to the pastor, she asked. "Will they be staying with your family?"

"Yes, my wife has prepared a place for them and is cooking food."

"Tamara was a sweet Christian girl and a hard worker. I loved and appreciated her." Liz's voice cracked, "I'm sorry that she died. I miss her, but you will feel her absence much more than I do."

When the pastor finished his tea, he set the cup on the table. "We need to hurry or we'll be late for the evening service. We'll stop at her grave before we go to my home, but you can spend more time there tomorrow. My wife and I will try to make your stay as comfortable as possible."

After the visitors left, Mercy cried, so Liz fed soymilk to the baby. "She is such a beautiful little girl."

"How long will you keep her?" Henry asked.

"She'll stay until I find her family. I couldn't keep her forever here in Africa because I'm under scrutiny."

"What's that mean?"

"It means wherever I am and whatever I do, I'm being watched all the time."

"That is true. We keep our eyes on you because you are a stranger. We are trained to observe outsiders in case they want to harm us." Henry hesitated. "I thought you didn't want to keep Mercy because you thought she was cursed."

"I couldn't keep her because I'm here on a temporary visa. If the government changed hands and didn't renew my papers, I would have to leave. I couldn't take Mercy because I have no legal documents proving she is mine. I'm not married, so the church would never approve of me keeping her. Every child deserves a mother and a father, if possible." Liz lifted Mercy to her shoulder. "I'll love her and care for her while she is here."

"Aren't you wasting your love?"

"Love is never wasted."

"There's a limited supply of happiness, love, and peace like there's a restricted supply of food and water. If you squander your love on this child, you might not have enough for your own children." Henry scowled.

"God's bounties of love, joy, and peace are endless. I love this child and can have ten children and love them with the same intensity."

Henry raised her eyebrows. "It seems to me when a mother gets to her tenth child, she has run out of love."

"Genuine love can never run out."

"Women seem to love their first children more than their last ones."

Liz stroked Mercy's cheek. "Maybe the mothers are exhausted after years of pregnancy and nursing babies. A mother's love might not be as obvious later as it was when she was younger and had more energy."

Henry crossed her arms. "In my opinion there's not much love left when those last children arrive."

Liz clutched Mercy tighter. She had lots of love for babies. Liz looked at Henry. "Would someone kill a helpless baby if he thought the child is cursed?"

"There are secret sects that still practice human sacrifice throughout West Africa. Everyone knows the Dahomey did it more than anyone else."

"Didn't the British condemn it?"

"Yes, but evil men do it in secret. The witch doctors use the blood and heart of babies in sacrifices."

"I heard stories of people who leave cursed babies in the bush to die or bury them with the dead mother." Liz took a deep breath before asking, "How would you kill Mercy?"

"Me!" Henry yelled. "I wouldn't hurt a baby."

"You said that Mercy was cursed and I wondered what you wanted to do about it."

"If I believed in my heart Mercy was cursed I wouldn't do anything about it. I'm a Christian and God commands us not to kill even cursed babies." Henry cocked an eyebrow. "But some people who aren't Christians might try to hurt her."

Liz shuddered.

CHAPTER SEVENTEEN

Liz used the long hours during taxi rides to pray. It had been three weeks since she had seen Andrew. If he'd moved on to another woman or forgotten her, she could accept it, but she worried about his safety. Andrew had claimed she was impulsive, but he flew into danger throughout a world filled with perils.

She no longer worried about Henry hurting Mercy. Henry cared for the baby as if she was her own child and even talked to Mercy. It had startled Liz when Henry laughed one day while playing with the baby.

When they arrived in the city, Liz hired a local vehicle to take them to the mission guesthouse.

The hostess handed Liz a letter. "This came for you."

Liz smiled. "Thank you." Her breath caught as she glanced at Andrew's return address. She ripped the envelope open and scanned the contents. Andrew was safe. It had been sent two weeks earlier. She took her time to go back and read more slowly.

"Dear Liz, I hope you are well. I've been praying for you. After my time in the States, I'll be going to Ethiopia to carry out a survey for HOW. I didn't want to be gone so long, but I promised Mr. Sloan to make this trip for him. I miss you and look forward to spending many weekends with you, even with a chaperon. Stay well. Please pray for my trip. Yours in Christ, Andrew."

She slumped forward in relief. Her lips parted in a sigh. He'd soon be coming back. She crushed the letter to her chest and her heart fluttered.

"Did you receive bad news?" Henry asked.

"Brother Andrew had to go to Ethiopia and wants us to pray." Liz smiled. "I'll keep the baby with me while you go shopping. Mercy will be going home fairly soon."

"You are a bizarre woman. How do you know where her home is, if she was abandoned?" Henry asked.

"The Lord will show me."

"It sounds strange." Shaking her head, Henry left.

Liz tied Mercy to her back, picked up her bag, and walked to the curb. Liz hired a taxi to take her to the clinic. When the taxi stopped, she stepped out and went inside.

Dr. Tomi looked up from his desk. "Good afternoon. It's nice to see you. Dr. Luke is at the hospital today. We were shocked and sorry to hear about Tamara's death. She was one of our best student nurses and more sincere in her Christian walk than any of the others."

"I miss her." Liz's eyes moistened.

"How is Henry doing?"

"Tamara was helping round the rough edges off Henry." Liz sighed. "I guess the job falls to me now."

"You can do it, Sister, Liz."

"I'll try, but Henry has a mind of her own."

Mercy fussed and stretched on Liz's back so she untied the baby and put her on her lap. "This child was abandoned, and I'm looking for a home for her." Liz took the milk out and began spoon-feeding the infant. "I often meet childless couples in my clinics, but I haven't met any recently."

"If a couple is unable to conceive, I refer them to the fertility doctor at the hospital."

"Do you know any couples in the church who have been trying for a long time to have their own child and don't have one?"

"I can introduce you to a couple, who will be attending church tomorrow."

"Thank you. I'll be there."

***

Sunday morning Liz followed Henry to their usual seat on the women's side of the large evangelical church.

As the service was about to begin, every pair of eyes turned back to the main door. Liz looked around, too.

Andrew, dressed in a navy-blue suit, stood in the doorway. He was looking over the women's section of the church.

Liz suppressed an urge to run and throw her arms around him. She lifted her hand only enough for him to see her and waved it slightly. As the only other white person in an ocean of dark-skinned people, all her actions drew attention to her.

He nodded in her direction as an usher escorted him to the men's side of the sanctuary.

She spent the next hour thanking God for Andrew's safe return. Liz never heard the sermon.

After the service, Dr. Tomi approached Liz. "Come with me so I can introduce you to the couple."

Liz wanted to speak to Andrew, but it was important she check out the couple. Liz turned to Henry. "Please go find Brother Andrew and invite him to join us for lunch. I need to take care of business."

"What kind of business? We are not supposed to work on Sunday."

Sometimes Henry's comments and questions got on Liz's nerves, but she smiled. "I'll explain later. Wait with Brother Andrew for me." Liz dashed away with Dr. Tomi.

Liz and Dr. Tomi stopped in front of a man in a black suit and an attractive woman in an elegant gold and white African-style dress.

The doctor smiled. "This is Mr. and Mrs. Isaiah."

Liz shook their hands. "It's nice to meet you. Do you live here in the city?"

Mr. Isaiah picked up his wife's purse from the church pew and handed it to her before turning to Liz. "I'm the principal in the secondary school. My wife owns her own sewing shop."

"That's wonderful. I've wanted to find a seamstress to make me some church clothes. Can you give me the address of your shop?"

The wife opened her purse and took out a little slip of paper. After writing on it, she handed it to Liz. "Here is the location of my shop and the hours I work."

Liz slid the paper in her bag "Thank you, I'll visit you soon."

She turned and bumped into Andrew. Her heart beat faster as his hand reached for hers. Stepping back in a formal manner, Liz shook his hand. "I'm happy to see you. I prayed for you day and night."

He asked, "Can you join me for lunch?"

"Yes, I sent Henry to look for you."

A moment later, Henry approached. "I am sorry, but it wasn't possible to get through the crowd to give the message to Brother Andrew."

He reached for Liz's backpack, but she shook her head. "I'm looking forward to lunch."

Andrew took off his suit jacket. "What's your recommendation for lunch?"

"It's nearly time to feed Mercy." Liz sighed.

He grinned. "I could go to the hotel and bring fried chicken and rice for everyone. We could eat together in the dining hall of the guesthouse."

"What a lovely idea." Liz nodded. "We'll go ahead and wait for you there."

By the time Andrew arrived, Liz had fed Mercy and put her to bed. Andrew handed two bags to Liz. Henry helped her unpack the food and set it on the table. Then everyone sat down.

"Brother Andrew, would you like to pray?" Liz asked.

He bowed his head. "Lord Jesus, thank you for watching over Liz, Henry, and Mercy. Keep them safe. Thank you for bringing me back. Thank you for giving us this nice time to visit and eat. Amen."

"Henry, I forgot the drinks. Would you get us sodas from the refrigerator?" Liz asked. "Write my name down, so they can put it on my account."

Andrew reached in his pocket and took out a bill. "Take this and pay for them."

Henry took the money and nodded. "There's only three flavors, Coca Cola, orange, and Sprite. What do you like? Sister Liz drinks Coca Cola."

"I'd like that, too, please." Andrew said.

After Henry left, Liz slid her chair a little closer to Andrew and whispered. "I had a terrible nightmare that something awful happened."

"After I landed to collect the water samples, I was detained by police."

Liz swallowed. "Did they hurt you?"

"No. they locked me inside a house for a week."

"That must have been horrible." Tears moistened her eyes. "How did you get released?"

"Another American who worked for the US Embassy was arrested with me. He had political connections and was able to get us both free."

Liz blinked several times. "I'm glad you're safe." A tear escaped her eye and ran down her cheek

If he was going to fly in dangerous countries, she had to trust God to keep him safe.

The baby cried. She jumped up and left.

***

Andrew's heart tightened at her distress. He cared for her deeply and had fallen in love with her.

When Liz returned, he stood. Then Henry came around the corner from the opposite direction. He wasn't sure if holding a chair for a lady was a taboo, so he kept standing.

His heart clenched at Liz's red eyes and smeared make-up. She'd changed out of her church clothes and into a blue dress with a form-fitting top and drop-waist that emphasized her curves. It was the shortest dress he'd seen her in, but it still covered her knees. He loved her walk and the way her gathered skirt swayed.

Henry interrupted his thoughts. "Why are you standing? Is something wrong with the food?"

Liz giggled. "A man, to show his respect for a lady, stands up when she comes into the room and stands when she leaves. It makes us ladies feel special."

Henry frowned. "Give me the baby and I'll tie her to my back. She must have been lonely in the room."

Liz sat down and passed the rice to Andrew who served himself. He handed the bowl back to her. "I wish there had been a way to send you a message."

"Communication is a challenge without phones and an adequate postal system." She passed the food to Henry.

When they finished the meal, Liz and Henry stacked the dishes, cleared the table, and left.

Liz returned with a cup of coffee for Andrew. "Henry is washing the dishes."

"Thank you." He took the mug. "I arrived this morning, but I have to leave in a few minutes. It's a long drive. I need to get settled into my quarters and pick up my work schedule."

"I have an idea." A light flickered through her face. "I need what they call a high-class tailor to make church clothes. I'll be coming to the city next weekend to order an outfit."

Seeing Henry return, Andrew didn't stand up. He had to be careful around Henry, who had strong opinions on American customs and talked far too much. The girl's chattering sometimes gave him a headache, so he didn't always listen.

What if she said something that he needed to know about Liz?

CHAPTER EIGHTEEN

Henry ran into the house. Sweat covered her face. She gasped, "My father is on his way with two wicked sorcerers."

"Let's go and speak to them." Liz picked up the baby.

"No, let's hide in the house and lock the doors."

"We're going outside. I don't want warlords in my house."

"That's a smart idea. Those evildoers might hide a vile fetish in here."

Henry walked behind Liz to where Henry's father waited under the shade of the mango tree. He was dressed in the same soiled clothes from the previous visit and smelled worse.

The tattooed warlords shook their spears and glared at Liz and Henry. Pouches of foul-smelling herbs hung from their waists.

Liz's nostrils flared from the wretched odor, but she suppressed the urge to pinch her nose. "Good afternoon." After greeting them, she pointed down the trail. "Can you gentlemen come with us to the pastor's house so we can have a man to man discussion?"

Henry whispered in Liz's ear. "Let's stay here so they can go for the man to man discussion. We're not men."

"Maybe you're right." Liz lowered her voice. "Still they are strangers, so we ought to be polite and escort them to the pastor's house."

The visitors followed Liz down the footpath. Henry was last. At the pastor's house they sat down under a baobab tree and waited for the minister.

Pastor Ebenezer stepped out of his house and walked toward them. He gripped the Bible in front of him like a shield as if to ward away the dark spirits from the witch doctors.

After exchanging more salutations, the pastor took a seat. "What do these gentlemen," he pointed to the sorcerers, "have to do with Henry's wedding?"

Mr. Bellolare turned to the minister. "If Henry refuses to come home to marry her fiancé, these sorcerers will proclaim maledictions on the ladies."

The pastor's eyebrows lifted. "You claimed she was marrying a Christian man. How can you bring these sorcerers to do evil to Sister Liz and Henry?"

Henry's father remained silent. His black eyes darted left and right. Beads of sweat dotted his forehead.

Watching the man's distress, Liz swallowed a smile. She waited for the proper moment to excuse herself. As seconds rolled by, Liz shifted her weight on the uncomfortable log.

At last she stood up and tried not to appear eager. "It's best that Henry and I go home so you gentlemen can have a proper discussion without us ladies."

The pastor frowned at the men. "We need time to pray."

"We cannot give you people any more time," Henry's father growled, "We came today to take my daughter back to her wedding. She is coming with me now."

The men stood. Mr. Bellolare grabbed Henry's arm. Tears filled her eyes and her lip quivered. Then she twisted out of his clutches and ran down the trail.

The situation wasn't funny, but watching Henry run with a baby bouncing up and down on her back was hilarious. Liz swallowed her laughter and pasted a serious expression on her face.

Then Liz crossed her arms and glared at Henry's father. "Mr. Bellolare, go ahead and tell your men to put their curses on us."

The pastor gasped and raised his voice, "No, Sister Liz, you do not want evil hexes on you."

"They can put all the spells they like on me because the blood of Jesus Christ covers me. The Son of Almighty God protects Henry and me." She wanted to walk away from the men but that was considered rude, and she mustn't anger them too much. "Greater is He that is in me than he that is in the world. God in me is greater than any sorcerer."

The two warlords shook their spears at Liz, and growled sharp words. Lowering her head to conceal her grin, she clamped her jaws closed.

Mr. Bellolare yelled, "Henry must come back home. If she does not come willingly we will use force."

Liz scrunched her face up into her meanest expression. Hoping she looked fierce, she raised her voice. "Your daughter is not coming with you today."

Or any other day, if Liz had a say in the matter.

Henry's father whispered something into the ears of the men. They turned toward Liz's house and marched down the trail.

The pastor asked, "What are they going to do?"

"They will put a little curse on them." Mr. Bellolare scowled.

A small malediction was nothing to Liz, but it would terrify poor Henry. So Liz took off running down a short cut to her home. She leaped over large roots and boulders on the unused trail. Gasping for air, she jogged as fast as she could. As she jumped over fallen trees and hurdled over the huge rocks, she kept up a reckless pace to reach the house before the men arrived. Her mad dash reminded her of the one with Andrew to save the baby.

Sprinting along the path, she prayed, "Lord, keep Henry safe inside the house with Mercy."

When she reached her home, Liz tried to open the door. It was locked so she pounded on it. "It's me, Sister Liz."

The iron bar grated in the brackets and the door banged open. Liz stepped inside, closed the door, and bolted it at the top and on the bottom. Then she replaced the metal lever in the middle of the teakwood frame. Liz thanked God that Henry and little Mercy were safe, and Liz had arrived ahead of the sorcerers.

Seeing Henry's terrified expression, Liz didn't want the witch doctors' words to frighten her more. "Let's go to the closet. They are coming to curse us." She reached for a bottle of water and two cups from the counter. "We are quite safe, but I don't want to listen to them."

Inside the tiny chamber, Liz whispered. "Do you know the story in the Bible about Elijah and the prophets of Baal?"

"I've never heard that one."

"It's in first Kings Chapter 18 of the Old Testament."

"The Gideons gave me a New Testament. I've wanted a whole Bible but never had the extra funds."

"The next time we go to the city, remind me to buy you a complete Bible."

Hoping to keep Henry distracted, Liz went on with the story. "Elijah was a prophet of the Lord God who challenged the prophets of Baal. They were like the witch doctors here in Africa. They decided that whichever god called down fire from Heaven would be declared the real God. Those evil worshippers of Baal and Satan tried everything. They cut themselves and screamed but weren't able to call fire down from their god to burn their sacrifice."

Henry whispered. "You mean they didn't have any power."

"That's right. They didn't. Elijah rebuilt an altar to God, and killed a bull to sacrifice. Then he poured lots of water over the animal to show that only the true God could burn up a sacrifice covered in water. Elijah reminded everyone again that the god that sends fire is the true God. The Lord sent fire and burned up the bull sacrifice, the wood, the stones, and the soil. All the people dropped to their knees and cried that the Lord God was the true God. Elijah and his companions grabbed the 450 prophets of Baal and killed them. Many people turned to the Lord."

Bang! Clang! Bam! The girls jumped.

Liz let out a ragged breath. "It sounds like they're throwing rocks on the metal roof."

Henry's teeth chattered. "Are they coming in to get us?"

"No, they can't get inside. Let's pray." Liz bowed her head. "Lord, we thank you for your sacrifice and your protection. Show these idol worshipers that you are God Almighty. Amen."

"I do not hear anything." Henry sniffed.

"I'd like to creep out there and see what's happening."

Henry stood. "I am afraid, but I will not let you go by yourself."

Liz pushed open the door slowly. Then she turned and took Mercy from Henry's shaking arms. "I'll put her in bed. She'll be fine."

On hands and knees they crept to the kitchen. Liz raised her head and peeked out the window.

As she watched the sorcerers hurl curses and tramp around the house, Liz started giggling. Then they threw dirt in the air and stomped in the ground. Liz could no longer restrain her laughter and clamped her hand over her mouth so they couldn't hear her chuckles.

Henry's father screamed. "You have not seen the last of me. I will return with more power."

Liz whispered into Henry's ear. "Do not worry. Their curses are worthless. Jesus is greater than any evil they want to do."

The men stomped down the trail.

Henry's hands shook. "We must never do anything to anger them."

"I'm not afraid of these workers of iniquity."

Henry's eyes widened. "You are a brave woman."

Liz smiled. "Christ in me gives me courage."

But even with Christ, there had been times that Liz had felt real terror.

CHAPTER NINETEEN

Andrew stood and waved at Liz and Henry as they came inside the lounge of the mission guesthouse. Liz flashed him her brilliant smile, but Henry scowled at him.

"We're late because our bush taxi stopped every few miles to drop a letter, discharge a passenger, or pick one up. Are you free to join Henry and me to meet the new seamstress?" Liz asked.

"Can I drive you ladies there in my vehicle?"

Liz turned to Henry. "What do you think?"

"Yes, it will save us taxi money." Henry lifted a small suitcase off her head. "We should put our bags in the room first."

The girls left and returned a few minutes later. They followed Andrew outside to the parking lot to a white pick-up truck. He unlocked the doors and opened them.

Henry handed the sleeping baby to Liz. Then Henry climbed into the back seat. Liz gave Mercy to Henry and clamored into the seat next to her assistant.

Andrew chuckled. "I guess I'm the chauffeur. Where are we going?"

"Here's the address for the seamstress." Liz handed him a slip of paper. "Did you get a room here in the guesthouse for the night?"

"I'm staying upstairs in the men's barracks because all the single rooms were occupied. I enjoy meeting the Christian guys working here." He turned into traffic. "My official job starts on Monday."

"Are your new quarters in Carmi?"

"Yes, they gave me an air-conditioned villa there."

Liz asked, "What's it like?"

"The walls are brown, the furniture is gray, and the floors are black. It feels like a cave. Your little home is cozier and more inviting than mine, but my accommodations are comfortable with running water and a flush toilet."

"I assume there's electrical power."

"Yes. There's even a back-up generator." He stopped for a red light. "I feel guilty having a good vehicle while you walk everywhere."

Henry said. "You wouldn't need to feel guilty if you drove Sister Liz and me where we had to go."

"Henry," Liz gasped. "Brother Andrew has to work every day, so he can't drive us. Besides I enjoy walking."

"I don't." Henry frowned.

"Henry's right. When I'm here in the city with you ladies, I could drive you to do your errands."

"Thank you. That would be lovely." Liz turned to Henry and whispered, loud enough for Andrew to hear. "Say thank you."

Henry spoke in a monotone. "Thank you, Brother Andrew."

Liz said. "I chose to live in a mud house in the village so I could be closer to the people. The church headquarters wanted me to reside in the city on their compound."

"Sister Liz, you are a foolish woman to refuse a nice house in the city." Henry shook her head.

Andrew clamped his mouth shut so he wouldn't say something he'd regret. He didn't like Henry's harsh words toward Liz, so he changed the subject and asked, "How did you start your clinics?"

"I hiked to the villages close to my home with a basket of medicines and set up a clinic under a big mango tree."

"You have no overhead expenses."

"I charge a little bit more than cost for all the treatments. A Tylenol is 4 cents, but I charge a nickel because there are no one-cent coins."

"Is there anyone who can't afford your treatment?"

"Maybe one or two people a month? I leave the medicine on the table, and if no one pays for it by the time I'm ready to go home, I ask the pastor to take it to the patient. If the sick person doesn't have the money, the pastor gives the pills and tells him it's a gift from the Christians in the church."

"That's a clever tool of evangelism. I like it."

"Health programs must be affordable, acceptable, and accessible. Importing fancy British medicines, which are dependent on regular shipments and require extra funds are a waste of time and money."

Andrew stopped the truck and turned right. "If the people became accustomed to them and the European volunteers were evacuated because of civil unrests, the poor people wouldn't have any medications."

"If they depended on them, they could die without them. With the unstable political status it's better if people were used to drugs that were readily available."

Henry raised her voice. "Your American pills are better than local ones. Those high-class medications are stronger."

"Sometimes they are, but many are more expensive and with more side effects. Give me a couple of aspirin any day for a headache."

Andrew drove down a side street and parked next to the curb. A sign reading 'God's Miracles Sewing' dangled from the entranceway. Stepping out of the truck, he slid the front seat forward. He offered his hand to help them out, but they refused it.

Liz flashed him one of her happy expressions that made his heart squeeze. Then he looked around and frowned. Why was Liz visiting a back street tailor? He followed the ladies up the uneven steps and swallowed his disgust at the cracked walls, water-stained ceiling, and packed earth floor. Magazine pictures of different dress styles plastered the walls.

Liz approached an attractive woman and shook her hand. "Mrs. Isaiah, it's nice to see you again."

"Sister Liz, did you bring your cloth for me to sew?"

"No, I didn't. There aren't any fabric shops in my village. Could you buy some green cotton brocade for me?"

"Yes."

Straightening her outfit, Liz looked up at Mrs. Isaiah. "Would you be able to copy this dress I'm wearing?"

"It's a simple pattern. My junior apprentice can sew it for you." The woman flipped open a small notebook and used a broken pencil to sketch a rough image of Liz's outfit. Opening a drawer of her sewing machine, she pulled out a tape measure. Mrs. Isaiah stretched it around Liz's chest. "It looks like your bust is about 90."

Mercy wailed. Liz glanced at the baby in Henry's arms. "That's strange. The child never cries for anything. Excuse me a minute." Liz moved to the baby and knelt. Then Liz put a hand to little Mercy's forehead. "Her head is cool, so I'm not sure what's wrong." Liz glanced at Mrs. Isaiah's concerned face.

Henry scowled. "I fed her so she's not hungry, and I changed her clothes so she is not dirty or wet."

Mrs. Isaiah whispered, "May I hold her for a moment?"

Henry handed the baby to Mrs. Isaiah, who asked, "Whose baby is she?

"She was abandoned. I've no idea who the parents are, or where she is from. Many people give me unwanted children."

"I've often seen you with an African baby. I thought you were giving a special medical treatment to a sick infant." Mrs. Isaiah rocked and sang to the child. She put Mercy to sleep. "Has anyone shown an interest in keeping this beautiful girl?"

"No." Liz shrugged.

Henry stood and bent forward. "Put her on my back and she will stay asleep."

It was suddenly clear to Andrew why Liz was visiting the seamstress. He admired Liz's way of checking out a prospective parent for little Mercy.

After the baby was tied to Henry's back, Mrs. Isaiah picked up her tape measure and stretched it around Liz again. "Your waist is 61 and your hips 91."

Andrew memorized the numbers since they might be helpful later on. The country used centimeters, so he'd convert them to inches.

Mrs. Isaiah jotted notes. "After I measure the lengths of your shoulders, arms, and skirt we'll be finished. I thought you wanted several outfits."

"I do, but I haven't decided what other style I'd like. How long will it take you to finish this?"

"Is one week soon enough?"

"That's great. I can return next Saturday. How much will it be?"

"The type of cloth you want is expensive and specially made in the south. It will cost 10,000 francs and the sewing will be 2,000 francs."

"I left my backpack in the truck."

"I'll get it for you." Andrew turned to the entrance and shoved aside the tattered orange curtain that covered the doorway.

"I'll go with you." Liz headed toward the door.

Andrew reached in his pocket, but Liz shook her head. He could have easily slid a few bills into her hand, but someone might have noticed. Even he knew it wasn't proper for him to buy Liz clothes. As he unlocked the door, he whispered, "I'm glad there's no law against a gentleman watching a lady get her measurements taken. That was informative." He winked.

Her mouth fell open. Andrew smiled at her new look of surprise.

She opened her bag and took out her money. They returned to the shop. Liz handed the currency to the seamstress. "I see you have four young apprentices. Are any of these girls your daughters?"

"No, I haven't had any children."

"How long have you been married?"

"Ten years. I'm already thirty and want children."

"I'm sure God will bless you with them."

Several more ladies entered the little chamber. The extra customers made the room crowded. Andrew was uncomfortable watching women get measured. He stepped outside, but stuck his head through the opening in the curtain. "I'll wait for you ladies by the truck. Take your time."

A few minutes later Liz and Henry joined him. Andrew opened the door, so Liz and Henry could climb in the back seat again. Maybe it was forbidden for a lady to sit up front with him.

He caught Liz's eye in the rearview mirror. "Where are we going next?"

Liz smiled. "I'm hungry. Since the baby is with us, maybe we can stop and take food back to the guesthouse."

Andrew down-shifted and eased the vehicle into traffic. "Is there anything special you ladies want to eat?"

"Whatever you order will be fine with us." Liz said.

Henry frowned. "I'm trying to eat the white man's food, but not too much sugar."

Andrew chuckled. "I won't let them put sugar on the food."

He stopped in front of the hotel restaurant and went inside. He returned with two giant plastic sacks, which he set on the front passenger seat. Then he drove to the guesthouse and parked.

Andrew followed the ladies to the dining room and set the containers on the table. "I forgot to get plates and silverware. Take-out isn't the same in Africa."

"The kitchen's closed now, but I know the hostess. " Liz left and returned with the dishes and silverware. After the table was set, she took the covers off the food.

The tantalizing aroma of fried chicken in tomato sauce made Andrew's mouth water. He enjoyed Liz's company and was getting used to Henry's presence.

After his prayer, Henry stood. "Excuse me for interrupting, but we need drinks. Do you want me to bring you the same flavors?"

Liz nodded.

"Yes, please."

After Henry left, Andrew pulled a small tablet out of his pocket. "I need to take a few notes. I don't want to forget anything important."

Liz glanced at the numbers: 90-61-91. "Brother Andrew, isn't that against the rules."

"The seamstress announced the measurements for the world to hear."

Henry came back with two Cokes and an orange soda lying on a tray.

Andrew slipped the writing pad into his pocket and handed a bowl to Liz. "Would you like rice, Liz?"

Henry scowled. "She is Sister Liz."

That sounded like a warning to him, so he better be careful. He needed to behave himself especially under Henry's watchful eyes.

Liz cocked an eyebrow as she pointed to the serving bowls. "Did they give these to you, Brother Andrew?"

He laughed. "No, I had to pay for them."

"Of course you had to pay for them." Henry growled, "Everyone must buy containers the food comes in."

Liz smiled. "In our country, the waiter gives the customer a container to carry his food home."

Henry drew her brows together. "You people are rich to give away free boxes."

Andrew swallowed. "Giving containers to take away food can help the business. People carry it home or to work and share it with a friend. If others like the cuisine, the restaurant may get new customers."

Liz grinned. "Sometimes in shopping malls and grocery stores, the restaurant owners give away samples of food to customers. If it tastes good, shoppers may want to buy it."

"That may happen, but I think you people are wealthy to give it freely." Henry shook her head. "No one in business here gives anything away."

Andrew was wealthy, but not many people knew it. Many Africans assumed Americans were rich, so Andrew had told no one he was a millionaire.

Henry frowned. "In many homes, there aren't any leftovers. People don't have a refrigerator to keep the food, so they eat all of it at meal times. We don't understand how you Americans can give so much away and stay so rich."

"Maybe God blesses us because we share and give away things." Andrew shrugged.

CHAPTER TWENTY

On Sunday Andrew bought two fried-egg sandwiches and carried them to the guesthouse. Early morning breakfast sellers only prepared eggs with white bread or bowls of corn gruel. Neither he nor Liz liked the mushy cereal.

When Liz came into the lounge, her face lit up with joy. "Good morning."

He took advantage of every minute they could be together. After he sat down next to her, he prayed. Then he handed her a warm plastic bag.

Liz took the sandwich out of the sack. "Henry doesn't want to come to the first service."

"I'd prefer the later one myself, but I need an early start on the road. I have to collect my weekly schedule this evening because the office won't be open in the morning."

"I understand." Then Liz laughed. "I tried to bribe Henry with breakfast, but she was rather indignant and asked how could any human being eat at six in the morning? She never misses a meal and eats three times what I eat and doesn't gain weight."

Andrew took a small thermos out of his bag and poured two cups of tea. He handed her one.

Taking it, she asked, "Don't you drink coffee?"

"I do, but I had only one thermos and thought it would be easier for me to drink tea than for you to endure coffee." Andrew took a sip. "I've noticed how much Henry eats and she looks like she weighs about ninety pounds."

"How do you know so much about women's weight?"

"As a pilot I need to calculate the total amount the plane is carrying before I fly, so I've learned to estimate a person's weight. And you weigh one-twenty."

Her mouth fell open. "You're good. That's right."

When they had finished their breakfast, Liz stood to carry the trash to the bin. As she stepped away from the chair, a nail snagged her hem. She stumbled forward and pulled the chair behind her.

Andrew reached out and put his arm around her waist to stop her from crashing to the floor with the chair on top of her. Then he unhooked the hem of her skirt from the nail.

"Not again." She sighed. "This happened before and I still haven't learned my lesson not to sit there." She lifted the edge of her dress and examined the four-inch rip. Straightening up, she scowled. "I don't have time to sew it, but I'll get a piece of scotch tape to keep it together."

She left and returned a few minutes later.

Andrew picked up Liz's backpack. "Did Henry ask about us going in the truck alone together this morning?"

"Yes, I told her we'd get a taxi, so the driver would be our chaperon."

"We're not going to do that, are we?"

"Yes, we are. I can't lie to her."

Falling into step with her, Andrew shook his head. "I'm not looking forward to one of your dilapidated taxis."

"I'll try to get one that's not too broken-down." Liz giggled. "And I'll charter the whole cab for us."

"Don't you think that's a bit extravagant, Sister Liz?"

"No, Brother Andrew, after all it is the Lord's day."

The glimmer in her eyes indicated she wasn't serious. Andrew chuckled as Liz hailed a taxi and agreed to the price. A lifetime with her would be one long sweet adventure.

***

After they were seated in a new vehicle, Liz lifted the hem of her skirt and turned it inside out to make sure the torn edges were staying together with the tape. "This should hold until after church."

The driver pulled into traffic and made several abrupt turns. Liz tried to keep to her side of the seat, but without safety belts and door handles, Liz slid toward Andrew. She bumped into him every time the driver swerved around a corner.

After several more abrupt turns, Liz sighed. "I wish I had a seatbelt to keep me in my place so I wouldn't slide into you."

"I'd never want to keep you in your place." He squeezed her hand. "This is kind of cozy. Sometimes I'm off work in the middle of the week. Would it be possible to see you then?"

"I have clinics, but you could come with Henry and me." Her skin tingled. "We could go together in your truck." Then she wrinkled her forehead. "Can you handle sickness, blood, vomiting, and diarrhea?"

He nodded.

She grinned. "You could stay with the pastor and his family. They have ten children who can follow you around and report your actions to their parents."

"I'd need to be on my best behavior. No winking and handholding. With so many eyes on us, we'd never get in trouble. Would there be enough room for me to stay with them?"

"Africans always make room for one more." She slid into him again. "It's hard for me to stay on my side."

"Stop trying."

"Can you talk to the pastor about my coming to visit and make the arrangements? It'll give us a chance to spend more time together."

"I'll speak to him and his wife." Liz had given up staying on her side of the back seat and was wedged in close to him. "I need new clothes." Her eyes and mouth opened wide, like a lightbulb going off. "This is my Sunday dress, which is now torn. I'll need another new dress to replace it. Coming each Saturday to the tailor will give us many opportunities to get together."

The taxi stopped in front of the church, and they got out and walked up the uneven path to the sanctuary.

Andrew grinned. "I confess. The ride was rather pleasant."

All heads turned to them as they entered the sanctuary. Liz's heart plummeted. She groaned inwardly because when they stepped into the church they didn't have a chaperon. She was in serious trouble. Her hands shook.

She wished Henry would have come to the early service with Andrew and her. Liz should have insisted that Henry join them, but Liz could never do that.

Liz couldn't concentrate during the sermon. Out of the corner of her eye, she tried to see the features of the women around her, to determine if they showed displeasure. They looked like they enjoyed the service.

After it ended, Liz ran out the side door close to where she had sat. Then she walked around the outside of the church and stood near the main entrance to wait for Andrew.

"It's already ten o'clock." Andrew frowned. "Let's hurry back to the guesthouse so I can collect my bags."

As they went to the road to get a taxi, they met several people who asked, "Where's Henry, this morning?"

"Brother Andrew has to report in for duty late this evening so we came to the early service."

By the time they found a taxi, Liz was tired of explaining to everyone why Henry wasn't with them. She didn't tell Andrew that she was worried about their appearance.

At the guesthouse, Liz made sandwiches and handed a bag to Andrew. "Here's a snack for your trip."

"Thanks for thinking of me. It's a long ride. There aren't any burger stands along the way." He opened the refrigerator and took two bottles of water and then put money in the donation box. "You never cease to amaze me. For an impetuous lady, you do a lot of planning ahead."

"How many hours is it to Carni?"

"It's about ten, so I'll be on the road all day." Andrew put the lunch in his briefcase.

She walked with Andrew to his pickup truck.

He grinned. "Staying for church and being with you was worth every minute of reaching Carni when it's dark."

Andrew unlocked his truck door and put his briefcase and bags on the backseat.

People, dressed for church, left the guesthouse. They nodded at Liz and Andrew as they walked past them.

"It was good to see you, Brother Andrew. I hope to see you again." She wanted to throw her arms around him and tell him to careful, but she mumbled. "We're being watched."

Liz put her own palm to her lips and kissed it. Then she reached for Andrew's hand and used her free hand to press her palm into Andrew's.

He looked at his palm, grinned and put it to his lips.

Then he reached out and shook her hand again.

As they looked into each other's eyes, Liz wanted to tell him not to leave. Her heart pounded faster as he climbed into the driver's seat. Liz couldn't shake the horrible feeling that something awful was about to happen. Rubbing her forearms, she suppressed a shudder. Her premonition that Andrew was flying into danger was stronger than last time.

CHAPTER TWENTY-ONE

Andrew drove his truck to the small airfield and parked it. He'd never flown to the villages on his flight schedule, but as long as he was cautious, he should be fine. He grabbed his emergency bag and carried it to the plane. After looking his aircraft over, he checked the fuel level, engine, brakes, and undercarriage, and then he climbed inside the fuselage and ticked off every item on the pre-flight checklist.

After starting the engine, the control tower asked him to wait until two helicopters landed and a larger plane took off. He used the time to pray.

Something bumped the undercarriage. He leaned forward, looked out the window, and checked the controls again. Rubbing his forehead, he concluded it was only his imagination until he spotted a dog coming from behind the aircraft. He breathed easier. The animal must have banged the plane.

He drove to the end of the runway and turned. After guiding the plane down the center of the asphalt, the aircraft lifted. Andrew smiled at the perfect takeoff.

He wished he had a photo of Liz to keep in the cockpit. Andrew needed to get a picture of her the next time he saw her, so he'd have her image in front of him. And maybe another photo for his wallet and another for his room and another for his desk. He sounded like a man in love, was he?

The flight was smooth and perfect until ten minutes before his scheduled landing when the plane jerked. What was that? Andrew's fingers tightened. Then his hands shook as they griped the vibrating stick. What was happening? The plane was fairly new and everything had been in perfect order when he left.

The instrument panel failed. The engine died. His heart stopped. For a moment.

No, he couldn't crash.

Lord, please help.

The motor started up again.

Thank you Lord.

The engine spluttered and hiccupped. He nursed the failing plane past a grove of treetops and aimed the nose straight for the water where it was safer to land. The aircraft dipped and rose several times. When it dropped into another cluster of trees, his heart plummeted to the pit of his stomach.

Lord, please help.

Then the plane miraculously lifted once again but fell a moment later. The small aircraft soared over more trees. Then it dropped and landed with a heavy thud, five hundred yards before the river.

His chest slammed forward and crashed into the control panel, and his head banged into the windshield. Pain exploded in his temple. Fragments of glass, like razors, sliced his face. Lifting his hand, he wiped a sticky, warm fluid from his forehead and cheek. Blood.

He blinked several times to focus on his surroundings. The bolts that had held the seat to the floor must have loosened, because he was still buckled in but leaning forward into the controls. Sparks from the fading engine flashed and popped all around the aircraft. Diesel fuel ran out on the ground and pooled in large puddles. The gas fumes chafed his nostrils. He gagged. Flashes of fire shot out in front of him.

He had to move and get out of the plane.

Lord, give me strength.

Agony tore through his head and chest as he shoved the seat back. With shaking hands he unbuckled the belt. Then he pushed open the door, leaped, and cleared the aircraft. He tripped and landed in a pit. Electrical jolts shot through his right foot. He pulled himself out of the hole and hopped on his good leg. Then he lost his balance and tumbled to the ground. After forcing himself to stand, he was knocked down again by the inevitable blast.

The world turned. Sky, clouds, and land swam before him. Trees swayed and the river moved left and right. Blackness took over, and he closed his eyes.

He took a breath and forced his eyes open to calm the dull roar of his blood. Sweat dripped off his chin and chest. Lifting a hand to his head, he prayed the pounding would stop.

Andrew choked on petrol fumes and it was hard to breathe. So he crawled closer to the river on hands and knees.

Another explosion shook the ground. Perspiration covered his skin and soaked his clothes. He breathed faster and harder as he crept away from the heat of the flames and got closer to the water. The stench of diesel fumes filled the air and nauseated him. Out of breath, he let himself collapse next to the river.

Where was he going and who was he?

He rolled over onto his back, but it didn't ease the thudding in his head. Dizziness took over. His right foot must be broken, so he tried to stand on his good one, but it went out from under him. If only the earth would stop spinning. He put his hand on his head hoping the lightheadedness would leave. Then he turned away and vomited. The whole world went black.

Sometime later the chatter of little children roused him. Two charcoal-skinned girls walked to him. Seeing their naked bodies, he kept his eyes half closed. Both of them dropped their baskets, and papaya leaves spilled out. The scent of wood smoke grew stronger as the girls tiptoed closer to him. He attempted to guess their ages.

The taller girl, about ten years old, knelt on his right side. Not wanting to frighten her, he kept as still as a chameleon and held his breath. The shorter girl moved to his opposite side and squatted. Behind the slits in his eyes, he watched as each girl took one of his hands.

They raised his arms straight above his head and held them there for a few seconds. Was it a form of resuscitation? Then they let his arms fall to the ground. No, the girls were playing a game with him. Then they shook their heads as if something was wrong. He remained limp as the little ones lifted and dropped his arms over and over again. Not wanting to frighten the children, he remained motionless.

He wanted them to know he was still alive, so he groaned and moved slowly. He hoped he hadn't scared them. The children jumped, backed away, and ran to their baskets, about twenty yards from him. The younger girl, about six, stopped and stared at him. He pressed his left elbow in the dirt and forced himself to a sitting position to assure them he was alive, but they ran off.

He tried to halt his tears. "Wait, please, don't go."

Looking toward the thick trees, he shuddered. He was alone.

Sometime later, the jabbering of three ebony-skinned men woke him. Seeing their spears, he played dead. He couldn't suppress the chills racing through his limbs. Perhaps if they thought he was injured, they wouldn't stab him. Taking in a deep breath, he tried to calm his racing heart. Through his half-open eyes, he watched the men circle him. He pressed his shaking arms into his sides.

They took up positions next to him and lightly pressed the tips of their spears into his chest. The sharp blade of one hit a nerve. He jerked and groaned.

As the natives leapt away from him, they shouted and prattled in another language. The youngest man positioned his spear again as if to strike, but the gray-haired man put his hand out. Then all of them jumped farther away, shrugged their shoulders, and shook their heads.

The oldest native, wearing torn shorts and a pointed straw hat, put his spear on the ground, knelt, and touched the injured man's bloodied face. The elderly man rubbed his reddened fingers together and slid backward. He extended his blood-covered hand for the others to see. They nodded and grinned.

Why were the nomads happy about his blood? He tried to hold back the shivers that ran up and down his spine. If they planned to drink his blood, he didn't have the strength to stop them, and he was outnumbered. Lifting his hand to his face, he hoped to convince them he was no threat.

They shook their heads and kept chattering. The oldest man pointed to the black smoke. The smallest native pinched his nose and wrinkled his forehead. The heavy-set one waved his hand in front of him as if to get rid of the stench.

The wounded man clutched his pounding head. Then he pressed his trembling hands into the ground and sat up.

The three natives sprinted away, halted thirty yards from him, and turned to look again at him. He lifted his blood-covered hands from his face. Seeing the men come closer again, he moaned. They kept grinning and pointing to his bloodied face. The injured man didn't like their excitement over his wounds.

They aimed their spears at the smoke-filled sky. The littlest native squatted a second time and touched the wounded man's face. The small man took his reddened palm away and held it up and showed it to the others. All three of the nomads beamed from ear to ear again, and this time revealed perfect sets of white teeth.

The bleeding man kept trembling. Were they cannibals or headhunters? He closed his eyes but couldn't relax for his heart pounded faster and faster. What did they intend to do with him?

Then all three warriors dashed off in the direction of the black smoke.

Not much time passed. The stench of greasy, sweaty bodies returned with more chatter. He heard the word, "toluuda" repeated several times. He shrugged and shook his head.

The cannibals made flapping motions with their arms and elbows as if flying and pointed to the smoke.

"Airplane." He whispered.

The oldest man turned to him. "Eeehhh-plan."

"Airplane."

The two younger natives repeated, "Eeeeehhh-plannnn."

"Airplane."

One warrior stood on each side of him. Reaching out, they gripped his upper arms and pulled the injured man to his feet. When they let go, his legs gave out, and he slumped to the ground. The men shook their heads. After three attempts to get him in an upright position, they left him on the ground. The heaviest native bent over and backed up close to him, while the gray-haired man and the smallest one slid him onto the lowered back.

As the hurt man bounced on the back of the robust fellow, dizziness overwhelmed the injured man, so he closed his eyes. The stench of diesel fuel, wood smoke, and body sweat nauseated him.

The heavy-set native stopped in front of the burned-out plane. The stout fellow bent his knees and shoved the wounded man to the ground. He groaned as he landed with a thump.

The oldest warrior pointed to the plane. Using his arms, he flapped them like wings and ran around in a circle. Then the other two natives joined him and waved their arms and elbows as if flying and ran around in circles.

"Airplane." Struggling to his knees, the injured man crawled closer to the burned-out craft. Perhaps the natives expected him to fly the plane away, but the plane was burned to a crisp, and he was hurt. Creeping closer on hands and knees, he stared at the blackened fuselage.

He passed out again.

A few minutes later, body stench roused him from his faint. He was on the native's back again, bouncing along the rough ground. Then he was lowered with a thud, next to the river.

His eyes grew round as the three men dashed away into the jungle. Why did they abandon him? He held his head in his hands. His shoulders quivered. Maybe, they were no longer interested in his blood, and he was better off. But how could he survive without provisions?

Devoid of hope, he stared into space. He wished the natives would come back for him. His head throbbed and his foot pounded. He rubbed his legs and arms to calm the shivers, but his bones ached.

How had he come to be with Stone Age people?

And who was he?

CHAPTER TWENTY-TWO

Liz was feeding Mercy at the table while Henry washed the dishes.

Henry put the last plate in the cupboard and turned to Liz. "My father is coming back."

"You can't hide. It's best to confront your problems."

"He will carry me away to his house."

"I won't allow him to take you."

"You can't stop it. My father will bring strong men to haul me off."

Liz couldn't imagine anyone carrying off Henry. She may be small, but she could carry a load of charcoal equal to her weight on her head, and she was a fighter, who would kick, bite, and scream.

"Let's talk about what to do when your father comes." Liz handed the baby to Henry.

Tying the baby to her back, Henry shook her head. "Sister Liz, there is nothing to do."

"We can pray and devise a course of action."

"What is a course of acting?"

"It's a plan we carry out"

"My father will never agree to any plan."

Liz suppressed a chuckle. "The plan is for us. What will we tell him?"

Henry snapped, "I'll tell him to go away and leave me alone."

"Let's talk about this tomorrow." Feeling her headache return, Liz rubbed her brow. "We need to find a way to stop him and make him leave you alone. With God all things are possible."

An hour later, Liz was surprised to see Pastor Ebenezer at her door. She invited him in and sat across from him. "What brings you here?"

"I need to speak to you about the Henry problem."

"What problem?"

"Henry's father came to see me last evening about her wedding."

Liz tilted her head toward the pastor. It was none of his business, but Henry was a member of his church, so everything that involved Henry was his concern.

The pastor lifted his hands as if pleading. "He asked me to escort Henry home for the marriage."

Henry came into the room carrying a glass of water for the pastor.

"Stay and sit down with us." Then Liz turned to the pastor. "Her father threw her out of the house. He let her fend for herself since she was twelve years old."

"That may be true, but she is bound by duty to go home and meet the man her father has chosen. He said the fiancé is a Christian."

"Why would my father find a Christian husband for me?" Henry's lips curled.

"I wondered about that myself." The pastor shrugged. "What do you think?"

Henry's lips trembled. "My father is lying and full of tricks. He wants me to go home so he can lock me in a room and force me to marry this man to collect the bride price for me. I am now an educated lady, so he will receive a lot more money."

"You are commanded by God to honor your parents and must go to your father."

"I will not go." She glared at him.

Liz's eyes widened at Henry's insolence. Liz had never seen such willfulness in an African lady, but Liz kept her mouth closed. All her other assistants had been complacent and obedient.

"You are a stubborn girl." The pastor said. "I'm telling you that you must go with your father."

"If you insist I return to him, I will run away where he will never find me." Henry handed the baby to Liz. "I do not want to cause you problems, so I will pack my bags and leave now."

Liz took a deep breath. "Pastor, it's best if we discuss this later. I'll walk you to the door."

He nodded and went with Liz. Turning back he said, "This is not over yet."

Henry put her hands on her hips. "It will never be over unless my father becomes a Christian. It's best I go far away and hide."

Shaking his head, the pastor left.

"Henry, I'm on your side and will do everything I can to help you. Stay here with me. Please don't run away. We'll figure something out together. Let's talk about the options and a possible plan of strategy."

"What is a stray-gee?"

"A strategy is a line of attack."

"My father is wicked, but we must not attack him."

"It's not a real attack. It's a plan for us."

"My plan is to run as fast as I can before my father comes back with the police or the witch doctors."

"If you run away, your father will find you again. What if I'm not there to help you?" Liz took a deep breath. "If you stay here with me, I'll do my best with God's help to support you."

"What's your plan?" Henry asked.

"If your father returns with the police and sorcerers, we should all go to the pastor's house. I have a little authority, but it's the men who run things. They respect the pastor as a male authority."

Henry moaned, "We can't go to the pastor because he is against me. He wants me to go back to my father's house."

"Maybe so, but the pastor is also against witchdoctors and sorcerers. If we keep taking your father and his sorcerers to the pastor's house, Pastor Ebenezer might be more sympathetic to you."

Henry nodded. "I'm willing to try it."

Liz stroked Mercy's cheek, and the child smiled. Then Liz tickled the baby's tummy. She lifted the giggling infant. Raising and lowering her, Liz made clucking noises to keep Mercy laughing.

"You are a soft-hearted and intelligent lady. Sometimes I wish you were stubborn like I am. I had to defend myself and stand up for what I believed. If I didn't, no one was there to help me. It's been me against the world, so I had to be tough."

"What about God?" Liz asked as she changed Mercy's diaper. "Shouldn't it be you and God against the world?"

"God's in my heart." Henry furrowed her brows. "Are you saying that if God's on our side, we can fight the world?"

"If the Lord wanted us to fight the evil in the world, with His help we can stand against it."

"I will try, but it won't be easy." Henry reached out, took the baby, and tied Mercy to her back.

Fighting evil is never easy. Liz loved Henry and understood why she had a hard time trusting people. Running away, rarely solved anything and often put off the inevitable.

If Henry was considered a child under the rule of her father, maybe he could force Henry to marry.

Liz shuddered. So how could she help Henry?

CHAPTER TWENTY-THREE

Chief Tiolare faced his village elders in his judgment hut. "My brothers and I found a stranger by the river."

"Where is he now?" A wrinkled man asked.

"He is near the grove of papaya trees." The chief stretched his legs out in front of him on his grass mat.

"Who do you think he is?" The ancient man asked.

The chief's head moved from one man to the next. "We do not know."

"I went with my brother." Sitou took a deep breath and puffed out his chest. "It seems to me as if this stranger was inside a big bird that flies in the sky. The iron bird caught fire and burned."

"Yes, I agree he was in that metal bird. When it caught fire, he jumped out of it." The heavy-set Doditu sharpened his cutlass on the stone.

Sitou smacked a fly. "The flames burned all of the stranger's skin off."

Several men moaned. Others covered their faces. A few clicked their tongues.

The oldest man stared ahead as if in a trance. "Have any of you ever seen someone who lost all of his skin?"

Shaking their heads, the village men frowned.

The chief shrugged. "Let's call him Kiki, which means no skin. I checked his blood, and it is red like ours, so he is one of us.

Doditu nodded. "His face is covered in bright flowing blood. Since he is injured and bleeds like we do, it is certain he is one of our people."

"The red blood confirms he is not a white man." Another man scowled. "Those fellows have blue blood. I saw a pale fellow in the city when I was young."

Sitou stared. "How do you know that white men have blue blood? Have you ever watched one of them bleed?"

"I never saw one bleeding." The man turned to the chief. "The canals that carry blood pop out of white people's limbs and look like blue strings on their white skin. I saw many of these on the skin of a white man in the city market."

Sitou shrugged. "Kiki does not speak our language so he must be from a faraway tribe."

"I agree." The chief nodded.

"It must have been a terrible fire to have burned his black skin off." Doditu looked around at the other men. "We searched inside the bird and there is nothing left."

Chief Tiolare took a breath. "I am concerned about his blue eyes."

"Blue eyes?" A village elder gasped and shook his fist. "We should all be worried. It means he is not human. He may be an evil spirit sent from the master of wickedness to torment us."

The village leader had to convince the men to let the stranger stay in their village. Several responses ran through the chief's mind, as he tried to formulate the best words to persuade them.

"I do not believe Kiki is a bad spirit. Ghosts do not bleed. He is bleeding red blood, like ours."

"Our leader is right. He is one of us because he has red blood." The ancient man said.

Chief Tiolare shrugged. "The fire in the iron bird could have been so powerful it turned his black eyes blue?"

The wrinkled elder pointed south. "Remember that lady back there, who kept falling into the fire because she had the brain sickness? The skin was burned off her face, but her eyes always stayed black."

"Have you men ever seen any of our people with blue eyes, anywhere?" The village leader asked.

Sitou shrugged. "I am more worried over his weapons than his blue eyes."

"Weapons?" Chief Tiolare raised his voice. "What are you talking about? Kiki has none."

"That's my point." Sitou shook his right fist. "Do you know any man who travels without any weapons?"

"I'm worried." Doditu put his cutlass on the ground. "If he is coming from a faraway village he carried weapons."

One of the elders turned to the chief. "Maybe they were burned up inside that bird? Did you and your brothers overlook the weapons? We must search again for them. He can have dangerous bludgeons and knives to harm us."

Chief Tiolare didn't like the way the conversation was going. He needed to convince them that Kiki was no threat to them, but how? "There is nothing inside that burned-out bird."

A village elder turned to the chief. "How did you find Kiki?"

"My granddaughters, Tio and Eilo, were picking leaves when they discovered him by the river. They came and told me right away. My brothers and I collected our hoes, machetes, spears, and slingshots."

"We carried our arsenal with us and headed down to the river." Sitou puffed out his chest. "We did not know if the stranger was an enemy of our people."

Chief Tiolare sensed no danger from Kiki and needed to take their attention away from the weapons, so he said. "He wears two sets of shoes, inner soft shoes and outer hard ones. His clothes are strange, and he is wearing more garments than I have ever seen on anyone. He may have come from a far away, cold village on the mountains in the north where it's so chilly it turns people's eyes blue."

Sitou frowned. "Do you believe that people from far away villages have blue eyes and wear many different clothes?"

"It's possible. I think the land goes farther than any of us ever traveled. Maybe it is very cold in that distant country." The chief shrugged his shoulders. "I've seen no signs of aggression from Kiki. When my granddaughters were alone with him, he did not harm them. He is injured, and we should bring him here to the village."

"We elders have not agreed to allow him to come here," the ancient man proclaimed.

The chief extended his palms up. "He is injured so we can't take any risks by leaving him. If the stranger's god is more powerful than our god and we do not help him, his deity may become angry and harm us."

"I agree." Sitou stood. "If his god is more powerful than ours, maybe he will bless us for helping the stranger."

"My granddaughters are very compliant. If they had seen or even collected his weapons, they would have told me. Kiki is hurt and has no weapons. Maybe he had them, but they were destroyed inside the bird. He is no threat to us."

Doditu shook his sharpened blade. "We do not know, do we? After all, he is a stranger. We know nothing about him. Maybe he came in that bird to hurt us."

Chief Tiolare had already decided to ask his daughter to watch Kiki. If Kiki's god was stronger than their gods, he'd bring wonderful blessings to their village. Give everyone good health, plenty of food, and productive animals. And maybe his daughter would get a new husband.

If they let the stranger die, his god might curse them.

CHAPTER TWENTY-FOUR

When he woke, the injured man still didn't remember who he was. He glanced at his wristwatch. He'd been by the river for five hours, since the natives had dashed off into the jungle. Longing for a drink of water, he licked his lips to moisten his dry mouth.

Lord God, please a little mercy.

The chatter of men coming from the trail gave him hope. Their voices grew louder. He moaned to alert the warriors he was still there. The same three, nearly-naked men, glistening with sweat, halted in front of him. They grabbed his arms and pulled him to stand. When they let go, the wounded man fell to the ground. The robust native bent over and the other two lifted the hurt man onto the heavy one's back.

As the native carried him through the bushes, the injured man tried to keep his eyes open to see where they were headed. But his eyelids snapped shut to cut off the dizziness. He wished his lightheadedness would go away.

The Stone Age men halted and the wounded man forced his weary eyes open. He was in the middle of a small settlement of ten thatched huts. Half-naked people surrounded him. He shuddered. Several hands shoved him off the native's back, and he landed with a thud on the ground.

A group of children came closer to him. He sat up and peered at the youngsters. All of them shrieked and ran off except the two little girls who wanted to hold his hands by the river. His bloody face must have terrified the others. Why weren't the two little girls afraid of it?

Then the girls, shaking their heads walked away but returned with a woman who handed him a calabash of water. He shuddered at the tiny particles of gray, black, and brown floating in the liquid. He needed a drink to ease his parched throat, but if he swallowed the contaminated water, he'd probably die of a fatal illness. He'd wait until he was offered safe drinking water. But what if no one ever gave him any?

The stench of the water gagged him. It smelled like it came from a swamp. Maybe it wasn't for drinking so he put his left hand in the calabash. The villagers screamed and shook their fists at him. Using his hand, he splashed water on his face. He put his left hand in the calabash a second time, and the people shrieked again. Then he used his right hand to finish washing his face, and no one shouted at him.

The same topless woman returned with a bucket of water and a larger calabash. The taller girl carried a clump of rough straw. The smaller child clutched a black, waxy-looking ball. What was it?

He tried to keep his eyes open to watch them. The woman knelt in the dirt next to him and took the ball from the little girl and rubbed it on the straw that the other girl handed her. Suds bubbled up. She swiped the straw on his face and stopped. He shivered from the stinging cuts.

Opening his eyes wide, he looked straight at the woman. She jumped up. Her hands shook and she dropped the sponge, soap, and calabash of water. He reached for the soap, but a wave of dizziness swept over him, and he fell back.

The hurt man looked up at the adults who surrounded him. His vision blurred, but he concentrated on focusing. The sun had already set and it was getting dark. The woman stepped close to him a second time and pulled on his shirt. He felt hot and overdressed, so he'd be glad to give them his shirt. He unbuttoned it and handed it to her. Without the shirt, he'd fit in better with the Stone Age people.

Maybe the woman wanted his filthy shirt to use as a rag, and he'd never see it again. Christ said if anyone asked for a shirt to give it to the one who asked.

His headache had eased up a bit but not the dizziness. The people seemed to float around in circles.

The woman threw the shirt over her arm, picked up the calabash, soap, and straw sponge, and then dashed off. The two little girls ran after her.

The hurt man held his painful face in his hands. Sticky, warm blood seeped from the wounds and ran down his fingers. Closing his eyes, he lay back and rested. Then he turned his head, vomited, and passed out.

When he recovered, it was almost dark. The woman came up to him and handed him a man's wallet, a small notepad, a pen, and a little

New Testament. She patted her chest and made motions as if she was pulling them out of a pocket.

He opened the pad and read the numbers, 90-61-91. What did they mean?

The billfold looked familiar, so he opened it. Taking out a HOW identity card and a driver's license, he scowled at the photos. He stared at the name, Andrew Thomas. His eyes widened, and he looked again at the pictures. Was he Andrew Thomas, a pilot for HOW?

He opened the small Testament. On the first page was written. "To Andrew Thomas, presented on his baptism." He read the words, "Took Jesus Christ as my Savior and Lord on April 10, 2000."

He flipped to the ribbon bookmark at Psalms 142:1 "I cry aloud to the Lord; I lift up my voice to the Lord for mercy." The first verse of Psalm 143 was also marked. "O Lord, hear my prayer, listen to my cry for mercy, and in your faithfulness and righteousness come to my relief."

Then he bowed his head. "Lord Jesus please help me. Be merciful, or give me a little mercy to get me through this. Amen."

He must be Andrew Thomas, so he'd start thinking of himself as Andrew until his mind cleared. Why else did he have that identification in his shirt pocket? He stuffed the pen, cards, and notebook into a pants pocket. Then he put the Testament in the opposite pocket. At least he had something to read when his dizziness left.

The oldest man Andrew had ever seen approached him. The wrinkled fellow chanted an eerie dirge. He wore yards of colorful stringed beads and a loincloth. He had shiny grease on his face and feathers sticking out of his hair. Was he the village medicine man?

He knelt by Andrew's head and stared into Andrew's eyes without flinching. He took a black glob of dripping slime that resembled feces but didn't smell as bad. Then he pressed clumps of it into Andrew's wounds.

Each application stung. Andrew shivered from the pain. He squeezed his tear-filled eyes shut.

After the medicine man left, Andrew rolled on his stomach, lifted himself to his knees, and stumbled to his feet. Staggering for a moment, he maintained his stance.

He bowed his head and closed his eyes. "Lord, Jesus. Give me favor with these people. Use them to help me. Protect me from whatever evil is here. Amen."

Looking at the men who had found him and the little girls, he asked. "Where am I? What is the name of this place?"

Everyone shrugged.

Squatting, Andrew rubbed his painful, swollen foot. Then he lay back on the mat. His head pounded and the dizziness was worse. It looked like the people spun around in circles. The thatched homes rose up and down as trees lifted toward the sky.

Then everything went black.

CHAPTER TWENTY-FIVE

Andrew swallowed several times to wet his dry mouth, but his throat still burned. He turned to the large cooking pot that sat over the fire, put his hand to his lips, and mimicked drinking.

A woman dipped a plastic cup into the black kettle and poured the fluid into a calabash. Handing it to Andrew, she smiled a huge toothless grin.

He took a sip of the warm drink and gagged. It was the foulest beverage he'd ever put to his lips, but the steaming alcohol soothed his parched throat and lessened his thirst. The repulsive drink had been boiling, so it wouldn't harbor any dangerous sicknesses. At first he couldn't tell what the brown flecks were that floated in the last remaining swallows, so he stopped drinking. Then he spotted the stalks of millet near the fire and suspected the husks were what floated near the bottom.

The quarter moon offered a little light, but the four campfires lit up the dark-skinned figures enough for him to see them coming and going.

Maybe the millet beer had medicinal properties for the pain in his head, joints, and limbs eased up a bit, but he'd give anything for a glass of cool water.

The taller girl took his calabash and refilled it. She curtsied and handed it to him. The smaller girl gave him several handfuls of roasted peanuts in the shells. The smiling children were the only ones who didn't appear to be afraid of him.

"Thank you."

The taller girl opened her mouth wide. "Tuk yu."

Andrew lifted his tongue to the bottom of his upper teeth and pulled it back to show them how to say it. "Thank you."

"Tunk yu."

Thank you, Jesus. I'm alive and have food and drink. Andrew shelled the peanuts and munched on them. Maybe it was the only food the natives had to give him.

Rubbing his head, he tried to recall what food he'd eaten earlier that day. When was the last time he'd eaten and where was it?

The shorter girl brought him a ball of white dough in a calabash and red sauce in a small plastic bowl. It smelled like tomato gravy. She curtsied as she handed the dishes to him

He glanced at a group of men eating with their fingers. So Andrew broke off a bite of the paste and dipped it in the red sauce before popping it into his mouth. He coughed, choked, and coughed again.

Grabbing a calabash, the taller girl ran and dipped water out of a large clay jar. She handed it to him. Andrew shook his head and closed his eyes. As thirsty as he was, he couldn't bring himself to drink the dirty water.

The child went to the women stirring millet beer in large tubs. The girl dipped out a goblet of the boiling alcohol and brought it to him.

He sipped the pink liquid. The hot drink helped the globs of the heavy white clay go down. His stomach stopped growling. Perhaps the little fluid and food would sustain him.

As he finished eating, rain drops hit his naked chest. He held the container forward for rain to drip into it. As the drizzle increased to a heavy downfall, it filled the bowl and drenched Andrew. Gulping down the water, he sent a prayer of thanksgiving to the Lord.

Men and women ran into the thatched huts while Andrew shivered under the chilly downpour. Sitting in the middle of the compound, he looked around at the abandoned village. Everyone had left him in the storm. He hunched over, trying to keep as dry as possible while the rain pounded on him.

The two little girls stepped out of a thatched dwelling and ran to him. They grabbed his arms and pulled him to his feet. He hopped on his good foot and went with them inside one of the primitive structures.

The woman, most likely the girls' mother, bowed as he entered the shelter. She had beautiful white teeth, and he recognized her as the one who tried to give him a sponge bath. She stepped back and curtsied as if he was royalty.

Andrew plopped down in front of the small fire. The cool, rainy shower had soaked him, and he was chilled to the bone. He slumped closer to the glowing embers, but he couldn't stop trembling.

The topless woman spread a mat on the packed earth floor next to him, and she pointed to it. What did she want?

Since the thatched carpet was drier than the floor, he moved to it. Wood smoke filled the tiny shelter and stung his eyes. Squeezing his eyelids shut to avoid the thick smoke, he massaged his painful head. Every bone in his body throbbed. Still wearing his soaked trousers, he curled into a fetal position as close to the fire as possible. Tears ran down his cheeks.

Lord Jesus, please mercy.

A blanket landed on his shaking body. The woman stood over him and opened the cloth wider to cover him. The small act of thoughtfulness made him cry again before falling asleep.

Later in the night, snoring woke Andrew. He squinted in the darkness. By the light of the campfire, he saw two ebony-skinned men, one sleeping on each side of him.

Andrew was a prisoner.

CHAPTER TWENTY-SIX

Seeing the three visitors in her doorway, Liz took a deep breath. Then she snapped her mouth closed and remembered her manners. She stepped aside and pointed toward the living room. "Please go in and have a seat. Would you like coffee, tea or water?"

"Nothing, thank you. We're here on business." The older gentleman in a brown suit extended his hand. "I'm Andrew's boss, Larry Sloan, director of the Health Organization for the World. Are you Miss Elizabeth Connor?"

Her heart beat faster and her voice wobbled, "Yes."

The stocky man, wearing a button-down shirt and jeans, shook her hand. "I'm Stan, a helicopter pilot with HOW. Andrew's a good friend and I work with him."

"I'm Lieutenant Brown from the US Embassy." The marine nodded.

Liz's stomach churned. Something awful had happened to Andrew. In Africa, the larger the group to bring news represented the size of the problem. Three officials meant they brought a distressing report. Was Andrew dead? No, he couldn't be. She swallowed to slow her racing heart and brace herself at the inevitable bad news.

Her brows furrowed at their grim faces. "Is something wrong with Andrew?"

Stan removed his baseball cap. "Andrew asked us to inform you if he was ever in an accident."

Liz slumped in the chair. "Is he... Is he..."

"We don't know. There was an accident." Mr. Sloan opened his briefcase and took out a map. "Andrew was flying to the village of Magaou, which is on the northeast border of Tamago. It neighbors Genta and Norgia. His plane exploded."

Tears filled her eyes. Liz put her hand on her fluttering heart. "No, I can't believe it."

Lieutenant Brown stood and touched her shoulder. "Are you alright? Can I bring you a glass of water?"

She sniffed and shook her head.

A few moments later, Henry came into the room carrying four glasses of water on a tray. She put the platter on the coffee table and handed each of them a drink.

"I'm sorry to tell you, there's no sign of him." Mr. Sloan moved the map toward Liz and pointed. "The plane crashed here. Andrew's aircraft was burned to a crisp."

With the back of her hand, she brushed the tears off her cheek. "Couldn't Andrew have climbed out of the aircraft before the fire?"

"Several teams have investigated the site of the crash. Some of us thought he might have left the plane before it burned." Lieutenant Brown shook his head. "But we've searched the surrounding area extensively. He is nowhere in the vicinity."

"What if he landed because of a mechanical problem, ran to get help, and later the plane exploded. That would account for his absence at the crash. Perhaps he's on his way to a town to get transportation." Liz sniffed.

The men looked at each other and shook their heads.

"Miss Connor, we don't think that's what happened." Mr. Sloan grimaced. "We've checked out the closest villages, twenty miles from the crash. Andrew was not seen in any of them."

Liz took several deep breaths. "Did … did … you find his burned body?"

"There wasn't any charred body inside the plane. The door was open, but passing natives may have gone inside of it."

"If local people could enter, maybe they carried Andrew somewhere, since you didn't find a corpse."

"We'd all like to see Andrew alive, but we don't think that happened." Stan frowned.

Mr. Sloan closed his briefcase. "There's more. Andrew's plane may have been tampered with in the airport before he left."

Liz asked, "Who would do that and why?"

"We don't know. Andrew always checked out his plane. He departed early Monday morning and an hour later, he crashed."

"That was three days ago."

"If there were no burned remains," Lieutenant Brown sighed, "he must have gotten out of the aircraft, but if so, where is he?"

"If he did survive," Stan grimaced. "Maybe some locals carried Andrew away from the crash site."

"If someone took him, they must want him to fly one of their planes." Liz brightened. "Andrew flew for the national airlines during the military coup. Perhaps opposition parties kidnapped Andrew to fly them somewhere."

"If that's true, then why didn't someone take him at the airport? Why blow up a perfectly good plane and risk killing the pilot?" Mr. Sloan folded the map.

Liz put her hand on her heart. "I believe he is alive and trying to find help."

"Don't get your hopes up." Mr. Sloan shook his head. "There have been border conflicts with several groups in that region and the area is dangerous."

The marine looked at his watch and stood. "Miss Connor that is all the information we have. We will keep you informed if we hear any news."

Liz's vision blurred as tears ran down her cheeks. "Thank you for coming."

Stan nodded at Liz, "I'm free today and plan to return to the site of the crash. Maybe my buddy and I can find something that was overlooked in the other searches."

With shaking hands, she took the business cards the men handed her. As they turned away from her home, Liz's heart squeezed. Then she shuddered.

Andrew can't be dead, but what if he was?

CHAPTER TWENTY-SEVEN

Andrew rubbed his throbbing head and wished the pain and dizziness would leave. His foot hurt just as badly.

He remembered the plane crash, but where had he been going? Looking around the primitive dwellings, he wondered where his home was and if he'd ever find it. The primitive iron hoes and blackened copper pots proved he'd crashed in a Stone Age village. Thank God the people were friendly.

The woman who had to be the mother of the two girls called, "Tio." She handed the taller child a large, red bowl. Then she called, "Eilo" and gave the smaller girl a calabash.

He had heard others calling the older girl "Tio." People always addressed the younger one as "Eilo." Were those their names? Even if they weren't, he'd think of them that way.

Tio carried the bowl of corn meal mush to Andrew and curtsied. Eilo brought him tomato sauce with a fish tail. Then she curtsied, and so did the mother who handed him a warm millet beer in another calabash.

He pinched off a bite of mush and dipped it in the sauce. Andrew couldn't decide what was worse, the alcoholic drink or the food, but he was grateful for both. Thirty minutes after eating and drinking, his dizziness had reduced.

A flock of scrawny chickens pecked at the ground. Three black goats pulled cloth from the single line strung between two acacia trees. Andrew felt like the mangy dog covered in flies that rested in the dirt and ashes.

An ancient woman handed him another calabash of millet beer. She gave him a toothless grin and nodded with vigor. Andrew averted his gaze from the topless lady's chest. The warriors didn't seem to be bothered by the women's nakedness, so he tried to ignore it, too.

Several ladies poured fresh milk in a large pot and stirred it over the fire. They added powders and herbs which made it smell like burnt rubber. After lining a small basket with a cloth, they put the hot liquid in it. The milk separated so the whey ran off. It looked like a form of cheese. A few old women unwrapped the cylinders and coated them with a dark orange-colored surface. They gave these to the younger ladies, who layered them in baskets. If it was cheese, why didn't anyone ever eat it?

Several ladies cooked food or beer while others scrubbed clothes in large tubs. Young girls stained little girls' hands and feet with red and black. Looking around, he wondered why he'd been left alone in the village with only women and children.

His head pounded again, so he stretched out on his mat.

When the sun set, he was relieved to see the men return. He nodded to them as they took their places around the campfires and waited for their evening meal. Andrew was always left alone. The men ate together but apart from Andrew, as if he was contagious.

Later that night, like other nights, Tio and Eilo pulled him toward the hut. If he put weight on his swollen ankle, unbearable pain ran up and down his leg, so he hopped on his good foot.

Andrew stared up at the sky.

Help me get home. But where is it?

***

When a groggy Andrew woke the next morning, his guards were gone. Hopping out of the hut on his good leg, he went to the big pot of water boiling over the campfire. He waved at the girls' mother and mimicked drinking. Taking a plastic cup, he dipped out hot water and lifted the cup to his lips. The villagers screamed and shook their fists. What was wrong with the water? If it was poison surely someone would have knocked the cup out of his hand.

The woman who had been taking care of him furrowed her brows and scowled. She rubbed her arms and chest as if she was bathing.

Andrew kept sipping the boiled liquid, even though it tasted and smelled like swamp water.

An older woman brought a bucket. She dipped cups of water out of the cooking pot to fill it. Then she carried it to Andrew and handed him a yellow ball of soap, the size of a golf ball, and a straw sponge. She rubbed her arms as if she washed herself and pointed beyond the village and into the bush.

Andrew glanced at his filthy chest. Then he stared down at the pail of scalding water and shook his head. The woman pointed to a large clay jar, so he hopped over to it. A calabash floated on top of the cool water. Using the broken gourd for dipping, Andrew added the cold liquid to his own bucket until the water was no longer red-hot.

Just to hear his own voice, he spoke out loud. "Do you want me to go that way and bathe?" Andrew pointed beyond the village and pantomimed bathing.

The women nodded, so he carried the filled pail, waxy ball, and straw outside the village and searched for a large, tall clump of grasses to use as cover.

The giggles of Tio and Eilo followed him. He hoped the girls didn't stay and watch him bathe. Maybe he should ask for one of the men's loincloths before he undressed, but only the elderly men wore them, and he'd never seen a man without the garment. He stopped and turned slightly. With his arm he made a sweeping go-away motion to the laughing girls, but they kept coming.

He stepped behind a thick hedge and set the bucket down. The girls came around the shrubs with him and handed him a plastic cup, a pair of old flip-flops, and a cloth. Then they ran off.

That had been simple. Maybe he could bathe alone and in peace.

He had abandoned his right shoe, when his foot started swelling. Unlacing his left one, he leaned against the tree and replaced the shoe with a flip-flop.

Andrew took off his filthy pants and remaining sock. As he stepped out of his undershorts, the bushes swished behind him. Blushing, he kept his back to the movement. Naked under the sun and out in the wilderness, he had never felt so vulnerable.

He lifted cup after cup of water and poured it over his body. Then he lathered up the soap and scrubbed away the filth. The suds and water loosened dried blood and the medicine man's concoction from his face. Glancing down at his foamy torso, he scraped away filthy bubbles of soap covering the black and blue blotches on his skin. He took several deep breaths and checked if his ribs were fractured. They didn't seem to be broken. *Thank God.* He poured more water over him with the plastic goblet. Except for the scent of the local soap that smelled like cooking grease, he felt clean.

Loud chattering and giggling reached his ears. He turned his head to look behind but saw nothing. So he finished rinsing off the soap with more cups of water.

A few minutes later, the laughter started again. He'd been surprised the girls had stayed to watch him bathe, but in the village there had been no privacy. He swiveled his head to the side to see the girls, who pointed with their index fingers at his buttocks. They jabbered and waved their arms frantically back and forth toward his backside. What was wrong?

Andrew twisted his neck farther back and saw an isolated glob of soapsuds clinging to his derriere. The girls kept pointing toward it. He left the soapsuds and snatched the cloth from the bushes. After wrapping it around him, he turned and growled loudly. He hopped toward the moving bushes. The laughing girls squealed and ran away. Andrew put the soap, straw sponge, plastic cup, and his shoes into the bucket. He picked up his clothes and limped back to the settlement.

The girls were chattering on and on in their language to the man whom Andrew assumed to be the leader. Tio and Eilo pointed to their buttocks and the bar of soap. Were they reporting to the village leader that he hadn't rinsed off all the soap? The chief scowled and clicked his tongue. Then he waved the girls away.

The girl's mother reached for Andrew's clothes, which he had wadded up into a ball and held in his left arm. He wondered what had happened to his shirt and hadn't seen anyone using it for a rag. A few minutes later, the woman brought his clean, folded shirt. She curtsied African-style with one leg back and a little dip of her knees.

Andrew took the garment and smiled. "Thank you."

Why would a strange woman wash and fold his shirt? The thoughtful gesture made his heart squeeze with guilt for thinking someone had kept it. He ran his fingers over his laundered garment and then swiped a tear off his cheek. After slipping the clean shirt on, he buttoned it. He pressed his palms down over his chest and tugged his shirt over the wrap-around skirt he'd tied around his waist.

Bathed and in clean, dry clothes, he would have felt better if the exertion of the walk and bath hadn't fatigued him. The pain in his head was worse and the dizziness had returned. So he sat down on the mat by the cooking fire.

Maybe Andrew should have camped by the burned-out aircraft, until he regained his strength to head home, but where was home? Could he get there without the plane? Or did he need the aircraft to travel home?

Or would he be with the smiling natives forever?

CHAPTER TWENTY-EIGHT

After sprinkling cinnamon sugar over her French toast in the frying pan, Liz covered it with a lid.

She turned to Henry, "My breakfast is almost ready. Have you prepared your corn meal?"

The girl brought her bowl to the table and sat down while Liz transferred her own breakfast to a plate.

When Henry saw the French toast, she wrinkled her nose. "You white people love to eat sweet food. The missionary who helped me with my classes ate sugary doughnuts every morning."

Liz sat down. "Sometimes I eat peanut butter bread for breakfast and other times scrambled eggs and toast or yogurt. I only put a small spoon of sugar on my French toast. There are people who pour syrup on it."

"The missionary used to do that, and then she got sick and left Africa." Henry finished her mush. "Can't you get a disease like diabetes by eating too much sugar?"

"It's complicated."

"You should take care. We don't have medicine for diabetes in our country."

After breakfast, Henry tied Mercy to her back and followed Liz to the taxi station.

Liz hired a vehicle to Taaluta. When they reached the village, the local pastor brought a table. Henry set out the bottles of medicine.

Patients arrived and handed their health cards to Liz. The first woman brought an emaciated child. The mother sat down and put the skeleton-like boy on her lap. She took out a rag and wiped her son's dirty face.

All the tree branches were too high, so Liz couldn't attach the scale. She turned to the pastor. "I need to hang this so it is eye level."

"There's a nail in the wall of the church. Follow me and I will show you."

The mothers carried their babies into the church and stopped behind the pastor. He pointed to the wall.

Liz shook her head. "A tiny nail on the wall will not support the weight of a baby."

The pastor pointed up at a beam in the ceiling. "That is strong."

"I'm sure it'll hold the weight of the heaviest child here today, but how could we read the scale if it was tied six feet up in the air?"

"We can push the offering table under it and stand on it. I will show you." He shoved the table under the lowest beam and put a wooden chair next to it. Then he climbed on the chair and up onto the table. "Hand me the rope, and I'll fasten it for you."

After he tied the scale to the beam, he pulled the balance to confirm the knot held well. "See, it works fine."

Liz shuddered. People would get the wrong impression if she weighed infants from ceiling beams, but the pastor had gone to so much trouble.

"Let's start work." He jumped off the table.

She climbed up on the table and looked down at Henry, who handed her the child to be weighed. When Liz put the boy in the scale, she read the weight at eye-level.

Liz called to the mother. "How old is your baby?"

"He is one year."

"Your boy only weighs five kilograms. He is too lean. What food does he eat?"

"He eats corn meal mush."

"His blood is weak. Can you add an egg and a tablespoon of red oil to the gruel every day?"

"I will try, but can't you give me medicine to make him fat?"

"The only foods to make him better are those rich in protein like eggs, meat, fish, green leafy vegetables and fried bean cakes."

Based on the weight, Liz calculated the dosage for a malarial treatment. After handing it to the mother, she counted out worm pills and multivitamins for the child.

Another woman brought her little son, who appeared to be about three-years old. He was too large to fit in the trousers to be weighed.

Most children enjoyed swinging in the air like Tarzan, so Liz leaned over to speak to the child. "You look like a brave little boy. Can you hold onto this rope and step off the table? Your mommy will catch you."

Henry frowned but handed the child to Liz. "You shouldn't do this. This is too dangerous."

"It's not dangerous. It only looks that way."

"It's the same thing. If it looks dangerous, the people will think it is."

"We need to weigh the child. How else can I calculate the dosage for the treatment? Please explain to the mother what we are doing. Stand to the right of the mother and catch the boy if she doesn't."

Henry spoke to the woman and her son.

Liz kept her hand close to the child as he grabbed the rope and stepped off the table. Screams filled the church. Liz glanced around at the toddlers and their mothers running out of the sanctuary and down the trail.

The mother and Henry had caught the child and set him on the floor.

"What happened?" Liz frowned at the empty sanctuary. "Why did the children run away?"

The pastor shook his head. "Everyone thought you were going to push children off the table. The mothers yelled that you expected their children to swing in the air like gorillas."

"Our little ones are tied to their mothers' backs." Henry shook her head. "They are not swingers."

Liz sunk down on a nearby pew. "Our children sit on seats and glide back and forth. They hang from branches or bars and swing all the time because they enjoy gymnastics."

"Our children are not used to swinging around like monkeys from vines." Henry put her hands on her hips.

Liz bit her lip. "Is there any way to call the mothers back?"

The pastor shrugged. "They're too terrified. You'll not do any more work today. After you leave, I'll talk to the mothers. Maybe the next time you come, they'll be willing to try again."

"We need a better spot to attach the scale so it doesn't look frightening." Liz sighed. "It must be able to move freely without knocking into a wall or tree trunk."

Henry answered. "I can hold it."

"You are too short, but you've given me an idea." Liz started packing up her medications. "If I tied the scale to a pole and two people held it, they can stand on chairs. That might be the right height to read the weight." She wrinkled her brow. "I have a shovel at home. The long handle would support the scale."

"If we take a shovel with us every day to our clinics, people might get the wrong impression." Henry frowned.

"Maybe someone locally has a solid pole we can borrow." Liz furrowed her brow.

"Everyone has a hoe."

"That's a great idea. Thank you Henry."

Liz was beginning to appreciate her assistant's unique suggestions.

***

As they approached the house, Liz turned to Henry. "Thank God Stan is here. Maybe he is bringing good news." Liz shook Stan's hand. "Come inside and have a seat while I get the coffee."

After giving Stan a steaming mug, Liz sat facing him. "I've been praying for news."

"Gary, another ONCHO pilot, and I visited the site of the crash three different times to look for clues, but there's no trace of Andrew. The storms obliterated all the signs, and without footprints leading anywhere, I'm not sure how to proceed."

Liz slumped back in the chair. She blinked quickly to suppress her tears.

Stan patted her hand. "We need to accept the fact he may be gone."

Tears ran down Liz's cheeks as she shook her head. Andrew wasn't dead. She'd have felt his absence in her heart. Taking a deep breath, Liz sniffed. "I can't do that."

"What do natives do with the dead? Do they bury the body?"

"I don't think a local inhabitant would bury a stranger. They are too superstitious."

"If they wouldn't bury outsiders, what would they do with bodies?"

Her heart beat faster. No, she couldn't think about it. She needed to convince him Andrew was alive. Taking a gulp of air, Liz tried to sound positive. "Please don't give up." Liz wiped away the tears on her face.

"We've gone inside the burned-out aircraft several times. During the last search, we found Andrew's keys to his truck and his apartment which means he left the plane in a hurry or was carried out of it by others. If he had been able to leave under his own power, he would have taken his bags."

"If the plane was on fire, Andrew may only have concentrated on getting out of it. Isn't it a good sign you didn't find a charred body? Doesn't that prove he is alive?"

"Not necessarily, he could have been carried out of the plane." Stan sipped on his coffee. "Andrew's carry-on bag was a scorched clump of melted plastic and metal buckles, and the first aid kit was ruined beyond repair."

Liz sniffed. "Maybe the plane was about to explode, and Andrew leaped out of it with only the clothes on his back, and he didn't have time to take anything?"

"Can someone survive in the jungle without drinking water or food?" Stan asked.

"The Lord will take care of Andrew. He is a child of God."

"He's a good Christian, but many good Christians die." Stan puckered his brow. "We looked more closely at the safety belt. It was unbuckled with the metal clasps dangling on each side of his seat. We don't know if Andrew unfastened it or someone else did."

Liz yelled. "That's a good sign!"

"What's good about an unfastened seatbelt?"

"Only Andrew could have opened it. There are no seatbelts in public taxis. One time I saw a missionary fasten one around an African. When the car stopped to let the man out, the villager lifted his machete to cut the belt because he didn't know how to unfasten it. This proves Andrew had to be alive and conscious to unlatch the seatbelt."

"None of this is a guarantee that he's alive today. Suppose he unfastened the buckle, was carried out, and then died. Or what if the explosion injured him after he got out of the plane? What would an African do with him, or where would a villager take him?"

"They'd take him to their home."

"We checked all the surrounding villages. There's no sign of Andrew. Face reality, Liz. Andrew may be dead."

Liz blinked several times hoping to stop the tears. Her heart throbbed with turmoil. Andrew wasn't dead. Gulping down a sob, she had to convince Stan to keep searching for Andrew.

"Your seatbelt theory has possibilities. Since we haven't found his body, we'll keep looking for him."

She sighed in relief and dried her eyes. As long as they kept searching there was hope.

Stan patted her arm. "We'll go back and look through a wider area."

Through tears she nodded. "Thank you."

But what if a more extensive search was inconclusive?

Would they give up?

CHAPTER TWENTY-NINE

Chief Tiolare motioned with his hands for the elders to enter his judgment hut. Sitting down, he counted the men. All were present, so he began. "Is anyone worried about Kiki being a threat to us?"

Doditu shook his head. "We left him all day alone with the women and children. None of our females are afraid of him, and he never bothered them or took away their food. He has shown no signs of aggression."

"He appears stronger and has not vomited or passed out." Sitou shrugged. "He did not get angry when we excluded him from the men's circle."

The chief nodded. "He doesn't object that we men eat before he does."

"I called off the guard in Milo's hut at night, but I've been watching him." Doditu smacked a mosquito. "He's made no effort to return to the iron bird to get any weapons he may have hidden nearby."

The village leader still needed to persuade his men that Kiki posed no threat. The chief even liked Kiki. Chief Tiolare wanted his people to support and care for the injured man, but he had to convince them.

"His weapons were destroyed, and he has not tried to make more of them." The chief sighed. "Kiki seemed annoyed and raised his voice when my granddaughters watched him bathe, but he never struck the girls and he should have. We must stop thinking of him as hostile."

"It was improper of the girls to watch him bathe." The oldest man grimaced.

"Yes, I shouted at them for that, but they wanted to see if he was white all over his body." The chief shrugged. "I've never heard of a man losing all of his skin."

"Neither have we. Was his skin burned completely off?"

"Yes." Chief Tiolare let out a ragged breath. "The girls said all his black skin is gone."

The chief's heart raced and he swallowed several times to calm himself. Kiki's clothes had not even been scorched, so the skin under his clothes should have been black, but it was white. It could only mean Kiki was a white man. The chief's heart pounded faster. If he was a white man why didn't Kiki's people come to take him home? Chief Tiolare would keep his own counsel.

The oldest man rubbed his swollen, arthritic knees. "Let's give him more freedom among our people. We'll allow him to eat with us."

"No, he must eat separately since he is from a tribe we don't know." Doditu raised his voice. "We should keep watching him. He might be a spy waiting for the right time."

"Right time for what?" The chief asked.

"The Houtajiji people have tried for years to steal our cattle. Kiki has no tribal markings, so we do not know where he is from. He might be one of their warriors who came here to take away our herds."

"If that is true, why hasn't he made any effort to learn more of our people?" The chief scowled.

"He might be lingering to gather as much information as possible."

"I do not think so." The chief chuckled, "They should have sent a spy who spoke our language and asked questions about the cattle."

"I've wondered why he hasn't asked about our cows or the rest of the herds." The oldest man took a deep breath. "If he is not a spy, who is he?"

Doditu sighed. "We must learn why he came here."

"Maybe he was headed to another place but got lost. Unless he learns our language, we may never know." The chief glanced at his elders. "I sent scouts to search for new pastureland for our herds, and they brought the report last evening."

"That was wise." Sitou nodded. "Our cows need fresh grasses."

"What should we do with Kiki when we move to a new place? We do not know his people." The oldest man frowned. "If he is lost, why hasn't he made an effort to leave and look for his family?"

"How can he leave?" Sitou shrugged. "He can hardly walk."

"Maybe he doesn't know how to get home." The chief looked out of the hut toward the mat where the white man sat.

"That is my point exactly." Doditu scowled. "If he is lost, how can we help him get home? We don't know the way."

"We could allow him to live with us." The chief smiled.

"What if his brothers are searching for him?" Sitou asked. "If they all came here it might be dangerous."

The eldest man shook his head. "Our ancestor spirits and gods would not be pleased with us if we abandoned a helpless man alone in the bush, especially when he has done us no harm."

"So far he hasn't hurt us, but he could be waiting for the right time." Doditu crossed his arms. "We must take him back to his bird and leave him there. Then we can go on to the new pasturelands without him."

"He needs food, water, and shelter and could never live in a burned out carcass." Chief Tiolare lifted his hands in supplication. "Besides, no man can survive without a woman to chop firewood, cook food, and fetch water."

"That's true, and we cannot leave one of our ladies alone with him to do these chores because our women are respectable."

"He needs extra help because of his sick foot. The limb is large and the disease is powerful." The chief's youngest brother shrugged.

Chief Tiolare looked from one elder to the next. "Our cows have eaten all the grasses and we can no longer stay here. To survive we must move but cannot leave Kiki. He must come with us. Do you men agree to this action?"

Each of them nodded. Then they left the judgment hut.

The chief went to his daughter, Milo, who handed him two plates of rice with okra gravy. He carried the food and sat on the mat with Kiki. Smiling, the village leader handed one plate to Kiki and then started eating with his fingers from the other one.

Tio brought two calabashes of the local brew. She knelt in the dirt and bowed to her grandfather with her head nearly touching the ground. Then she handed the gourds to the men, who sipped the alcohol between mouthfuls of mush.

When they were finished, the chief pointed. "Kiki."

Andrew nodded and put his hand on his chest. "Kiki."

The chief pointed to the setting sun. Then he raised and lowered his hands hoping to indicate the passing of the night.

Andrew pressed his palms together and put his head on them and closed his eyes. Then he opened his eyes and smiled at the chief.

Chief Tiolare nodded and put his palms flat in front of him and moved them forward one after the other as if walking. He tapped Kiki's shoulder and motioned for him to come. The chief placed his palms open and face down, one after the other again.

Then the chief stood and waved everyone closer. "We must avoid the great Foulunda people. If they see our herds, they might try to steal them. We will leave early tomorrow morning." He stopped and pointed. "Kiki will come with us."

Doditu approached the chief. "What if Kiki cannot walk and keep up with the rest of us? We men cannot carry him and supervise our herds."

The village leader went to his daughter. "If Kiki can't keep up on the trail, will you take care of him?"

"Yes, he is a tender man. Since he's been staying with us each night in our shelter, he hasn't shown any hostility. If this is what you wish, I am happy to obey."

"It is what I want."

Milo whispered, "Do not worry, father. A few of the women will travel with me and watch over him."

"Kiki cannot survive alone in the bush." The chief patted his daughter's arm. "We do not want his death on our hands."

"I understand." Milo's eyes widened. "That would anger Kiki's god. If his divinity is bigger than ours, his god might bring disaster to us."

The chief turned to the villagers and announced. "The neighboring region will be safer for our people. The scouts informed me there are tribal conflicts, so we will travel around them. No one will object to us journeying through the land if we do it quickly. We must keep watch on our herds and not allow them to eat the local crops. That might cause a war." Chief Tiolare glanced at the women. "We will dismantle our village and carry everything with us to our new home."

Then Chief Tiolare walked to his hut and went inside of it. He came out carrying a wooden cane. "I will give Kiki my great grandfather's walking stick." He handed the cane to Kiki, who rubbed his hands over the exquisite carvings that ran up and down the length of the polished wood. The chief helped Kiki stand to test his weight on the hand-carved cane.

Kiki shook the old man's hand. "Thank you."

The chief nodded. "Tunk you."

CHAPTER THIRTY

The following Sunday morning, Liz was surprised to find Mrs. Isaiah seated in the women's section of the village church. Liz and Henry took their own seats in the third row from the back.

After the service, Liz approached the seamstress. "It's good to see you. Did you travel here to attend the service?"

"No." Mrs. Isaiah smiled at the baby in Liz's arms. "You didn't collect your dress at my shop, so I wanted to bring it."

"Please come to my house so we can talk." Liz handed Mercy to Henry, who tied her to her back.

They walked single-file down the trail.

At the house, Liz unlocked the door. "Henry, can you prepare tea and biscuits?"

Mrs. Isaiah asked, "May I hold the baby?"

Henry gave Mercy to Mrs. Isaiah, who sat and held the baby on her lap.

When Henry brought a tray, Liz served the refreshments. "I'm sorry I didn't come yesterday to collect my dress."

"They announced it in my church."

"What?"

"Brother Andrew's plane crashed. I remembered him because he attended our service. I wanted to come and offer my condolences."

"Condolences!" Liz gasped. "What are you talking about?"

"They announced he died in the fire."

Liz felt the blood leave her face. Why would they say he was dead when the men were still searching for him, or had they stopped looking? With the back of her hand, she wiped the sweat that beaded on her forehead, before it ran down her face.

"I appreciate your concern, but Brother Andrew isn't dead."

"The plane exploded, and they never found his body."

"I believe in my heart," Liz put her hand on her chest, "that Brother Andrew is alive. I think he got out of the plane before it caught fire."

Mrs. Isaiah's gaze clouded. "This is confusing to me."

"I believe Brother Andrew is still alive."

"How? Are you saying that you have faith to believe?"

"Yes, I do, and I am sorry I didn't pick up my dress, but I wanted to stay home in case members of the search team brought news of him."

"I thought you were in mourning and unable to travel."

Liz's voice wobbled, "I'm not in mourning."

"I see that now. You have faith to believe a man can survive an explosion."

Henry brought a cup of soy milk and set it on the coffee table.

Liz said. "Give Mercy to me and I'll feed her."

Mrs. Isaiah asked. "May I feed her?"

"Yes, of course. Put Mercy in the crook of your arm and keep her head high." Liz handed a spoon to the seamstress. "Unlike bottle-fed babies, she doesn't need to be burped. Use the spoon and let her sip slowly. I've had her almost two months, and she enjoys being held and fed like this."

Mrs. Isaiah picked up the spoon and dipped it in the milk. "I like holding her and love the way she feels in my arms."

Mercy, as always, grinned when she was drinking her milk. Tears filled Mrs. Isaiah's eyes. "The baby smiled at me."

"She's an agreeable and happy infant."

After Mercy had finished her milk, her eyelids closed. Mrs. Isaiah sighed. "May I put her to my back?"

Liz nodded.

Mrs. Isaiah stood and tied the baby to her. Then she gently rocked back and forth and reached behind her to pat the child. When Mercy was asleep, Mrs. Isaiah sat down on the couch and lifted a package out of her bag and handed it to Liz.

She opened the wrapping and held up the blouse. Liz squealed, "It's beautiful. You've done a good job." Then she looked at the skirt and her eyebrows narrowed for a moment. "Why is the waistband so large?"

"Aren't all your waistbands big like this?"

"No, they aren't."

"Doesn't your stomach get larger when you eat?"

164

"Yes, but I don't eat so much that my waist gets this big." Liz giggled.

Henry came into the room and took away the tea tray. "You white people eat four or five little meals daily. We eat one or two giant meals each day. Taking in that much food at one time makes our stomachs big. Haven't you seen my own stomach get larger?"

Liz had noticed it but didn't think it polite to say anything. She'd no idea their eating habits required seamstresses to put extra inches in the waists of their clothes.

"Would you be able to make another outfit like this using purple brocade?" Liz asked.

"I can have it ready for you next Saturday."

"If I don't get to the city, can you hold it for me? I'll collect it the next time I come."

"Yes, but it's getting late. I need to go, so I can get a taxi home." Mrs. Isaiah bent forward, untied the knot at her waist and handed the sleeping baby to Liz. Then she left.

Liz would need to give little Mercy to someone one day, but was Mrs. Isaiah the right person?

***

Towards suppertime, a truck pulled up in front of the house. Liz recognized Stan's vehicle and went outside to greet him. "I hope you're bringing me good news. Did you find anything?"

"Gary and I took a longer look inside the burned-out plane. After taking lots of pictures, we filled a large trash can with the scorched first aid box, burned water bottles, Andrew's melted carry-on, the seatbelt, and ruined bag of emergency supplies. We'd like to send them to a British crime scene investigator who may be able to put the pieces of the puzzle together."

Liz raised her eyebrows. "That's a good idea."

"If we never find Andrew, we want to know how the plane exploded and why."

Her heart dropped. Never find Andrew? Surely they would find him, but when and in what condition would he be?

"None of this makes sense." Stan took the cup of coffee that Henry handed to him. "If Andrew is alive and looking for help, why doesn't he go to a nearby village? It's the most likely place to get food, water, and medical treatment."

Liz took the tea from Henry. "I don't know."

"Andrew unfastened the seatbelt, and then he passed out or died. Maybe the villagers found him and carried him away."

"It must have happened too fast. He saw fuel and sparks and ran for his life. After that, maybe the explosion injured him. The local people found him and carried him to their village." Liz willed herself to be calm.

"That makes sense, but why wasn't he in any of the villages?" Stan asked.

"Are you going back?"

"Yes, but we need to be cautious. This is the rainy season, and another storm is coming." Stan set his empty cup on the table. "I need to be going."

She walked him to the door.

After he left, Liz got her needle and thread to put several tucks in the waist of her new skirt.

What if Andrew was dead?

No. She couldn't believe it.

CHAPTER THIRTY-ONE

Giggling children woke Andrew. Using the cane as support, he hobbled out of the shelter. The cool breeze refreshed him. Andrew always felt better each morning after a night of resting his painful foot.

Tio brought him a calabash of corn gruel. The Africans drank the watery cereal, so he did, too. The tasteless liquid slid down his throat.

After breakfast, the women stacked their bowls and rolled up the sleeping mats. Older ladies heaped clothes and towels on blankets and knotted the corners together to make a bundle. People slung them from poles balanced over their shoulders.

The men lifted the thatched roofs off the homes and set them on the ground. Then they wound the grass coverings into tight bundles, which they secured to the backs of donkeys. The older women tied firewood in bunches and fastened it to the backs of cows. The teenage boys rolled up the thatched walls. Younger boys pulled up the stakes that had held the walls in place. Children gathered the posts and tied them together.

From his mat, Andrew watched the nomads dismantle their community. Where was the village going and would he be able to keep up with them? He understood that he'd be traveling with them. What if he was supposed to stay with the plane? His identification said he was a pilot for HOW, but he couldn't remember. If he left with the village people, he might never find his way home, but where was it?

Young girls spread open large pieces of cloth and set plastic plates, calabashes and cups in the center. They gathered the corners, knotted them, and hung them from poles which resembled loads that hobos carried. After the younger men left with the herds and laden beasts, the older men stayed with the women and children.

Tio and Eilo pulled on Andrew's hands to help him stand. Putting his weight on his good leg, he began hobbling along with the children. Several times he stopped and caught his breath.

Had he done something that required the nomads to leave the community? As he followed them down the winding footpath, he prayed that he hadn't put any of the smiling nomads in danger. On slow, unsteady steps, Andrew limped along with the help of the antique cane. When his good leg cramped, he tried to use his injured one but agony tore through his ankle and foot. Tears of pain filled his eyes. Even with the walking stick he was scarcely able to endure the excruciating throbs in his limb. Beads of sweat broke out on his forehead as he hiked behind the villagers into a teakwood forest.

By noon the arthritic old women had limped past him. Milo and her daughters lingered with him. With every excruciating step, Andrew gripped his cane tighter. His breath caught. Sweat soaked his shirt and pants as he leaned on his walking stick and hopped down the path.

As the sun set, the wind howled and the skies opened up.
Shivering, he pulled his shirt closed to fasten it, but another button was missing. His teeth chattered. Forcing himself forward, he attempted to hobble faster. He shuddered as the frigid air chilled him to the bone, but he had to keep going or maybe they would leave him.

Should he have camped out by the plane until he regained his strength to hike home, but where was it?

***

Liz and Henry arrived home from the clinic and found Stan waiting under the mango tree. Liz set her basket down. "It's good to see you."

He frowned. "Let's go inside and talk."

His serious tone troubled her. Her hands shook as she opened the door. Had they found any clues? Her heart beat faster. If they'd located his body, they would have sent a large delegation to inform her.

Stan took a seat and Liz sat facing him.

Reaching into his chest pocket, Stan pulled out a button. "Have you seen this?

Liz picked it up and turned it over in her palm. "It looks like a button from his gray shirt. I noticed them because they were unusual with the little A on them. Where did you find it?"

"Today when I flew around the site of the crash, I spotted a smoldering thread. It looked like a campfire, so we landed close to it."

"Was it a village?"

"It looked like it had been, but it wasn't on the map. The dwellings were gone. They'd left behind two falling-down shelters of bamboo and banana leaves and four dying campfires. The ashes were still hot. I picked this button up because I, too, recognized the A on it."

"Andrew must have started walking down the trail and stopped in the village."

"Or he was carried by someone." Stan shook his head. "I circled around the abandoned town. Why do you think the people left?"

Henry came into the room with a tray.

Liz turned to her assistant. "Why do entire communities leave their home?"

Henry set the platter on the coffee table. "If there was sickness in a neighboring village, they might be afraid it would come to them, so they would leave. They'd also leave if their wells went dry."

"Why did Andrew go with them instead of staying with the plane?" Stan asked.

Henry shrugged. "He'd have to remain with them to get food and water."

"Why couldn't they give him supplies?" Stan took the glass of water.

"Our people are poor. They only have one or two pots or a few containers for water, so everyone shares them. If they gave one to Brother Andrew, they might not have enough for their families." Henry left with the empty platter.

"I had no idea people were that destitute." Stan sighed. "We extended the search several miles away from the abandoned community but didn't see anyone."

Liz clutched the button. "If he was injured, the local people might have taken him to their village."

"Would they have carried an unconscious white man to their home?"

"They might have thought Andrew had fallen asleep. If they weren't able to wake him, they'd have waited."

"Why?"

"Many rural people believe if they don't help a stranger, and his god is stronger than their god, the stranger's god might get angry and hurt them."

"They sound religious."

"Some tribes are quite superstitious." Liz glanced again at the button. "This must have fallen off recently. No one would have left this button on the ground. They're scarce."

"I can't convince the officials at HOW that Andrew is still out there. They suggested a native took Andrew's shirt after he died."

"You haven't found a charred body or a newly dug grave." Tears formed in her eyes. "Shouldn't that convince them that Andrew is alive?"

"They admitted he may have escaped the explosion, but they said he died of burns, internal injuries, or smoke inhalation." Stan shrugged.

"If that's true, where is his body?"

"What would the African people do with it?"

Liz put a trembling hand to her chest. "All the tribes I'm familiar with bury their dead in their back yard or in the center of their compound. There are a few isolated tribes who may use a white man's body parts in their witchcraft preparations."

Stan raised his voice. "You mean they'd cut up the body and boil it in a pot?"

She nodded. Tears blurred her vision. "Andrew is a Christian. Even if he's dead on earth, he's alive in Heaven."

"I wish I could believe that."

"Trust Jesus and He'll give you faith to believe."

"No." Stan clasped his hands together. "I'm my own savior. There is no one who will ever save me, except me. I'm responsible for myself. I respect you, Liz, but I don't want to talk about religion."

"That's fine. Thank you for searching for Andrew." Using the back of her hand, Liz wiped several tears from her cheek. "Suppose he jumped out of the plane and started walking. As he hiked through an abandoned village, this button fell off. If Andrew were uninjured and strong, what is the greatest distance he could walk?"

"Without injuries at four miles an hour for eight hours, he might travel thirty miles a day." Stan slapped his forehead with his palm. "Liz, I should have circled a radius of thirty miles or more."

"Can you go back and do that?"

"Yes, I can, but you've given me a fresh idea. Without injuries and with food and water, he might have hiked fifty to sixty miles. He's been gone ten days, so we should be searching a wider area." Then he frowned.

"So what's wrong?"

"That makes no sense. If he was hiking, he should have run into people. I'll take another trip and search a greater radius."

"Do you need money for the helicopter?"

"Andrew means a lot to me. I'm glad to fly on my days off, but when the copter is used for a personal mission like this, I have to pay all the expenses. I've gone through my funds."

"What would it cost to rent the helicopter and hire trackers to search?"

"I have a few ex-marine buddies who might like to do it. The cost of a helicopter would be about a thousand dollars a day."

"Can I write you a check?"

"What are you talking about?"

"I want to hire a professional rescue team to search for Andrew. He's still alive, and you, too, must believe, otherwise you wouldn't be looking for him."

Liz left the room and returned with a slip of paper. She handed Stan a check for ten thousand dollars.

He stood and put it in his pocket. "I'll keep you informed."

She walked him to the door.

Liz believed Andrew was alive, but where had he gone?

CHAPTER THIRTY-TWO

Andrew shuddered at his image in the tiny mirror that Milo and her daughters used. Staring at his unshaved, dirty face, he tried to comb out his filthy hair with his fingers. He resembled an old, homeless man with sunken eyes. Scabs covered the gashes on his forehead and cheeks.

Throughout the day Eilo and Tio brought him bananas and roasted peanuts. They gave him energy, but he was always thirsty. If only he had a glass of cool water.

The villagers had left Andrew alone on the trail. Even Milo and the girls had disappeared. He stopped and leaned on the antique stick to ease the pain and catch his breath.

It was twilight, when the bushes up ahead moved, but there were no giggles of little girls. Andrew quivered as a wildcat darted out from the shrubs not far from him. The animal stopped in front of him. It weighed about fifteen pounds and was a yard long with short, brown fur and black stripes on its foot-long tail. Although it wasn't too big, it looked fierce. Suddenly the animal's hair stood on end. Was the wildcat coming after him? His heart beat faster. Andrew might be able to drive off the beast with his cane, but he couldn't outrun him.

Andrew kept still and let his eyes run along the grasses on the trail. The wildcat looked away from him. He didn't see any other animals. With stealthy movements, the wildcat skulked across the path as if approaching a prey. Three yards away, Andrew spotted the huge rodent. The cat pounced on the grass cutter. The attack startled Andrew and he dropped his cane. As the cat clawed the smaller animal to death, Andrew shuddered. The wildcat used its sharp jaws to lift the grass cutter. Then the feline ran off with its victim in its mouth.

Andrew thanked God and breathed easier the wildcat hadn't been after him. If it had been hungry and unable to find any mice or birds, it would have attacked Andrew. Then he recalled that wildcats roamed West Africa and never traveled alone, so Andrew took a moment to look for the animal's mate. The animals lived in the savannas which could only mean that Andrew must be in Africa. He gasped, but why was he there?

Picking up his walking stick, he tripped down the dim path. It was too dark to see the trail clearly. He wished he had a light, but even the nomads didn't have matches or flashlights. They shared everything, including the hot charcoals to start one another's fires.

He stopped to rest again. Had the people left him or were they waiting up ahead? The throbbing in his swollen leg never stopped. Exhaustion overcame him. His head pounded and his joints ached as he shoved his good leg forward. He had to keep stumbling along the path or he'd get lost in the dark. His life depended on it. The natives might leave him if he fell too far behind the others, and then what would he do? He couldn't survive in a damp jungle without a fire, an ax, or a pot to boil water.

Tears moistened his eyes. He shouldn't slow down, but he already had. Maybe he was too far behind the others to reach them. He halted again to catch his breath. Agony ran up and down his injured leg and foot.

God, please help me. A little mercy is all I need.

"Lord, I can't survive without you. Thank you for saving me. I rededicate my life and surrender everything to you. I promise to serve you all the days of my life, even if there aren't many left. I'm all yours."

The Lord's presence was with him, but he felt so alone. His shoulders shook as he wept. In the silent night, God answered him through the voice of the chief.

"Kiki. Kiki." Footsteps crunched on the path up ahead.

The village leader was looking for him. Andrew had never been so thrilled to see anyone as he was that man. Wiping his face, Andrew put on a serious expression. The chief might not respect him if he found him crying like a little boy.

Drying his eyes, Andrew called. "I'm here."

He breathed a sigh of relief as the chief rattled on and on in his language. Andrew didn't understand a word of it, but hearing the man's voice, comforted Andrew. The older man pointed to the trail as if he wanted Andrew to keep hiking. Shaking his head, Andrew lowered his eyes to his swollen foot.

The chief took a kola nut out of his pocket. Breaking it in half, he popped a piece in his mouth and chewed on it. Then he handed the other half to Andrew, who put it in his mouth and bit into it. He was surprised at its bitterness, but the more he chomped on it, the less offensive it became. The chief motioned Andrew forward. He tried to take a step but faltered and fell to the ground.

Chief Tiolare picked up the antique cane and pulled Andrew's left arm around his shoulder. Then the chief wrapped his right arm around Andrew's waist. Taking most of Andrew's weight, the chief moved Andrew forward down the trail. They met Doditu, who swung Andrew's right arm around his shoulder and grabbed Andrew's waist above the chief's arm. Together the men carried Andrew to the camp.

By the time they reached the temporary settlement, the caffeine in the kola nut had calmed Andrew's headache and lessened the pain in his foot.

The chief and Doditu set Andrew down on a mat in front of a campfire. Andrew stared at his leg. Black patches covered places on his ankle and foot.

Was his leg gangrene?

***

The next day as Andrew hobbled down the path he was no longer worried and thanked God for the chief. If Andrew fell behind, the chief would find him and help him get to the camp.

Andrew recalled the biblical story of the good shepherd who had left the flock to search for one lost sheep. When the shepherd found the animal, he lifted it to his shoulders and carried it home.

Tears of joy moistened Andrew's eyes. God loved him, and the Lord showed His love and mercy every day through the strangers who cared for him.

Eilo and Tio ran to him. The older sister grinned and handed Andrew a calabash filled with dirty water, which was intended for drinking, but he splashed it on his face and poured the rest down his chest. His heart swelled with pleasure at the girls' thoughtfulness. He wiped his eyes with the back of his hands.

The little girls giggled. They pointed to his enlarged foot and scrunched up their faces.

After hopping a couple of steps, Andrew stopped to catch his breath. He leaned over and rubbed his painful foot. Then he waved his hand to indicate the girls should keep going. They laughed as they ran down the path.

By the time he arrived in camp, he was exhausted. They had stopped hiking earlier than usual. The sun hadn't gone down yet.

As Andrew rested on his mat, four boys, around ten or twelve years, sat down in front of Andrew and gave him a handful of smooth, round stones the size of marbles. The tallest boy scooped out five holes parallel to another strip of five holes each about four inches in diameter. The boy took Andrew's stones and put four of them in each of the holes leaving one hole on each side empty. He smiled at Andrew and motioned for him to come closer.

The biggest boy patted his chest and said. "Tarli."

Andrew pointed to himself and mimicked. "Tarli."

The boy tapped his chest a second time. "Tarli." And then he pointed to Andrew. "Kiki."

Andrew pointed to himself, "Kiki." Then he pointed to the boy. "Tarli."

The lad nodded and lifted the four stones from the first hole and dropped one into the second hole, another in the third hole, the third in the fourth hole, and at last the fourth in the fifth hole. Then he collected all the stones from the sixth hole. The boy kept dropping and lifting stones consecutively from all the holes.

Andrew wondered why they were playing with stones. If it was a form of gambling, what were they wagering?

Tarli pointed to Andrew to take a turn dropping and lifting stones. Andrew reached out for the stones in a hole and dropped the pebbles in the other holes until he had no more left.

The boy pointed to Andrew's feet. "Koogi."

Andrew had a feeling it meant sneakers. He was the only one who wore them in the village. The people either wore flip-flops or were barefoot.

Andrew suspected the boys were gambling for his sneakers. He was exhausted, didn't understand the game, and didn't want to gamble. It would be best to give them his shoes. So he untied his right sneaker from the loop in his waistband, and then he took off his left one. He handed the shoes to Tarli and laid back on his mat and slept.

***

Chief Tiolare shouted. "Tarli. Come here."

Carrying the sneakers, the boy went to the village leader.

The chief asked, "What are you doing with Kiki's shoes?"

"He gave them to me."

"Why did he give them to you?"

"I don't know."

"What were you doing when he gave them to you?" The chief asked.

"We were playing our game with the stones."

"Kiki needs these shoes to keep walking with us." The chief scowled.

"I thought he gave them to me." Tarli shrugged.

"Did you buy them or do something in exchange for them?

The boy hung his head. "Nothing."

"So he has no reason to give you his shoes. Kiki must want you to take them to Milo to clean them for him." The chief scowled. "Go give them to Milo."

After Tarli left, the chief turned and stared at Andrew's sleeping form. Chief Tiolare had to keep a closer watch on Kiki. It would be a terrible offense to their gods if anyone took advantage of the sick man, while he was in their village.

The chief couldn't do everything and be everyplace at the same time. He couldn't instruct his leaders, direct his people to the new pastures, and still look after Kiki.

CHAPTER THIRTY-THREE

Early the next morning before getting started on the trail, Milo brought Andrew's sneakers to him. Seeing the clean shoes he was full of shame. Guilt sliced through him as he tugged on his left shoe and laced it. The villagers hadn't taken anything from him and had shared everything they had.

Lord forgive me.

As he stumbled along the path, an engine noise startled him. He recognized the whirl of a helicopter. Looking up, he searched for an aircraft, but the thick foliage of trees blocked his view. Hoping to get a better look at the sky, he hopped forward. Raising his arm, he tried to wave, but too many leafy trees were in the way. An agonizing jolt shot through his swollen foot, and he tripped. As he tumbled to the ground, he passed out.

When he opened his eyes, he searched the confines of the thick forest. The pain in his foot was worse and his head still pounded. He couldn't go on any more. Tears of hopelessness filled his eyes.

Then he remembered flying his plane until it crashed. Maybe one of his friends at HOW was searching for him. He glanced at his single footprint. His Nike sneaker made a different track from the barefoot natives and the few who wore flip-flops. Sitting up, Andrew leaned forward and untied the other shoe dangling from his waist.

The chief jogged toward Andrew, who was still on the ground. The older man pointed to the sky and flapped his elbows like wings.

Andrew nodded and smiled at the village leader. Taking out both shoelaces, Andrew used a chopping motion with his right hand in the palm of his left hand and pointed to the leader's machete.

The chief handed Andrew the blade. Getting to his knees, Andrew stretched a lace over a fallen branch. He chopped his shoelaces into two-inch pieces. Then he carefully put one on the ground next to his footprint. Maybe the people in the plane would find his imprint with a piece of shoelace. He stuffed the rest of the sections into his pants pocket. Pointing to the piece on the ground, he lifted his hand to the sky. He made a flapping motion with his elbows. Using his index and middle fingers, he pointed to his eyes and up to the sky. The chief nodded and repeated the motions.

The older man pulled Andrew to his feet and handed him the walking stick. Andrew hopped along while the chief ran ahead shouting orders to the villagers. Andrew lagged farther behind in the forest and stopped to rest.

Popping sounds cut through the air. He scanned the area for danger. More explosions. The bangs grew louder, and Andrew recognized gunfire. The shouts of the innocent nomads alarmed him. Were soldiers shooting down the unarmed villagers?

Bang! Bam! More explosions. Women and children turned back and raced toward him. Others ran helter-skelter into the tall grasses and bushes on the side of the path. Loud rifle blasts echoed around him. Villagers halted in their tracks, dropped to the ground, and covered their heads.

Where were the gunshots coming from? Who had rifles and used them against the herdsmen? It made no sense, unless the nomads had left their village to escape evil men.

Staring down the trail, Andrew frowned at the women and children face down on the ground. A moment later they rose and followed other villagers into the crushed grasses and shrubs that lined both sides of the path.

Tio and Eilo came to him and took his free hand. They pulled him down the path and into the thick grasses. The little girls led him onto a freshly stomped trail. Behind him, men lifted the shrubs and arranged them, so it appeared nothing had been disturbed.

About five hundred yards up ahead of him was a camp. Andrew, out of breath, collapsed on the ground. He couldn't take another step. Weak and in excruciating pain, he glanced at his leg. It looked blacker than before. It had to be gangrene, and if so, it would soon kill him. If only he could have a glass of cold water before he died.

The women started the fires. When the water in the pots boiled, Andrew hopped to one and poured the steaming water the people used to bathe, into a calabash. He hopped to his mat and sipped it as it cooled. The hot water tasted awful but was safe to drink.

Milo rubbed her arms as if bathing. Then she pointed to the dirty water in the clay jar that villagers drank and mimicked drinking.

He shook his head. It made no sense to him. Why did the people take swamp water and boil it for bathing but pour water from stagnant streams into clay jars to drink? If they boiled the water they drank, they'd be better off.

Milo filled a calabash with a dipper from the clay jar and carried it to the chief.

Chief Tiolare sat down next to Andrew, drank half the water and handed the calabash to Andrew.

He took it and stared at the squiggly insects floating in it. Andrew preferred drinking the boiled bath water. At least nothing moved in it. Then he shook his head at the chief.

Milo spoke to the chief, pointed to the clay jar, and the calabash. The chief talked to her. Then Milo went back to the water container, poured several calabashes into a small cooking pot and set it on the fire. After she boiled it, she filled a gourd and carried it to Andrew.

"Thank you." He sipped on it.

She beamed. "Tunk yu."

Then Milo brought two bowls of corn meal mush with a dab of green, slimy sauce. She handed one to the chief and the other to Andrew.

He was getting used to eating with Chief Tiolare. People in the tribe didn't speak while eating, but Andrew was accustomed to the silent companionship of the older man next to him.

After they had eaten, the chief went to one of the cows. Untying a bag, the village leader took out a liter-sized plastic Clorox jug. He unscrewed the lid and lowered his face to the opening. As he sniffed he wrinkled his nose. Then the chief shook his head as he gave Andrew the empty container.

Andrew caught a whiff of chlorine bleach. He smiled and nodded. At least it was a clean container. Chief Tiolare took the calabash of boiled water from Andrew and poured it into the bottle, which he handed to Andrew.

Sipping the bottled water, Andrew didn't like the lingering taste of chlorine but with the powerful bleach scent, the container would be safe. Screwing the cap on, he beamed at the chief and clutched the jug to his chest. "Thank you. Thank you."

A liter of water a day meant the difference between survival and death. At least he'd no longer have to drink boiled swamp water that the people used for bathing. If he carried the bottle, he could drink throughout the day rather than only in the morning and evening.

***

Andrew hobbled behind the string of nomads up ahead of him on the trail. He stopped every few feet to massage his throbbing foot, swollen three times its size. Forcing one foot ahead of the other, he shuddered from the agonizing pain.

He could rest when they arrived at their destination, and maybe then his leg would stop throbbing. Each evening when he stopped, his leg didn't ache as badly. By morning, the swelling was always down a little bit.

Even with the use of the sturdy cane, he wasn't sure he could go on much longer. The pain in his head and the throbbing in his leg grew worse daily. Too bad he didn't have a couple of Tylenol to ease his misery. The cola nut containing caffeine that the chief had given him had taken the edge off his pain. He wished the chief would give him another one.

Andrew started to crawl on hands and knees to keep up. Even then, he stopped often to rest. He rubbed his aching head and shivered. His dizziness increased, and so did the up and down movement of the trees. He couldn't remember how long he'd been lost.

Each evening he sat on his mat and watched the women prepare the meal. He enjoyed their camaraderie and pleasant chatter after the long day. It was beginning to feel like home, but then he remembered he was from Oregon.

If his leg gave out and he stayed behind, he couldn't ask for a pot to boil water. Even if one of the families gave him a small skillet, he had no idea where to get water and wasn't in any shape to carry it. Nor was he able to chop firewood.

They lived off their cows, goats, sheep, and chickens. Having meat, milk, and eggs, they could survive. They had no rice or corn of their own, but each day a couple women left the trail and returned with giant bowls of ground corn to prepare mush.

The ladies plucked green leaves, which they chopped and put in the sauce. He tried to help them by picking leaves, but they scowled at the foliage he plucked and tossed it to the ground. Andrew had seen no difference in their leaves and his.

He was getting weaker and weaker each day as the villagers hiked deeper into the bush and farther away from civilization. Could Andrew keep marching on his injured leg? And if not, would he be left behind?

Without the help of the people Andrew would already be dead. He wasn't afraid of death, but he didn't want to die alone. God had sent the nomads, so he wouldn't be by himself.

Each evening, the old medicine man applied the green slime and leaves to Andrew's foot. It didn't help, but Andrew didn't think it hurt him either. The witch doctor beamed broadly as he spread the sticky treatment on the deformed foot. The old man was only trying to help. Andrew said thank you, but no pomade cured gangrene. His leg was getting blacker and blacker. Maybe if the light had been better he could see how much of his leg was rotten, but he really didn't want to know.

Andrew was grateful to spend his last days on earth with the friendly nomads.

Death come quickly.

CHAPTER THIRTY-FOUR

Liz and Henry arranged the medications on the treatment table in the village of Cioala.

When Mercy cried, Liz took out the soymilk to feed her. The women gathered around Liz and stared at the giggling infant.

One woman asked. "Where did the baby come from?"

"She was abandoned." Liz added milk to the thick corn cereal to turn it into a liquid.

Mercy no longer sipped from a spoon but had started drinking from a cup.

A mother, holding a child, shook her head. "It's hard to believe a baby that small can drink from a cup, but she should not wear a napkin."

Liz scowled. Little Mercy didn't wear a napkin, unless the cloth on her bottom was called a napkin. Liz didn't see anything wrong with an infant wearing a diaper. Liz had never seen African babies wearing them, so perhaps it wasn't acceptable.

"Your child should know how to urinate." A woman growled.

"She knows how to urinate." Liz shrugged. "She does it all the time."

"She does not do it the right way."

Liz turned to Henry. "Is there a right and wrong way to urinate? Can you train Mercy to do it correctly?"

"It's too late. You've ruined Mercy, so now she is lazy. But I'll try to teach her, if she hasn't wet the cloth." Henry removed the diaper. Then she positioned her feet and legs a few inches apart, and set Mercy on her ankles. Henry made a urinating noise. "Pishhhhh."

Liz's eyes widened when the baby urinated.

Another mother scowled. "Why does the baby smile all the time?"

Henry raised her eyebrow. "It's because the baby's mother, Sister Liz, is a joker."

"Why are you telling them that I'm a joker?"

"A joker laughs too much."

"Did you know that crying is a lot more work than laughing?"

"How can crying and laughing be work?"

"I didn't mean that they were real work." Liz sighed.

"Are you saying that crying and laughing are artificial work?" Henry had never smiled or laughed.

Liz bit her lip. "Frowning, being sad and crying require more facial muscles and energy than smiling and laughing."

"You're right. Ladies have cried themselves to death. Before they died they were tired from all the weeping, as if they had worked all day."

"That's true. I don't know anyone who died from laughing." Liz couldn't stop her playfulness, even though Henry didn't understand any of Liz's jokes.

Maybe one day Henry would laugh.

***

When they returned home from the village, they found Stan waiting.

Liz asked. "Did you see any sign of Andrew?"

Stan sighed loudly. "I flew in a fifty-mile radius from the place we found the button. I set the helicopter down by a thin column of smoke, which was an area that once supported people. It looked like another group left in a hurry without putting out their fire."

"Sometimes villagers leave their fires so people who come along can use the hot coals to build a new one."

Stan reached in his shirt pocket and opened his hand. "Take a look."

"It's another button." Liz grinned. "Where did you find this one?"

"At the abandoned campsite."

"Andrew must be traveling with these people."

"If so why do they keep packing up and moving on?"

Henry handed Stan a cup of coffee and mumbled. "No people leave without a good reason, such as war, famine, or epidemic. They might be searching for water."

"Should we look for bodies of water?" Stan asked.

"Yes, but people also need fuel, most especially firewood." Liz said.

"Andrew would be an extra mouth to feed, so wouldn't it be better to leave him behind?" Stan took a sip.

"People will take care of strangers. Remember, they are fearful of the gods of foreigners. They don't want strange gods to curse them. " Liz rolled the button in her fingers. "What's next?"

"My team of professional trackers will arrive this afternoon. I'll take them straight to the crash site and start from there." Stan pulled out a pack of cigarettes, glanced at Henry, and returned it to his pocket. "Why do so many of the foot trails and cow paths go nowhere?"

"When local people pack and leave, the trails to their homes are still there." Henry kept standing.

"If Andrew is traveling with a group, they are most likely headed to a specific destination, but where?"

"I don't know." Henry shrugged and left.

Liz took a breath. "I believe Andrew is alive and we'll find him."

But when?

***

Chief Tiolare found Kiki crawling on the path. The poor white man was getting sicker and sicker. The medicine man's treatments hadn't helped Kiki, but some herbs took longer to heal than others and a few diseases were stubborn.

The chief wished he could send Kiki home but didn't know where Kiki lived. Even if the chief knew the way, how would he get Kiki there? Could the chief do it without running into any of their enemies? His biggest worry was that Kiki's death might bring disaster on his people.

The village leader lifted Kiki to his feet and took most of his weight as he helped him to the settlement. "We are preparing for our celebration of independence." Why did he bother speaking to Kiki? The poor white man didn't understand anything.

Reaching the camp, the chief helped Kiki sit on a mat. His people shouldn't take time for a party, but they loved celebrations. They had worked hard with the herds and deserved a day off.

The men lugged buckets of water into the bushes to take baths and returned with towels wrapped around their waists.

The women dressed in festive red, orange, and purple clothes and decorated their necks and arms with chains of gold and blue, yellow, and green bracelets. Others wore sparkling earrings with matching nose rings.

Milo squatted by her father and Kiki. "Do you think a bath will help him feel better?"

"Yes." The chief stood. "I'll help you take him to the bush."

The chief and his daughter lifted Kiki and took much of his weight. Kiki kept tripping, but the chief stopped him from falling. "He is getting weaker. I found him crawling along the path."

"He looks sicker than before." Milo kept an arm around Kiki's waist.

They headed outside the camp and stopped in front of a cluster of bushes. Milo pulled Kiki's shirt out of his pants. There were no buttons left on the garment. After she had him undressed, her daughters arrived with a bucket of water, a folded cloth, and a waxy ball of soap.

The older man called, "Let's leave Kiki alone to bathe."

Sometime later Kiki, wearing Milo's clean, wrap-around skirt, hopped into the camp. Milo ran to help him. Then she filled Kiki's empty bottle with boiled water and handed it to him. After that, she gave her father and Kiki each a plate of corn meal mush with spicy bitter leaf gravy.

Toward evening, Milo handed Kiki his neatly laundered clothes. "It was a hot afternoon, so they dried quickly." She turned to her father. "Do you think he understands anything we say?"

The older man shrugged.

A young boy carried a giant boulder on his head and set it in front of the chief.

Chief Tiolare left and returned with a miniature transistor radio. Putting it on top of the big rock, he turned the volume up as loud as possible. Other men brought drums and beat on them while the children danced. The adults spun around to the rhythm of the music. Young people laughed and leaped as they whirled about the radio.

Suddenly loud explosions shook the air. Women screamed. Young men jumped up and reached for cutlasses. Children halted in their steps and dropped to the ground. Bursts of machine gunfire jolted mothers forward to pick up their toddlers. They carried the little ones to the nearest bushes and hid behind them. Older men grabbed their spears and hunting sticks before racing to the trail. Smoke rose from the north.

Silence filled the camp.

***

Andrew's pounding heart was the loudest sound in the settlement. Someone was attacking the smiling nomads, and he could do nothing about it. He was sicker than he had ever been and shivered under the hot sun. Every bone and joint in his body throbbed, and it was difficult to breathe.

The bath hadn't cooled his hot body and only exhausted him. He'd barely been able to make it back to the camp.

Closing his eyes for a moment, he saw the burned-out aircraft. He relived flying it and the crash. Where had he been going and why?

Lord, please have a little mercy.

Something felt so familiar about a little mercy, but he couldn't remember.

The chief, Milo, and the girls came back into camp. A few minutes later, the other villagers returned. No one spoke and everyone sat down and hung their heads. What had happened?

The chief took a cola nut out of his pocket and handed it to Andrew, who broke it in half and put a piece in his mouth. "Thank you."

"Tunk you." Chief Tiolare took another nut out of his pocket and chomped on it.

The older man pointed to the cola nut in Andrew's mouth and then to Andrew's swollen foot. Twenty minutes later the caffeine in the nut had eased the pain.

Andrew had only seen the nuts in large cities. He suspected Milo had bought them during her last shopping trip to a market or from a passing trader.

Milo was dressed in shiny orange cloth threaded with silver. Her matching scarf was wound in layers a foot high on top of her head. She wore several gold necklaces and so many metal bracelets that she jingled as she walked.

Andrew's stomach lurched. Was she proposing marriage? The Bible was clear. He was a Christian, and she wasn't. Believers were forbidden from marrying unbelievers, so he shouldn't marry her, but he'd soon be dead, so what harm could it do? If he married her, at least he wouldn't die alone. She and her daughters had become family.

Andrew waved to the children around him and then stared down at his deformed, swollen foot. No amount of black slime and green leaves eased his suffering. He couldn't move his toes or his ankle. Most likely he had several broken bones. He shivered at the increased black color.

Every joint in his body throbbed. His skin was on fire. He'd lost his appetite and been nauseous for the last couple of days and hadn't been able to eat much.

He closed his eyes. Maybe he'd never open them again. Even if he did survive, a doctor would amputate his leg. If only he could persuade the nomads to let him die. Would God consider it suicide?

Lord, I can't go on. Please I need a little mercy.

He closed his eyes and saw a tiny black baby in the arms of a beautiful white woman, but who was she?

More blasts of gunfire ripped the air.

CHAPTER THIRTY-FIVE

Two days later, Stan and three other men arrived at Liz's home.

Stan led the way into the living room and sat down. "I'd like you to meet my buddies who are ex-marines."

"Thank you for coming to search for Andrew." Liz smiled.

"Gentlemen, this is Miss Elizabeth Connor, our supporter." Stan pointed to her.

"I'm Brian." The gray-haired man shook Liz's hand.

"I'm Tom." The youngest man smiled.

The giant extended his hand. "John."

Henry came into the room and stood as if waiting for an order.

Liz asked, "Can we get you coffee or tea?"

All the men nodded. Stan answered. "Coffee for all of us, please."

After Henry left, Stan leaned forward. "We hired the largest HOW helicopter. I'm using the rest of my vacation to fly it. These men were trackers in the jungles during the war. Brian retired from the army. We value his extra years of experience."

"We took a trip to the crash site." Brian leaned forward. "After investigating the burned-out plane, we set out in two groups. The storms wiped out every trace. We traveled south and southwest where there are many villages."

"We scoured the countryside, showing Andrew's photo to everyone in the market place and the officers at police headquarters." Stan sighed. "Some of those folks had never seen a white person. So when four white guys marched into their village it created a bit of a ruckus."

Tom chuckled. "The women and children screamed, but the policemen ran toward us."

"Surely they didn't think you were a threat to them?" Liz asked.

Brian shook his head, "No ma'am, but you can imagine their surprise and fear."

Henry carried a large tray into the room. She unloaded a pot of coffee, cups, milk, sugar, and plate of homemade peanut butter cookies onto the coffee table. After handing each of the gentleman a cloth napkin, she left.

Brian raised his eyebrows and chuckled. "Ma'am we didn't come for a tea party."

"It's the local way of showing hospitality. Before we eat, I'd like us to pray together for Andrew."

"Please go ahead." Brian bowed his head.

After Liz said, "Amen," she served the men coffee. "Please help yourself." She passed the plate of cookies. "I've been to villages in which children ran away from me."

"No one had seen Andrew." Stan shook his head at the plate of cookies.

Brian picked up a cookie. "We decided to go in the opposite direction, even though it made no sense. It looked uninhabited and the map showed no villages in that area."

"John and I headed north." Stan sipped his coffee. "Brian and Tom went northeast. Ten miles northeast of the burned out plane, Tom found a Nike footprint with a piece of white shoelace next to it." Stan reached in his pocket, pulled out the piece of shoelace and handed it to Liz. "It looks like it was cut with a machete. Brian believes Andrew cut his shoelaces and is leaving us a trail."

Her heart lurched. "If this is true, we'll soon find him."

"It was too dark to go on, so we made camp for the night." Stan shook his head. "Andrew may be hobbling around with a broken leg or foot and suffering other injuries. There was an indentation that appeared to be a walking stick."

"If Andrew is able to get around, he must not be too injured." Liz ran her fingers over the piece of lace in her palm. "This proves that Andrew is alive and clear-headed enough to leave us a trail."

"The bare toes of the right foot didn't make a strong print, which means it's sprained or broken since he's not putting weight on it." Brian took a bite of cookie.

Tom raised his eyebrows. "Do you think the natives coerced him to go with them?"

Liz shook her head. "There's no reason for it."

Stan clasped his hands together and leaned forward. "The plane was tampered with. Perhaps the men who did it, took him from the crash and are forcing him to go to another village to fly another plane."

"Or hostiles are holding Andrew for a ransom." Tom frowned.

Stan pursed his lips. "It's strange that he keeps hiking farther and farther away from civilization."

"The windshield was shattered." Brian grimaced. "I confirmed dried blood on the glass. He may have hit his head and passed out."

John set his empty cup on the table. "Maybe the natives are taking him wherever they are going."

"At least Andrew is limping along with a walking stick." Liz tried to smile but her lips didn't quite lift. "He's leaving us signs on the trail, like the cut shoelace. Since they gave him a cane, perhaps they are helping him reach civilization in the far north."

"Why up there?" Stan asked. "It's more reasonable to travel south where there are towns and a police station."

"What if the blow to his head made him lose his memory?" Brian asked.

Liz gasped. "If he had retrograde amnesia, it's possible he snapped out of it in a few days or a week. Or he still can't remember who he is, so he's going along with the villagers."

But what if he has a permanent brain injury?

***

That afternoon, Liz was surprised to see Mrs. Isaiah at her front door.

"I brought your dress." Mrs. Isaiah handed a bag to Liz.

"That wasn't necessary, but I appreciate your trouble."

After they were seated, Liz lifted out the garment. "This two-piece style is beautiful and you did an excellent job."

"Thank you. I'm glad you're pleased."

"I am." Liz held the ensemble up in front of her. "It looks like it will fit."

"I wanted to bring it, so I could see the baby again." Mrs. Isaiah looked around the living room. "Is she here?"

Liz's pulse quickened at what sounded like an excuse to see Mercy. It was a good sign.

Henry came into the room and untied the baby from her back.

The seamstress reached for the chubby infant. "She's more beautiful than the last time I saw her."

Liz nodded. "She's a sweet baby, and she's in perfect health."

"I'll be in the kitchen if you need anything." Henry left.

"Do you need someone to look after her for a while? I'd be glad to take her." Mrs. Isaiah clutched the infant to her chest.

Liz had always been cautious about prospective parents. She had prayed about Mr. and Mrs. Isaiah and was at peace about giving them the baby for a trial period. That way she could check on them.

"Has anyone claimed the baby since she was abandoned?"

"No one has asked about her."

Liz knew one day she'd need to give up the baby, and that would break her heart, as it always did. Still Mrs. Isaiah's offer was an answer to prayer.

"I want to go with the men to search for Brother Andrew, and I can't take Mercy with me. If you can keep her while I'm gone, it would be a big help."

"Everyone I know in church is praying that Brother Andrew will be found." Mrs. Isaiah ran her fingers along Mercy's arms. "You cannot go with a group of men. You'd ruin yourself and curse the trip."

"Henry." Liz called. "Please join us."

When Henry came into the living room, Liz asked. "Would you like to go with me to search for Brother Andrew?"

"I don't know. Can I think about it?"

"Yes, we'll talk about it later. If you come we can watch out for each other while we are with the men."

Henry scowled. "I'm not sure it's proper."

"You could chaperon each other, but who will keep an eye on the two of you?" Mrs. Isaiah asked.

"The Lord." Liz smiled.

"Everyone thinks so highly of you, Sister Liz. A proper lady like you must not follow men around the bush."

"If I go, I can pray."

Mrs. Isaiah tilted her head. "You can pray here at home."

"Yes, and I've been praying, but Brother Andrew is still lost."

"How do you know he is lost? There are people who believe he is dead."

Tears filled Liz's eyes, and she sniffed. "Brother Andrew is alive."

"Why do you insist on this?"

Liz put her hand on her heart. "I believe it right here."

"I see you care deeply for him. Maybe it's good that you and Henry go. It will put your mind at ease. You can pray for direction on the trail. But will those men listen to you, a woman?"

"Yes, they'll listen." Liz smiled.

"What makes you so certain?"

"I know more about African tribes and local culture than any of the men and Henry knows even more."

Mrs. Isaiah stroked the baby's cheek. "I'd love to take Mercy and watch her while you are gone."

"Thank you. I'll pack her things." Liz went into the bedroom and stuffed the baby's belongings into several sacks and carried them back into the living room. She smiled at Mrs. Isaiah. "Let's feed her now before you start the journey. Henry, bring her food, please."

Henry explained in another language how to prepare Mercy's soy milk and corn cereal. Mrs. Isaiah took out her little notepad with sewing measurements and dress designs in it. She wrote the instructions. "Don't worry. Mercy will be fine."

"Before she sleeps at night I add a spoon of red palm oil to her food." Henry stuffed the extra cups into the bag. "I added a spoon of peanut butter to this gruel so it will help Mercy sleep on the journey."

Mrs. Isaiah positioned the child in the crook of her arm and held the cup to Mercy's lips. The baby drank sips of the thick porridge. When the child was finished she grinned at Mrs. Isaiah. Tears filled the woman's eyes. "I love this baby."

After tying Mercy to her back, Mrs. Isaiah lifted the bags. Henry picked up the basket with Mercy's clothes and diapers. Mrs. Isaiah took it and set it on her head.

Mrs. Isaiah's eyes moistened from unshed tears. Liz sighed in pleasure for she'd made the right decision.

Now she was free to join the search party. She only needed to persuade the men.

CHAPTER THIRTY-SIX

Chief Tiolare touched Kiki's forehead and then jumped away. The chief recognized the most dangerous disease among their people, high fever.

He called his daughter. "How did Kiki get this sickness?"

"I don't know." Milo put her hand on Kiki's face. "He is hotter today than yesterday and looks worse."

"Can you prepare fever medicine?"

"Yes."

The chief swatted at a fly as his gaze flitted down the trail. He had tried to take care of Kiki and keep him safe but had failed. Maybe Kiki's god wasn't a nice one and gave Kiki the deadly fever.

"If our people stay here to care for Kiki, our cows may die without grazing fields." He squeezed his daughter's shoulder and smiled.

She was the best and most devoted child of all his wives and concubines. He couldn't let anything happen to her. She'd already lost her husband to the high fever. If the wrath of Kiki's god hit them, she could be hurt.

Milo put her hand on Kiki's neck and wrinkled her brow. "He smells like a wet chicken."

Crouching closer to the white man, the chief grimaced at the scent. "I've tried to care for you. Do you hold me responsible for this fever? Please tell your god that it wasn't my fault. My daughter has gone out of her way to help you."

Kiki opened his eyes and mumbled, "Jesus, help me."

"I don't understand what you are saying." The chief sighed.

Turning to Milo, he hoped she wouldn't reap the retribution of Kiki's god. Her children, Eilo and Tio, were the sweetest girls in the village. How could he stop a god's anger from hurting them?

Tears filled the chief's eyes.

***

Liz was working on her lecture notes at the dining room table a few nights later, when Stan arrived.

Seeing his despondent expression, she stiffened. "Come in, sit down, and tell me what you found."

After he was seated in the living room, he reached for his briefcase and clicked it open. "I've brought photos." He pulled a picture out of a thick envelope. "We made camp near this footprint."

He handed Liz the photo. She took it and moved it closer.

"Early the next morning we followed the signs and found another piece of shoelace next to the Nike print. Every quarter of a mile for five miles we found a part of a shoelace. We kept searching, but there were no more clues."

Liz sniffed and blinked several times.

Stan pulled a handful of pieces out of his pocket and lined them up on the coffee table. "You can see for yourself these are all the parts of the shoelaces."

Taking a tissue out of her pocket, she wiped a tear from her cheek. "If the shoelaces are finished, can't you follow the Nike print and the cane indentation?"

"We followed them until we arrived at a large country road, bigger than any I had ever seen. Cows, donkeys, goats, and sheep had stampeded the area. They wiped out Andrew's prints. After that, a storm hit us. Rain obliterated every sign."

"It sounds like a major junction."

"Yes, it was a well-traveled bush intersection. We needed to purchase more provisions so I suggested we return and give you our report."

Liz glanced at the stack of pictures. "May I see the others?"

He handed them to her. "Look at this photo of the foot impression and tell me what you think."

With a trembling hand, Liz took the picture from him. "By the indentation in the ground it appears as if his right foot is grossly swollen. He is using the cane to avoid putting weight on it."

"Yes, that's what my men and I thought. He may have other injuries because his steps waver as if he is in a lot of pain or dizzy."

Tears filled her eyes again. "Poor Andrew." Liz reached for the next one. Two hand prints firmly impressed in the ground and two round knob holes behind them.

Stan pointed to the photo. "Hands and knees."

Her breath grew ragged and her voice wobbled, "If he's crawling, Andrew must be terribly ill or out of his mind."

Stan grimaced. "It must be agony if he's trying to walk on a broken leg or ankle. Brian thinks Andrew may have temporary amnesia from the head injury, or he is escaping a local threat. There were tribal conflicts and gunfire in the region."

Liz's heart plummeted. What if Andrew had been shot and fell to the ground. She took a deep gulp of air. "Did you find any blood along the trail?"

"We didn't."

Liz stared at the last photo. "This picture confirms that I need to come with you."

Frowning, Stan shook his head. "What can you do that we haven't already done?"

"If I were on the trail with you, I could pray and ask God for direction. I might sense what was happening to Andrew."

"I thought you were praying here."

"Yes, I am. But it's been two weeks since the crash and he keeps going forward even with injuries. With his pain and possible memory loss, he might think he is one of the local people."

"Whenever the tracks turned onto small trails, Andrew's was the last print. I compared it with the shoes in his villa. It is positively his." Stan sighed. "Are there any tribes who are hostile to white people, or who kidnap foreigners and force them to go where they don't want to go?"

"Not that I know of."

Wrinkling her brow, Liz put a hand to her cheek and closed her eyes. She remembered the people who travelled with herds of cows, goats, and sheep deep inside the bush away from civilization.

Her eyelids fluttered open, and she yelled, "The Fuufuu are the cowboys of Africa."

"What are you talking about?"

"They are nomads who pasture large herds of cows. If they had found Andrew they'd have taken him with them. They never live in one place because their massive flocks need fresh grazing land, so their communities aren't found on any maps."

Stan asked, "What else do you know about these people?"

"For centuries they have owned the largest droves of cattle, goats, and sheep handed down for generations. They will not frequent cities and their children don't attend school because of their wandering life styles. They know less about the outside world than other tribes."

"My men and I will leave again tomorrow morning and try to pick up Andrew's trail."

"If you return without Andrew, I intend to go back with you to search."

"That's not a good idea. Hiking in the bush is strenuous."

Liz chuckled. "I trek every day to my village clinics."

"The men are up at the crack of dawn and search until nightfall. They are professional trackers and would resent you slowing them down."

"I walk quickly and have hiked many miles at a time. I'm in good shape and would not hinder the men."

"You'd have no privacy. Plus there are increased border conflicts and tribal fighting in the area where Andrew crashed."

Liz lifted her eyebrows. "I'm aware of the fighting and have been in dangerous situations."

"I cannot allow you to come."

"You've already admitted that I know more about the local people than you or your men do."

"I know Andrew cares for you. Suppose we found him but lost you through injury or sickness."

"Don't you think the supporter of your team should be allowed to take a look at the rescue operation?"

"Not necessarily. The men lug their own supplies. It would put an unnecessary burden on them to carry yours, too."

"I'll carry my own like I do every day to my clinics."

Shaking his head, Stan mumbled. "I'll ask the men. If we don't find Andrew in the next few days and they agree, you can come."

"In the meantime maybe you'll find Andrew. I'll pray that you do."

If not, Liz would go, no matter what his arguments were.

200

Andrew shivered at his deformed limb. The green slime and leaves covering his foot and leg hadn't helped. Still, the tender touches of the medicine man brought a smile to Andrew's lips, and the stinky concoction reminded Andrew that he was cared for.

He was hot, weak, and dizzy and had passed out so many times along the trail he lost count of them. In his delirium, he crawled on hands and knees. The agony in his head and leg increased. Sick and exhausted, Andrew wished the people would leave him behind, but he couldn't speak their language to tell them.

Andrew had thought of playing dead, but what if the people pulled him to his feet or put him on someone's back?

He was slipping closer to Heaven and prayed it would come quickly.

Milo brought him a black drink which he assumed was medicine. Squatting before him, she held the cup to his lips. Then she put her hand at the bottom of the container and tilted it, forcing him to drink the whole amount.

It was the vilest brew of herbs he'd ever drunk, much worse than the local alcoholic beverage they made. After he finished it, he collapsed back on the mat. Then he turned and vomited.

Lord Jesus, please a little mercy.

CHAPTER THIRTY-SEVEN

As Liz spread peanut butter on her toast, she heard men's voices coming closer to her home. She glanced out the window.

She put the knife down and called, "Henry, your father is here with two policemen." Liz looked out the kitchen window again and chuckled.

It looked as if Mr. Bellolare selected the biggest officials he could find. Each of them was twice the size of Henry's father and wore a gun belt with a pistol and a baton. Liz would need courage herself to stand up against them.

Liz opened the door and headed to the men, while Henry walked behind Liz. When she stopped in front of them, Henry stepped around Liz, and keeping her head lowered toward the ground, Henry curtsied.

Liz shook hands with the visitors. "Let's walk to the pastor's house so you men can discuss these important matters. Follow me and I will show you the way."

They met the pastor sitting under a giant baobab tree. After salutations were exchanged, he invited everyone to take a seat on the benches. Liz and Henry sat as far away from the men as they could while still being able to hear the conversation.

Henry's father announced, "I decided not to trouble you people any more with sorcerers and warlords."

Liz's mouth twitched, but she kept it closed. The evil men hadn't done any harm, except terrify Henry. There would be no point for him to buy more spells that didn't work.

Liz whispered into Henry's ear. "Remember God's faithfulness. Nothing bad happened to us after those sorcerers cursed us."

Henry murmured. "Should I tell my father that?"

"No, let's say nothing. It's best not to make him angry."

The pastor glowered and shook his head at them. He lifted a finger to his lips. It was rude to have a private conversation in front of men.

The pastor turned to Mr. Bellolare. "I see you've brought policemen. Has someone broken the law?"

"They have come to help me take my daughter home to marry her fiancé."

When the pastor started talking in a dialect that Liz didn't understand, Henry shuddered and shook her head.

Liz interrupted, "Excuse me, I'd appreciate your speaking the local language so I can be part of your conversation."

The pastor grimaced. "Each month that you keep his daughter and prevent Henry from getting married you must pay the father fifty thousand francs."

Liz's jaw fell open, but the words confirmed what she already knew. Mr. Bellolare only wanted money. He didn't care for his daughter.

"If Henry went home with her father today and got married, then Mr. Bellolare could collect the bride price. Since you are preventing this, it is only right that you pay the father every month."

Henry slid farther away from them on the bench, but her eyes moved from her father to the pastor to Liz and back to her father again.

"Is this a law in your country?" Liz's frown deepened. "I've never heard of such a decree."

One of the policemen said. "It is not a law."

Liz asked, "Do you have a written order from a judge that forces me to pay this amount?"

The policeman raised an eyebrow. "There's nothing like that."

"Then what right do you have to ask me for money?"

Henry's father snapped, "We have every right. You are supposed to love everyone. To prove you are a Christian, who loves us, you must give me the money."

One of the policemen glared. "We are pagans, the enemies that your God orders you to love. Now give the father the fifty thousand francs every month to show Christian love to him."

The pastor jumped up. "I've never heard of this being done."

The officer smirked. "Mr. Bellolare is a very intelligent man, and he is the one who thought of it."

Henry's eyes widened. Liz scowled. The pastor exhaled. "We need time to discuss this with the church leaders."

Mr. Bellolare stood. "We'll be back for the money or Henry."

After the men departed, the pastor sat down on the bench. "I've never heard of such a twisted version of God's laws."

Liz asked. "What do you think we should do?"

The pastor picked up his Bible. "Call a church meeting and pray."

Would giving the money be a testimony to win Mr. Bellolare to Christ? If he had been alone, it might work. But every policeman, warlord, and sorcerer accompanying Henry's father would demand money for being the enemy of Christ.

Liz gave the man credit. It was a clever idea.

**

When Liz and Henry arrived home, Stan was waiting for them.

"Good morning. Please come inside." Liz unlocked the door. "What is the news of Andrew?"

"We lost his trail again, but I need to learn more about the wandering cowboys."

Henry tilted her head. "What is a cowboy?"

"In our country anyone who travels with cows and leads the cattle to new places is called a cowboy. In Africa the Fuufuu do that work, so we Americans call them cowboys." Liz took a seat across from Stan but looked at Henry. "Can you bring coffee for our visitor, please?"

Stan spoke. "If Fuufuu live isolated from other tribes, how do they get their supplies? Where do they buy provisions? Or are they self-sufficient?"

"They sell one of their cows to purchase exquisite jewelry and beautiful clothes for their women. The men like to dress the ladies in expensive finery. They are a proud people, one of the oldest tribes in Africa, who consider themselves important because they own most of the animals. They have lots of body piercings and tattoos to make themselves more beautiful."

Henry brought a cup of coffee and set it on the end table.

Stan nodded and picked it up. "Why is this important?"

"They visit large city markets to purchase gold jewelry, silver earrings and necklaces. If we search the big African bazaars where people sell these expensive ornaments, we might meet members of the tribe."

"Do you know a place called she-bam?" Stan stuttered over the last word.

"Tish-baa-me?" Liz cocked an eyebrow. "It's a huge central marketplace about two hundred miles northeast from the plane crash."

"I've studied the map. I think these cowboys are headed there." Stan frowned. "If the men take care of the herds, what do the women, children, and old people do?"

"They stay in camp to cook, chop firewood, wash clothes, and prepare a local cheese which they sell in the market. They are the only people who make it because there is a secret in its preparation."

"What is the name of it, and what does it look like?"

"It is called rommy and it is sold in most African markets." Liz wrinkled her forehead. "The cheese is in the shape of a wrinkled cylinder about three inches high weighing several pounds. It is white but coated with a dark-orange substance to preserve it."

"Is it safe to eat, and do you eat it?"

"Yes. I cut it up in pieces and boil it for five minutes to kill germs. It's bland but takes on the flavor of what it is cooked in. Other people fry it with onions or put it in spaghetti sauce or gravy."

"Maybe Andrew is getting a decent diet." Stan sipped on his coffee.

Henry stood in the doorway and said, "Excuse me, Sister Liz. The Fuufuu never eat rommy. They prefer to sell it and collect the money."

"I've always wondered why those nomads are so skinny. They have plenty of milk, cheese, and meat but apparently don't eat much of it."

Stan looked at Henry. "Why don't they eat more of it to maintain their health?"

Henry glanced off to the side.

Liz sighed, "You may speak to Mr. Stan."

Not looking directly at him, Henry kept her head averted. "They like to sell all of it for money to buy beautiful jewels and clothes. They think if they eat even a little bit, it will deprive them of an ornament or a trinket."

"Will their campsite be close to the herd?" Stan took out his cigarettes, then glanced at Henry, who grimaced and shook her head. He put them back in his pocket.

"The herd will be near a campsite so they can keep watch over it," Liz furrowed her brows. "I've treated people from their tribes."

"How can you treat them when they move all around?"

"When I hold a monthly clinic, the Fuufuu in nearby camps send their sick to me for medicines."

"Sister Liz, the communities with large farms discourage the Fuufuu from coming near their villages because the herds can break away and destroy local crops. If those cows ruin a large crop, a tribal conflict may get started." Henry frowned. "To avoid trouble, Fuufuu try to keep far away from settled people, especially farming communities."

"Thanks for the information." Stan stood. "I need to be going."

"Did you ask the men about my coming?"

"They don't want you to, but since you're paying for the rescue operation and know a lot about these people, they agreed."

"I'm also a nurse and can treat Andrew when we find him."

"Brian was a corpsman in the war and can set broken bones, start intravenous lines, and give pain medications. He can care for Andrew if he needs medical treatment."

"When are you leaving again?"

"Early in the morning."

"Stop at the mission guesthouse first."

Stan turned to the door. "I'm not happy that you're coming."

Liz put her hands on her hips. "He's been gone over two weeks. It's time to join you."

"I didn't think you were serious."

"I'm determined to find Andrew." She walked Stan to his truck. "Goodbye. I'll see you in the morning in the city."

Liz breathed easier. It hadn't been as hard as she thought it would be to convince Stan. The Lord was working everything out. There were no scheduled clinics over the next few days, Mrs. Isaiah was taking care of Mercy, and Henry needed a distraction.

Henry had been sleeping on the floor next to Liz's bed instead of on the comfortable mattress in the sitting room because she didn't want to be alone each night.

Liz turned to Henry. "Do you want to go with me and the men to search for Brother Andrew, or stay here in the house, or take your vacation?"

"I'm coming with you. It's the safest place for me to be, but the men don't want any ladies with them."

"Don't worry about that. We're going."

CHAPTER THIRTY-EIGHT

Liz slung her pack over her shoulder and picked up a basket. She stepped out of the guesthouse and waited in the parking lot.

A couple minutes later, Stan's truck stopped in front of her, and he jumped out of it. He handed her a small stack of papers. "I'm sorry, but I forgot to give you these receipts. Are you ready to go?"

She took the papers and looked them over. Then she stuffed them in a side pocket of her backpack. "Yes, I'm waiting on Henry, who's coming with us."

"That's great. We can use another man."

"You've met Henry. She's …"

Henry had come and stopped next to Liz. "I couldn't find the can opener."

Liz smiled at Henry. "If you packed the machete, we can manage without the can opener."

Reaching up, Henry started to lift the giant basin off her head, and Liz turned to help. The packed tub was almost as tall as Henry and felt like it weighed as much.

When it was on the ground, Liz turned back to Stan. "As I was about to say, this is Henry. You've met my assistant and seen her many times."

Shaking his head, Stan pointed at Henry. "This woman is not coming with us."

Henry dropped to the ground and lowered her head. She screamed. "No! No! No!"

Liz wanted to pull Henry to her feet and tell her it was not the time to be dramatic, but Stan had insulted Henry badly. Her reaction was quite normal.

Henry wailed, "I'm not a woman."

Stan stiffened. "If you're only a child, you're definitely not coming."

Liz's backpack slid off her shoulder as she knelt beside Henry. "He didn't mean what he said."

"Yes, I did." He put his hands on his hips and glared. "She is not coming with us."

Brian, Tom, and John jumped out of the truck. Brian reached out to help Liz and Henry to their feet. Liz raised a hand and motioned them away.

Turning to Henry, Liz said. "Mr. Stan didn't mean to call you a woman."

Stan gave Liz a puzzled look. "What's wrong with that?"

Liz kept her voice calm. "Among her people only a wife or a prostitute is called a woman. Since she isn't married, you called her a harlot."

The men paled, so Liz took advantage of Stan's mistake. She turned to Stan and ordered. "You will apologize to Henry. And she is coming with us."

Stan turned to the men and asked, "What do you think?"

"Do it." Brian commanded. "The ladies are coming." Then he went to the huge basin piled high with pots, dried fish, and onions. Tom helped Brian lift it to the back of the truck.

Tom mumbled. "Sure is heavy. I hope it's not a bunch of stuff for tea parties."

Taking off his baseball cap, Stan said. "Miss Henry, I'm sorry for insulting you. I didn't know what I was saying."

With the corner of her scarf, Henry wiped the tears off her face. In a loud voice, she announced. "I forgive you in Jesus name."

Liz swallowed her laughter and breathed easier. She and Henry were going, and none of the men would say a word more.

Stan put his hat on. "Let's go."

Brian offered his hand to help Liz into the truck, and she took it. When he gave his hand to Henry, she refused it.

After they were seated, Stan put the key in the ignition. "It's not far to the airport where I left the helicopter. Once we lift off, it's an hour's ride to the site of the crash."

"If the rains hadn't wiped out all the footpaths, we would have found Andrew by now." John shook his head. "Every time we picked up his trail, it stormed and washed away the signs."

A few minutes later, Stan turned onto the airport road. "After every deluge it takes longer to start over or find where we lost the trail. We separate and go in different directions searching for tracks, but even with several sets of eyes, we can't follow the trail unless the weather is in our favor."

"I'll pray that we don't have any more storms until we find Andrew." Liz turned to Henry. "We are getting in a helicopter to fly to the plane crash."

"Fly? Did you say fly in the air?" Henry grabbed Liz's arm. "I can't fly up in the air, Sister Liz."

"Why not?"

"I'm too scared. I've changed my mind." Henry's grip tightened. "I can't go."

Liz reached in her bag and took out her keys. "You'll need these to get in the house."

"Why?"

"You'll have to go back to my house to stay there or collect your luggage for a vacation, if you're not coming with us."

"I can't stay there alone. It's too dangerous." She sniffed loudly. "I guess it's better to go with you. I only hope flying is safer than being kidnapped by my father."

"Don't worry." Liz patted Henry's hand. "We often fly in my country."

Stan turned into the airport and parked the truck.

After they stepped out, Henry went to the back to collect her washtub. Then she followed the others to the helicopter.

Liz let Tom help her inside, and then she turned to assist Henry. "At first it may be a little scary, but you'll get used to it."

After Liz fastened her assistant's seatbelt, she leaned over and whispered in Henry's ear. "I'm glad you're coming with me. It wouldn't be proper to go with four men into the bush alone without a chaperon."

Stan started the engine. Henry grabbed Liz's arm. Liz yelled above the roar. "Close your eyes tight."

Henry's body shook from head to toe. Her teeth chattered and lips quivered.

The roars of the engine and whirls of the blades were deafening, but after the noises quieted a little, Henry's eyelids fluttered open. As the shaking helicopter lifted from the ground, Henry screamed louder than the deafening motor. Henry's face had broken out in a sweat as she wrapped her arms around Liz.

"Please relax, we are quite safe. Keep your eyes closed." Liz put her hand on top of Henry's.

During the flight, the rumble of the engine prevented conversation, but the men kept glancing at Henry and shaking their heads.

Brian mouthed, "Is she okay?"

Liz nodded.

By the time they landed at the crash site, Henry had stopped trembling. After she got out, she wiped the sweat from her face. "I want to stay on the ground."

"Okay, but you'll have to walk home." Liz lifted her backpack. "There are no villages here and no taxis."

Stan led the way to the burned-out aircraft. "I wanted you to see this to visualize what happened."

Liz and Henry followed Stan into the cockpit. He turned and spread his arms. "It looks like nothing survived except Andrew."

Brian pointed to the broken windshield. "Don't be alarmed at the dried blood."

Liz clutched her lower arms to suppress a shiver. "It looks like Brother Andrew hit his head on the glass, was injured, and jumped out of the plane."

"We'll fly to where we last lost Andrew's prints." Stan led the way back to the helicopter.

"Are you coming with us or staying here?" Liz asked Henry.

Henry climbed into the helicopter. Liz showed Henry how to fasten the seatbelt. This time Henry didn't scream when the helicopter lifted off, but she kept her eyes closed and her hands clutched on Liz's arm.

Stan yelled above the roar, "I'm flying low so we can take a look around the area."

The men lifted their binoculars and peered out. Twenty minutes later Stan set the helicopter down in a small clearing and everyone got out. "Let's eat lunch and discuss strategy."

John moved some logs to make benches. Brian handed each person a ham sandwich. Tom gave everyone a bottle of water.

Stan said. "We'll search until dark and then we'll make camp and cook a meal."

After eating, Stan led the way to a narrow bush trail. "This is where we lost Andrew's prints."

"If we divide into three teams, we can check out more paths along the main trail."

Stan turned to Liz. "Will Henry mind going with Brian?"

"Since Brian has gray hair, it will be fine."

Stan scratched his head and furrowed his brows. "You come with me. Tom and John will make up the third team."

Liz explained the plan to Henry, who surprised Liz by agreeing without any fuss.

The men had cell phones with GPS. After they had hiked about fifteen miles, they decided it was too dark to search any longer, so they made camp. The men set up heavy logs around the outer encampment to use as seats. The searchers took out their military rations and offered the containers to the ladies.

Liz shook her head. "No thank you. Henry is cooking supper. She's used to preparing plenty over a campfire. Save your rations for another time and eat with us."

"Sounds good." John put the package away.

In a few minutes, Henry had started a fire. Over it, she set a small pot filled with aromatic tomato sauce and dried fish. Then she added rice and let it simmer.

Tom collected more wood for the fire. "It smells and looks good."

When Henry had supper ready she took out her plastic plates and metal soup spoons. She served each man a generous helping.

Brian took a bite. "Thanks Henry. This is tasty."

"Sister Liz, what's tasty."

"It means that is tastes delicious."

"It sure is delicious." Tom grinned.

After supper, the men unrolled their sleeping bags. Henry collected piles of leaves and spread open two thatched mats on top of them.

Sitting next to Liz on a boulder, Stan puffed on his cigarette. "The men take turns keeping watch. Although we don't expect trouble, we are aware of wild animals."

Brian swatted at a mosquito. "The African golden cat, which is much larger than the wildcat, is more common in this area. I'd like to see one, but I want to have my pistol cocked when I do."

"You can use my sleeping bag." Stan stood. "I'll sleep in the vacant bag while the owner is on watch."

"Thank you. When I was packing I imagined a shelter or a lean-to. I've never slept out in the open like this."

Stan moved to Brian and whispered in his ear. Then Stan picked up his sleeping bag and placed it closer to the center of camp. He turned to Henry. "You can double your mats. Sister Liz will sleep in this."

Brian whispered to Liz. "Can I use your fire to prepare coffee?"

Liz called. "Henry, can the men use your fire when you're finished?"

"I will boil bath water for the men." Henry washed out her large skillet.

"No, thanks." Brian laughed. "We don't bathe in hot water out here. I want to make coffee in my own small pot."

Stan stomped out his cigarette. "Brian's a coffee expert. He has a special brand and makes it a certain way."

Silently Henry handed Brian the jug of water. She sat down on a rock with a pan of soapy water to wash the plastic plates and silver spoons.

Nearby bushes shook.

The men reached for their guns and jumped up.

CHAPTER THIRTY-NINE

Liz stiffened and glanced at the men.

Brian whispered, "You ladies step back."

The bushes kept shaking until two teenage boys leaped out of them. They were barefoot, wore tattered clothes, and old straw hats.

The ex-marines chuckled and shrugged but kept their weapons by their sides.

Henry greeted the visitors using a lengthy string of salutations in three languages.

After the boys responded in one language, they carried on a conversation with Henry.

Liz understood the words but didn't comprehend the meaning. "My assistant speaks five languages." She whispered to Brian. "I know one of them well but only a few greetings in the others."

A few minutes later, Henry gave the pan of leftover rice to the boys. "Sister Liz, I told them we are searching for your brother."

The larger boy pulled up a rock and sat on it. The smaller lad pointed his finger at Stan. Henry nodded. "He asks if your brother is a white man like these men."

Liz smiled at the boys. "Yes. He was flying a plane near the border."

Henry said, "They heard one of those iron birds fell to the ground and burned."

The taller teenager raised his hand and pointed in the direction of the burned out plane.

Henry furrowed her brow. "Since then, the people have been talking of a man called "Kiki.""

"What's Kiki?" Liz frowned at Henry.

"It means no skin. Sister Liz, it's not polite to talk while eating so I have to wait until they finish the rice."

Clamping her mouth shut, Liz prayed the boys had good news. After they had eaten the leftovers, the taller boy stood and gave a speech. Henry put her hands on her hips and glared at him.

Liz mumbled for the men to hear. "Henry's very upset. Something is wrong."

Stan whispered to Brian next to him. The men moved their guns as if readying for a shoot-out.

Henry squatted by the campfire, filled a cup with water, and handed it to the taller boy. After he drank it all, Henry refilled the goblet and gave it to the other boy. Then the taller one spoke again.

Liz turned to the searchers and put a finger to her lips.

Henry translated. "There was a man inside a large bird with wings. It crashed to the ground and burned up. The man inside of the flying machine got all his black skin burned off. The people call him Kiki, which means no skin. They took him into their village."

Stan scowled. "They thought the man in the plane was an African."

"No one can survive if he had all his skin burned off," Liz frowned. "Ask them what language the man in the plane spoke."

After a lengthy discussion with the teens, Henry turned back to Liz. "The boys do not know his tribal language. Everyone believes he was an African man who lost his black skin so he no longer has any tribal tattoos or markings. They think Kiki has a disease, so the people are taking care of him."

"It has to be Andrew." Liz stood and paced. "He is the only white man who flies a small plane."

Henry asked. "May I tell the boys we are looking for Kiki? Maybe they know where the tribe is headed. Then we will be able to find him."

Stan nodded.

Liz mumbled, "They seem so certain he was one of them but lost all his skin."

"If they thought Andrew wasn't one of them, maybe he'd have been in danger." Stan turned to Henry. "Do the boys have any idea where the tribe is going?"

"Yes." Henry smiled.

Liz squealed in joy. "That's great. Where are they going?"

"They are headed to new pastures for their herds of cows."

Stan slapped a hand to his cheek and shook his head. "Where?"

"No one knows where they are going until they get there." Henry shrugged. "They are searching for fresh grazing lands."

Stan raised his eyebrows. "What direction are they traveling?"

After Henry relayed the question, both boys pointed northeast.

"How far?" Stan paced.

"They do not know."

As the boys turned to leave, Liz said, "thank you" in their language. Then she pulled two bars of soap out of her backpack and handed them to the teenagers.

Grinning from ear to ear, the boys left.

Tom chuckled. "They were real happy over that soap."

"You have no idea. I spent one Christmas day with the members of the church. During the exchange of gifts, everyone in the congregation handed bars of soap to each other."

"You're right." Henry nodded. "A bar of soap is a wonderful gift."

"I wanted to reward them but didn't know how. I appreciate you taking care of it Liz. Oops, I mean Sister Liz." Stan took a map out of his bag. "Here is what the region looks like."

Liz pointed to the map. "If we returned to where your men found the last footprint and cane indentation, we can start from there and head straight northeast to where the boys indicated."

"That's a good idea." Stan put his cigarette out.

Liz placed her hand on her chest. "I feel right here if we go back we'll find his trail."

"I agree with your logic, and since you're the one paying, we'll do it your way."

"Thank you, Stan. By the grace of God, we'll find Andrew."

"I'm beginning to believe in your grace of God. If we don't find him in the next few days, we can take this new information and persuade HOW to re-open the investigation. That way more people will search." Stan folded the map.

"The Lord sent these boys to us to confirm Andrew is alive." Liz's eyes widened. "If Andrew is struggling to hike on a broken foot and stopping often to rest, he may not be as far as the boys suggested."

Henry put the empty rice pan in the dish water. "If he is walking with the women, children and old people, he will move slowly. If he cannot keep up with them, they might leave several handicapped people with him."

Liz shivered. Handicapped people?

Lord, help us reach Andrew before it's too late.

CHAPTER FORTY

Andrew forced his eyelids open. The sun had set. He must have passed out again. He was grateful when he did. If he was alert, it felt like his head was bursting into a million pieces.

He rubbed his temple, but it didn't ease the throbbing and dizziness. The ground rose up in front of him. Every joint in his body ached. Even his stomach and back hurt. Nausea had kept him from drinking or eating.

Milo and the girls dropped their loads. The woman knelt next to him and touched his face. Her hand flew back. She picked up her jug and poured water on a cloth and wiped the perspiration from his forehead.

He shivered and groaned.

Lord, let me die quickly. Please mercy.

He closed his eyes and saw the tiny black baby in the white lady's arms. Then he remembered Liz. He'd wanted a future with her, but it wasn't supposed to be. He'd soon be in Heaven.

Andrew moaned as Milo sponged his face and mumbled strange words. He opened and closed his eyes several times. A group of villagers surrounded him, clicked their tongues, and shook their heads. One by one each nomad turned away and walked down the narrow path until only Milo and her two daughters were left.

Sighing in agony, he tried to sit up but fell back down. Everything went black.

When he woke, Milo was cutting branches from the nearby trees and constructing a lean-to. She picked up a large roll of woven thatch and unwound it. Then she dug holes in the ground and set the stakes for the walls. After chopping wood, she started a fire and set her small skillet of water on to boil.

Why was Milo setting up her home away from the rest of her people? Had he inadvertently married her and were they starting their own family?

Tio, Eilo, and their mother pulled Andrew under the thatched shelter. Milo took off his sneaker, unzipped his pants, and removed his clothes. Then she covered him with her wrapping skirt and put his shoes next to him. The girls ran off with his clothes, but he no longer needed them where he was going.

Why had they left the sneakers? That had been the only item the young boys had coveted in the village. Several had offered to trade their flip-flips for his shoes, but the chief had always interceded.

The world spun around him again and everything went black.

When Andrew woke, he peeked under the cotton cloth that covered him. He was still naked. It had been a long time since he last drank or ate and was grateful Milo hadn't offered him water or food because he couldn't stop gagging on his nausea.

Why had the woman constructed a lean-to for him? Was she trying to heal him and get him back on his feet? Or was building a shelter against the blazing sun her way of caring for him?

His life was slipping away, but he wasn't alone.

Lord, let me die quickly.

***

Chief Tiolare called his people. "Has anything bad happened to us since we took Kiki into our village?"

The oldest man said. "Nothing bad has caught us."

Sitou said, "We've had fewer difficulties traveling than we ever had and not as many problems buying supplies in the local markets."

"Milo has prepared Kiki to cross the river, so we don't need to sit around and wait for Kiki's departure." Doditu sharpened his machete.

"You are right my brother." Chief Tiolare nodded. "We will keep moving so we won't lose our herds."

"You are a wise leader. The animals are growing leaner and leaner," the oldest man frowned. "But that always happens on a long journey like this."

"Milo and my granddaughters have volunteered to wait with Kiki and see that he gets to the other side."

"You have a kind-hearted daughter, but it is not proper for her to stay with Kiki."

The chief looked at each female. "Would any of you women like to remain behind with Milo?"

All of them shook their heads.

Doditu glared. "None of our women can stay because we need them to chop firewood and cook for us in camp. Milo and the girls must come with us. Kiki is not from our tribe. He can go alone across the river."

"It isn't proper to let him cross by himself." The chief frowned. "Would any of you leave one of your relatives alone to pass over?"

"No, we wouldn't, but Kiki is not our relative."

Doditu pointed toward the trail. "Milo has built a lean-to to protect Kiki until his departure. She has done more than enough."

The chief sighed. "It would be wrong to let him go to the other side by himself."

"He is not one of us." The ancient elder said.

The chief's eyes pleaded as he looked at each of the men. "He never hurt any of us. Surely one of the females is willing to stay with my daughter and her girls."

"A crossover can take weeks. If we stayed and waited, all our animals could die. We need our women with us, so Milo and her girls should come, too"

Chief Tiolare didn't want to leave his daughter and granddaughters alone in the bush with a dying white man, but neither did he want to force another female to stay with them.

As always, he reached a compromise.

***

Liz and the rescue workers woke early and ate breakfast. After packing up, they left the campsite.

They divided into three teams again and found where they had stopped the previous day and headed northeast. They combed the countryside searching for tracks along the tapering paths.

Towards evening, Stan stopped to smoke a cigarette. "The sun is setting. I'll radio the other teams. We need to make camp before it gets dark."

They met in a small clearing.

John and Tom collected firewood while Brian and Stan arranged logs around the campsite. Liz helped Henry prepare spaghetti with dried fish in tomato sauce.

Liz filled the plates and served them to the men. "It's been two long days of searching and I'm disappointed we didn't find Andrew today. I've been praying all day as we've been looking."

After Brian finished eating, he made coffee. "I'm surprised we didn't meet anyone. Sister Henry, why aren't there any people here?"

"They don't have your special pills to put in the water to make it good. Without that medicine, they would get sick and die if they drank the swamp water." Henry poured hot water into her basin to wash the plates. "There are no fertile fields for farming and no pastures for grazing. It's a useless place except as a means to reach the good land on the other side."

After Henry finished washing the dishes, she and Liz went behind shrubs to get ready for bed. Then they took their places at the campfire.

As usual, Liz took out her Bible and opened it. "May I read the scripture again this evening?"

Brian nodded. "We'd like that." He was the only one who ever answered her.

After reading several psalms aloud, she asked. "Will you join me for prayer?"

All the men bowed their heads.

Liz prayed. "Lord Jesus, we thank you for giving us a pleasant day, be with us as we sleep. Lead our way and show us where Andrew is. Help us find him tomorrow. Amen."

Stan lit a cigarette. "Sister Liz, I respect you and Andrew as being religious."

"We aren't religious. Religion is doing pious acts. I accepted Jesus as my Savior and have a personal relationship with Him. I talk with Him every day."

"Praying, reading the Bible, and going to church sound religious to me."

"Reading God's Word and praying are the ways we communicate with the Lord." Liz put the Bible in her backpack. "We Christians love the Lord, want His presence in our lives, and desire to please Him."

Understanding the difference between being religious and being saved, wasn't enough. One had to believe on Jesus.

CHAPTER FORTY-ONE

Early the next morning Liz wrapped the supplies and handed them to Henry as she packed the tub. Since six people had eaten meals over the last few days, the basin was only half as heavy.

Stan slung his backpack over his shoulder. "Let's divide in the same three teams again so we can cover more ground."

Brian and Henry took the first path, Tom and John headed down the second trail.

As Liz followed Stan, she said, "Henry agreed to go with Brian because she considers him a father figure, but I'm surprised she hasn't raised a ruckus about me going with you alone on the trail."

"I never meant any offense by calling her a woman."

"She forgave you and that's the end of it."

"Most of the African ladies who work for HOW are quiet and submissive. I've never met a local lady like Henry." Stan squatted to cut bushes that had blocked the trail.

"All my assistants have been silent and compliant ladies, except Henry. Over the months, I've learned to like and respect her a great deal."

As they hiked on the narrow trail, a gentle breeze shifted the leaves on the nearby bushes. Searching for footprints, handprints, and cane indentations, Liz prayed for Andrew. She hoped he had some protection from the blazing sun. It was almost overhead, so it had to be nearly noon. She lifted her pony tail off her neck to get some relief from the heat. Then she twisted it with a clip to the back of her head. Taking a water bottle out of her bag, she drank.

Stan called. "Let's halt for lunch. I'll radio the others and tell them."

She could hike for days if only they'd find Andrew. It was their third day of searching. She tried to hold back her tears, but her heavy heart throbbed. Choking down some cheese and crackers, she waited for Stan to finish his cigarette. Then she stood, flicked sweat off her brow, and followed him down the trail.

Several hours later, Brian's voice shouted on the radio. "Sister Henry found a Nike footprint and a cane indentation."

Stan radioed back. "We'll be right there."

The searchers met at the print. Stan asked. "How did this indentation get so far off the path?"

Henry said, "I saw bushes out of place. Then I looked in the direction of the damaged shrubs and found this."

Tom walked ahead. "Here are two more handprints and they look fresh."

Henry ran forward, "There are many prints this way."

They walked slowly along the path without destroying the tracks. They halted at a cluster of barefoot prints, of various sizes.

"It looks like Andrew collapsed here and the people surrounded him." Stan frowned.

Liz closed her eyes and swayed as Brian reached out to steady her. Had the people beaten Andrew to death? Or had he died?

An unfamiliar female voice made Liz jump. Henry called loudly in several languages and started walking toward the woman's voice. They followed Henry as she led the way to a topless lady with two naked girls.

The woman stirred an offensive brew in a small cooking pot. She and the two children glanced at Liz and the men. Then the mother screamed, dropped her spoon, and grabbed the hands of her daughters. She raced down the narrow trail with the two little girls as if a lion was after them.

The men stepped closer to the tiny camp while Henry got down on all fours and crawled into the lean-to. "We found him. Sister Liz, come quick."

Liz ducked inside. Seeing the rise and fall of his chest, Liz thanked God. Then she crept on hands and knees toward the unconscious form. She put her hand on his head, face and neck. Andrew was burning up with fever, probably a hundred and five degrees. Tears filled her eyes. Gently she placed her finger tips on his wrist. She shuddered at his weak, irregular pulse. Pinching the skin on the back of his hand, she noted it stayed in place when pressed, a sign of severe dehydration.

"Brian, come inside and check Andrew."

Henry mumbled, "I'll go out, so he has room to crawl inside."

Brian took Andrew's pulse and shouted. "Sister Henry, can you bring my bag in here?"

Henry poked her head in the lean-to. "There's no room to carry anything in."

Liz called, "Can you men lift the sides of this shelter so we have better light and more space to work?"

Both sides of the lean-to lifted. With sunlight, Andrew's complexion looked whiter and deader.

Brian opened his bag and lifted out a blood pressure apparatus. He wrapped the cuff around Andrew's upper arm. "His blood pressure is 80 over 40. He appears to be going into shock or may already be in shock."

"He's burning up with fever, and his pulse is weak." Liz brushed a tear off her cheek and sniffed.

Brian took a bag of intravenous fluid, tubing, and a needle out of his backpack. Then he glanced at Liz's hands.

Liz stared down at her trembling fingers and shook her head. "I can't do it."

"Don't worry, Liz." Brian nodded. "I'll start the drip, but we need to get him to a hospital fast."

Tom and John crouched to watch while Stan puffed on a cigarette. "I'm glad we've been moving the helicopter to the nearest fields, but even so, it may take a couple of hours to get it. The closest landing space is about a mile back."

Brian nodded. "We'll bring Andrew to the clearing."

"I'll see you there." Stan left and jogged down the trail.

After starting the drip, Brian unrolled surgical tape to attach the bag of fluids to the top of the lean-to. Then he filled a syringe with a starting dose of antibiotics which he added to the fluids.

Liz sniffed. "Henry, please bring a bucket of cool water, so we can bathe Brother Andrew."

A couple minutes later Henry handed Liz a calabash. She picked up a large dressing and plunged it in the water. After taking a bar of soap out of her bag, she washed Andrew's face. Most of the dried blood clots and dirt came loose with gentle scrubbing. She unwrapped alcohol swabs and wiped the last bits of grime away. Then she sponged his neck and chest with the cool water.

"The wounds and gashes appear to be healing. His temperature indicates a severe infection or cerebral malaria or both of them." Liz covered the healed-over gash on Andrew's face with a gauge dressing.

Brian pulled another bag of fluids out of his pack. "He should have a second line in the other arm."

"I agree." Liz brushed a tear off her cheek. "If he has cerebral malaria, he needs an intravenous dose of quinimax or he can die. I have the medicine in my bag."

"You know more about tropical diseases than I do. If we gave it and he didn't have malaria, would it be harmful?"

"No, it's safer to give it." Liz called, "Henry, bring the quinimax from my backpack."

After Brian had started the second drip line with the malarial treatment, he lifted the cloth that covered Andrew's feet. "I've never seen a foot so swollen as this one. It's more than three times as large as his left one."

Liz's shoulders shook as she cried and prayed. "Lord, let it not be too late."

"It's probably broken." Brian said, "We could make a stretcher, but it wouldn't fit on these narrow trails."

John squatted. "I can carry him on my back."

Liz crawled to Andrew's feet and carefully removed the black and green mass from it. Then she washed his leg and foot with soap and water and cleaned it with alcohol.

As she examined the dirt-free deformity up closer, she shuddered. The tears flowed, but she thanked God that Andrew was still alive.

Henry glanced at the foot and shook her head. "I have never seen such a sick foot in my life." She picked up the exquisite cane by Andrew's mat. "This is very strong and if I put a notch in it we can use it to keep the fluids elevated. I can hold this staff with the attached bags and walk behind Brother John as he carries Brother Andrew." Henry turned to Tom. "Do you have a machete so I can notch this?"

Taking the staff, Tom flicked open his Swiss army knife. "I'll have this done in a few minutes."

Liz turned to Brian. "Can you set this ankle and foot? I cleaned all the witch doctor's concoction off."

"At first glance it almost looked like gangrene." Brian grasped the injured foot and tried to move it, but it stayed in place. "I can't set the ankle. He'll need surgery to break and re-set these bones. He's probably been walking on a broken foot. I'll stabilize and wrap it."

By the time Brian had dressed it, the first bag of fluids, antipyretics and dose of antibiotics had flowed into Andrew's veins. Brian replaced the bag and reinserted the antibiotics. He took out the blood pressure cuff and wrapped it around Andrew's arm. "His blood pressure has increased to 100/70. That's a good sign. His temperature has gone down to one hundred and three. I can't determine the extent of his head injury."

Liz kept swabbing Andrew's chest with cool water. "Andrew, it's me, Liz, open your eyes."

In slow motion his eyelids flickered. He opened, closed and opened them again. He puckered his brows and moaned.

"Can you see me?" Liz smiled. "The helicopter is on the way. You'll be fine."

He licked his cracked, dry lips. Liz held a cup of water to his mouth. He drank it, closed his eyes, and passed out again. Her racing heart slowed to normal. Her hands shook as she secured the intravenous site with several bandages to Andrew's arm to assure its flow during the evacuation.

Liz turned to Henry. "Let's leave our food, clothes, and provisions to show appreciation to the people who cared for Andrew. Besides we can walk faster without supplies." She kept her bottles of water, a few snacks, and medications.

Tom and Brian lifted Andrew and laid him on John's back. Liz arranged the fluid lines and attached both bags to the staff which Henry held. Brian led the way, followed by John with Andrew. Henry walked just behind carrying the staff and Liz followed. Tom took up the rear.

When they reached the clearing, they lifted Andrew off John's back and onto a sleeping bag. They waited an hour for Stan in the helicopter. Hearing the whirl of the blades, Liz thanked God.

After Stan landed, Brian leaped inside and prepared a mat of sleeping bags on the floor. Then he took the fluids from the staff in Henry's hands and tied them to the overhead window lever. Tom and Brian lifted Andrew and put him on the thick pad.

"There's not enough room for all of us in the helicopter." Stan turned to Liz. "What do you think?"

Liz smiled at Stan. "You men go with Andrew. Stan, you're familiar with the medical facilities at HOW and know the best and quickest way to get treatment for Andrew. Brian, you can monitor the medications."

"Tom should come with Brian and me, in case someone needs to run an errand and help with Andrew." Stan turned to John. "Can you keep an eye on these ladies until I fly back and get you? Do you have enough supplies in case I can't return tonight?"

"We'll be fine." John nodded. "I'll take good care of the ladies."

Liz smiled. "Don't worry, Stan. If something happens and you can't get back tonight we'll return to Andrew's camp and use the supplies we left. Henry speaks their language."

As the helicopter lifted off the ground, Liz let the tears of gratitude flow. Andrew would live, but when he'd opened his eyes, he hadn't recognized her. Did he have brain damage?

CHAPTER FORTY-TWO

Liz, Henry and John sat on logs and waited. By the time the sun had set, the helicopter hadn't returned. Liz thought it best to get settled at the campsite while there was a little daylight left.

She picked up her bag. "Let's go back to the lean-to for the night."

"Yes, we should do that." John took out a flashlight. "I hope there weren't complications with Andrew on the way."

Complications? She'd been so excited to find Andrew and have him evacuated she hadn't considered problems. What if there were complications?

"Don't worry." John encouraged, "I'm sure they made it to the hospital without problems."

Henry stood and hiked behind John and Liz toward the camp.

The radio buzzed. "John, are you there?"

"Yes."

"Can you and the girls manage tonight?"

"Yes. How's Andrew?"

"He's resting in a hospital bed and continuing treatment. There's a tropical storm here, and we can't fly. I'll be there early in the morning, if the weather permits."

"See you tomorrow."

After Liz had trekked about fifteen minutes, the chatter of the woman and the two little girls halted her. "Let's not startle them as we did earlier." She turned to Henry. "Go ahead and explain to them why we want to come into camp."

Henry left. Ten minutes later, she returned with the two little girls. "Their mother, whose name is Milo, has been taking care of Brother Andrew and agreed to stay with him until he got better or crossed the river. She is cooking supper for us."

John gasped. "I don't believe it."

Henry tilted her head. "What don't you believe?"

"That a stranger would cook supper for us."

"Among our people, it's normal." Henry shrugged.

"I'm famished." John grinned.

When they reached the campfire Milo spoke to her daughters, who left and returned with large rocks for John, Henry, and Liz to sit on.

Henry was a talker, but the two girls chattered more than Henry and in a language Liz didn't understand. The jabbering seemed to go on and on.

"These girls, Eilo and Tio found Brother Andrew by the river and performed the death exam on him." Henry translated.

Liz gasped and covered her mouth. "What's a death exam?"

"Lift the victim's arms, and if they fall to the ground it means he is dead. Brother Andrew's arms fell to the ground over and over again, but then he sat up and called to them, so the chief and his brothers came and did the blood test."

The corners of John's mouth lifted. "How can they do that out here in the jungle?"

Henry scowled. "The chief confirmed Brother Andrew's blood was red, like his."

Liz's lips twitched.

John chuckled.

"Everyone was frightened of Brother Andrew's eyes. They had never seen blue eyes and thought he was a spirit. The chief convinced them he had to be human because spirits didn't have any blood and Andrew had blood like them." Henry sighed.

Milo served each of them a steaming ball of white clay with a dab of green sauce. Liz's stomach growled, but she couldn't eat the slimy gravy. Out of the corner of her eye, she watched Henry devour the food.

"Sister Liz, this is delicious. I could eat yours and mine. I've missed my slimy sauce." Henry licked her fingers.

"I'd appreciate that, Henry." When Milo's back was turned, Liz lifted her plate and slid the food onto Henry's dish."

John put a bite in his mouth and choked. When Milo turned away again, he slid his supper onto Henry's plate.

Hoping they didn't understand English, Liz said. "After Milo finishes eating, let's share the cheese crackers. I need a little food in my stomach to be able to sleep tonight."

When Liz found the snacks, she said, "There aren't enough for everyone." Liz opened a package and gave Milo and the girls each a cracker, two to John and one for herself."

Milo and her daughters spit it on the ground.

Henry frowned. "You and Brother John should eat the last two packages of crackers. We can't eat your cheese."

Milo collected the dirty plates while Henry put water on the campfire to heat for washing dishes. "I gave Andrew's cane back to Milo because it belonged to her great-great-grandfather."

Henry put the washed dishes in her large tub, which she had carried on her head. "Milo wanted to know about our God. Her people have been worried that if Brother Andrew died, his God would punish their people. I told her about Jesus and how much He loves us and died for us. Milo wants Jesus to be her God. Can we pray with her to accept Christ?"

"Yes. I'll join you in the prayer."

John asked, "Can I pray, too, and ask Jesus to be my Savior?"

"Yes." After they had prayed, Liz smiled. "The Lord brought good out of Brother Andrew's plane crash. Milo and her daughters have now trusted in Jesus."

"Me, too." John grinned.

"Milo wants to know why we left our belongings because if we are giving them to her, we must show our appreciation in the proper manner, or it will offend them."

Liz rolled her eyes at John. "I need to present these one by one with a speech of gratitude." She picked up the bars of soap, "We present this valuable gift to show our appreciation for your care to our brother."

Henry dropped to her knees, lowered her head, and handed the soap to Milo. Henry looked like a servant bowing before royalty as she translated Liz's words and added her own flowery phrases.

Milo and her daughters beamed and clapped their hands after each presentation. Milo picked up the skirts and blouses, much too small for the large-boned woman, but held them up to the girls, who could grow into them. By the time Liz made elaborate speeches for the sack of food, a cooking pot, a knife, the clothes, and Andrew's sneakers, her throat was raw.

John mumbled. "African ladies talk a lot."

Liz clamped her jaw shut.

"Milo wants to know how far away Brother Andrew's village is because he wore too many clothes."

"There's a big water between Africa and America." Liz wrinkled her brow and rubbed her temple. "If Milo sat in a dug-out canoe and rowed day and night it would take three months in the boat on the water to reach our country."

Henry gasped. "Sister Liz, I didn't know you had to row a boat for three months to get to your country."

"It's an example." Liz turned to John. "Does that sound right to you?"

John laughed. "I've never heard such an illustration, but it shows the distance."

Liz covered her yawn. "Can we turn in now?"

Henry turned to Milo. "I'll get permission."

After Milo gave her consent for the visitors to sleep, John asked, "Can you ladies manage with only one sleeping bag. We used the others to make a pallet for Andrew in the helicopter."

Liz unzipped the heavy-duty bag. "This will be fine for us."

Milo pounded the stakes of the lean-to back in the ground while Tio and Eilo gathered leaves and spread them inside the shelter. Milo unrolled a grass-woven sleeping mat and put it on top of the foliage.

Henry spread another mat next to the first one and Liz placed the sleeping bag on top of the thatched mats. Eilo and Tio gathered a pile of leaves for John. Then Milo unfolded a cloth and covered the foliage for his bed.

"Thank you." He turned to Liz. "These people are hospitable. Wake me if you need me or in case of attack."

Liz giggled. "Who do you think will assault us?"

"Wild animals."

John tucked his gun under the corner of his mat near his head. "Better to be safe than sorry."

The ladies and girls crawled into the shelter.

An hour after everyone had gone to bed, John yelled, "Who's there?" Grabbing the gun, he jumped to his feet.

The females darted out of the lean-to.

Milo called, and a man shouted back. She grinned. "My father and his younger brothers have come to check on me and the children. It was the best compromise my father could manage since no one wanted to stay behind with us. Either my father or one of his brothers stays with me and the girls each night."

Three shirtless men approached the glowing campfire. Milo made the introductions.

Liz smothered another yawn. It had to be midnight, but it sounded like the Africans wanted to party as they talked on and on.

Milo picked up the gifts, one by one, and held them near the light of the fire. She chattered, most likely repeating the same speeches that Liz had given. The men beamed and nodded their heads.

Henry leaned closer to Liz. "Since he's the chief, we must give dignitary speeches of appreciation."

"Ask permission to do it in the morning." Sitting on the rock, Liz leaned forward. "I can't keep my eyes open."

Henry translated. The brothers shook hands with John and Liz before leaving, but the chief talked on and on.

"He wants me to tell him about our God. The chief is convinced that our God is very powerful to prevent Kiki from dying and bring you to find him here in the bush."

"We thank our Lord who showed us the way to Brother Andrew. Our loving God brought us here and we praise Him." Liz smiled.

Milo spoke to her father for a long time. Henry knelt. "He wants to believe on Jesus and trust Him as Lord."

Liz grinned for that was worth staying awake for. "Let's pray."

After the prayer, the chief beamed broadly as Henry gathered more leaves for the chief's bed. "He has taken Jesus as his Savior, but where will he go to church? They have no Bible to read, but it wouldn't do much good because no one in their tribe can read."

"We'll talk about it tomorrow." Liz led the way inside the shelter. The men lay on their sleeping mats. In a few minutes, John was snoring.

The whirl of the helicopter woke them. Everyone jumped up.

"John, where are you?" The radio blared. "Are you okay?"

"We're on our way." John grabbed his gun, the radio, and the bag he carried yesterday. "Time to go. Follow me." He took the lead down the narrow trail and jogged to the helicopter.

Liz slung her backpack over her shoulder and followed John. She glanced back at Henry, Milo, the girls, and the chief, who ran after them.

Reaching the helicopter, John helped Liz into it.

Henry climbed in. "Sister Liz, I can't leave."

"Did you forget something?" Liz leaned forward. "Stan, wait a minute."

"Yes, I did." Henry swallowed. "I made a promise to God that if He helped me through nursing school I would be a missionary. The Lord wants me to stay here and minister to these people. They are now believers and have no church, no Bible, and can't read. They need help so they will grow as Christians."

"I'm proud of you, but today might not be the right time to stay. These people are traveling and haven't reached their grazing lands. Go and ask the chief..." Liz looked up into the face of the village leader, who was climbing into the helicopter.

John patted the seat next to him, then turned to Liz. "Let's give him a little ride. It will be good public relations and show him that an iron bird doesn't always burn up and crash." He fastened the chief's seatbelt. "Henry, tell him what we are doing."

The chief and Henry talked for several minutes. Then she smiled, the first grin that Liz had ever seen on her assistant's face.

Stan flew over the terrain for ten minutes before he set the bird back down.

"Tell the chief that you will come back to his people and teach them more about God after they reach their new location. Find out where you should meet him."

Liz waited for Henry to finish talking to the chief.

"I'm so happy I can do what the Lord wants me to do. The chief gave me the name of the village, closest to their final destination. I will come back in three months and meet them."

As the chief climbed out, he beamed widely. Milo and the girls jumped and waved their arms. Then Milo took her daughter's hands. The chief waved with both arms as the helicopter whirled noisily. When it lifted, the chief stood proudly, grinning from ear to ear.

Liz's heart clenched. Without the chief's help, Andrew might not have survived.

CHAPTER FORTY-THREE

When the helicopter set down at the capital airport, Liz and Henry jumped out and hired a taxi to the mission guesthouse.

Liz could scarcely keep her eyes open. She hadn't slept much the previous night because Henry, as she slept, kept pushing Liz off the sleeping bag and onto the ground. Liz glanced at the clock and saw it was ten in the morning. After bathing, Liz ate a peanut butter sandwich and then collapsed on the cot next to Henry's bed and fell asleep.

Sometime later, a violent pounding on the door woke Liz. She got up and answered it. "Hello, Stan."

"I received a message from the clinic. Andrew will be leaving for England at five this evening. He wants to see you before he goes. My helicopter is here, so I can fly you there in thirty minutes."

"I'd love to see Andrew. I'll get dressed and meet you in the lounge."

Liz woke Henry. "Stan is taking me to the hospital to see Brother Andrew. Here's money to buy the supplies at the market this afternoon. Try to purchase replacements for everything we left in the bush. If you are scared to go out alone, get a taxi to the church and ask for an escort."

Henry stretched. "I'm not frightened."

Why wasn't Henry scared anymore? Her father was still out there with policemen and witchdoctors, who threatened to carry her away.

Shaking her head, Liz picked up her backpack and went to the door. "I'll be back tonight."

Stan led the way to his truck. "Brian came with me to see more of the countryside."

Liz asked, "How is Andrew?"

"Two bones in his foot are fractured. Walking on it caused more damage. He's being evacuated for orthopedic surgery. He also has malaria fever and typhoid"

"Please thank the men for me. Were there enough funds?"

"You were more than generous. I'm returning this five thousand with the receipts. HOW's insurance will reimburse you for the rest." Stan handed her an envelope. "Are you a secret heiress?"

"No, I earned a lot of money working at the hospital and never had time to spend it."

"The doctor says Andrew will need eight weeks to recuperate from broken bones, infection, and malaria. He would have died if you and Brian hadn't started the medications."

Stan parked his truck. He and Brian escorted Liz to the helicopter. After another deafening flight, Stan landed at the HOW clinic.

Liz followed them into Andrew's room. She nodded at John and Tom.

Her heart squeezed at Andrew's hollowed-out face and thin arms. She loved him and thanked God he was alive. His pale cheeks and clean-shaven jaw made him look sick. He was leaning back on a stack of pillows with his splinted leg elevated on a pile of cushions.

Moving quickly to the bed, she took his hand in a warm clasp. "I'm so happy to see you. Thank God we found you when we did."

"It's good to see you, too."

Her breath hitched in her throat. "You look thirty pounds lighter. How do you feel?"

"Much better since I'm taking pain medications and have had decent food and water. You would never believe the dirty water those poor people drink."

Liz sat in a chair by the bed. "What happened after you crashed?"

"I hit my head hard on the windshield. The glass broke and cut my face. My chest crashed into the control panel. I forgot who I was or why I was there. The Stone Age people took care of me."

"What Stone Age people?"

"The natives didn't wear many clothes." He winked at her. "Even the ladies were topless."

The men laughed.

"What's all this commotion? You should be resting." A middle-aged man in a white lab coat stood in the doorway. "I'm Doctor Morgan, who will be supervising your evacuation to England.

Considering everything that happened, you're in better shape than I thought you would be."

"We thank God for that." Liz smiled at the doctor. "But Andrew's not quite himself. He thinks he traveled to the Stone Age."

The doctor pointed toward Liz. "Here's a sensible woman."

Andrew squeezed her hand. "That's why I want to recuperate here after I have surgery."

"I understand why you'd want to come back here, but you'll need help getting around and bathing. Someone will have to give you meals and medications." The doctor smiled "The insurance and HOW authority will make the right decision for you."

"I don't know anyone in England." Andrew shook his head. "My friends are here."

Liz smiled. "I'd like to have you close by, but you need medical care. Besides, doesn't your foot have to be in a cast for two months?"

The doctor turned back to her. "He'll be able to get around with a walking cast and crutches, provided he has someone to help."

Stan scratched his head. "Andrew, if you're set on getting better here, I'll talk to our boss about letting you rent a suite in a city hotel. You were injured while working for HOW. Surely if you wanted to recover here instead of England, which is ten times more expensive, the boss will agree."

The doctor frowned. "It would be better if he stayed in his villa with live-in help."

"It's hundreds of miles away from her." Andrew pointed to Liz. "Besides, I'd be so lonesome there."

Two medical workers rolled a stretcher into the room. One of the nurses took Andrew's temperature, blood pressure, and pulse. The other one adjusted the drops of the intravenous line. They lifted Andrew onto the stretcher to wheel him out of the room.

He looked back. "I'll be seeing you, Sister Liz."

"Have a safe trip, Brother Andrew, and get well." She waved.

As the stretcher rolled out the door, each of the men shook hands with him.

When Andrew was gone, Liz turned to Brian. "Will you be free for a couple of months?"

"Free for what, Sister Liz?"

"As an experienced medical corpsman, you're accustomed to taking care of men." Liz took a breath. "If you don't need to get back for any commitments, would you be willing to stay with Andrew while he recovers? I'd pay you full wages."

Brian sat down on the vacated bed and rubbed his jaw. "I'm divorced and live alone. My daughters are grown. After thirty years in the military, I've been enjoying my retirement and don't need to rush back to the States. The extra money will come in handy. You folks are pleasant to work with. Sure, I'd be glad to stay with Andrew."

"Considering this is a third world country, I'd pay you hardship compensation."

"I trust you to give me what is fair. I don't think Andrew will be a demanding patient," Brian smiled. "And it will give me a chance to see more of Africa."

Liz sat on the bed. "I'd come every weekend to give you a break, so you'll have regular time off. If you had an adjacent room, you'd be close enough to help Andrew get around on his crutches, take a shower, shave, and get dressed. You can order meals from the hotel and wouldn't need to cook or clean since they have maids. You can keep him company and be around in case of complications or a relapse of the malaria."

"Sounds like a good plan."

"Would you like to go back to the States for a short rest while Andrew has his surgery or would you like to stay and wait?"

"Can I go with you to the capital now and check out the amenities at the hotel?"

Stan picked up Liz's bag. "Yes, come with us and get a room."

Brian said, "I'll check out the accommodations and services and get things ready for Andrew."

"I appreciate it." She reached out and shook his hand.

If Andrew recovered in the hotel, Liz could see him every weekend. At least that would give them time to get to know each other better.

***

Before returning home, Liz stopped at the sewing shop. She went into the crowded room and stopped. She was surprised to see a

242

clothesline full of miniature dresses. A pink-checked dress with exquisite ruffles caught her eye. It was gorgeous. Did Mrs. Isaiah have customers who wanted baby clothes, or were all the dresses for Mercy?

Mrs. Isaiah turned to Liz. "I am so happy for you. They announced at ladies Bible study that Brother Andrew was found."

"Yes, we thank God." Liz grinned.

Mrs. Isaiah untied Mercy from her back and handed the baby to Liz. "I am so glad to see you. I have important matters to discuss with you."

"Has Mercy been sick?"

"It's nothing like that. My husband and I love this child. Can we keep her?"

Liz tickled the giggling baby. "What have you been feeding her? It feels like she's gained two pounds."

"My husband and I feed her six times a day. We wanted her to be as big and strong as other children her age."

"No one has claimed her." Liz stroked the baby's cheek.

Liz loved Mercy and hated to give her up, but she had handpicked the parents and was at peace. "You may have her if you like."

A tear ran down Mrs. Isaiah's cheek "You have blessed me so much. You've no idea what it means to hold my own baby after years of barrenness."

Watching the happy interactions of mother and child, Liz had made the right decision. Her heart squeezed as she brushed a tear off her cheek.

CHAPTER FORTY-FOUR

Two weeks after his surgery and recovery from malaria and typhoid, Andrew was released. He was given permission to recuperate in Tamago.

Brian met him at the airport with a wheelchair and hired a private car to drive them to the hotel. Brian helped him unpack and get settled in the room.

Andrew thanked God Liz had the foresight to hire Brian. Without him, HOW would never have allowed Andrew to return to recuperate.

He was excited about spending more time with Liz and looked forward to seeing her on the weekend.

A few days later, when she knocked on his door in the hotel, Brian opened it.

Andrew's heart beat faster. "I've missed you."

"I thank God you'll be fine." She sat in the chair next to the bed.

Her slender fingers felt strong but feminine. As her warm palm settled in his large one, he didn't want to let go of her. Liz's golden-brown curls were twisted into an uneven bun clipped to the back of her head with a lopsided barrette. A few soft tendrils had escaped and framed her heart-shaped face. Her exquisite, green eyes appeared more luminous. He could stare at her for the rest of his life.

"Thank you for hiring Brian. He's a great help."

"I'm glad he's here." She paused. "How did the surgery go?"

"It went well. The surgeon re-set the bones, but they had to use pins." Andrew nodded toward Brian. "He was about ready to order a meal. Will you be able to eat with us?"

Brian took a room key out of his pocket. "I'll go down and order your food, then I'll stay in the restaurant so the two of you can be alone."

"No." Liz raised her eyebrows. "We can't be alone."

"Speak for yourself. I'd like to be alone with you." He'd been looking forward to spending time with her. Had her feelings changed so she no longer wanted to be with him? Or did she think of him as an invalid?

"Brother Andrew, perhaps the amnesia made you forget the chaperon law."

Andrew slapped his forehead. "It slipped my mind."

"If someone from my village found us alone in a bedroom, it would be the end." Liz rolled her eyes at them.

"I'll do my best to protect your reputation." Andrew had missed her teasing ways and cute expressions. "What do you want for lunch?"

"What are you having?" Liz asked.

"Pepper steak, mashed potatoes, and steamed carrots."

"I'll order the same, but I better go with you." Liz turned to the door. "It's not proper for me to be alone in Andrew's bedroom with him even for a few minutes."

Ten minutes later, they returned. Brian carried a cloth-covered basket, which he set on the floor. "I always bring drinks back with me after I order the meal."

Liz took out several one-liter bottles of filtered water, two beers, four cokes, and three glasses. "If you men want to wash up before dinner, there's time."

Andrew slid to the edge of the bed. Brian picked up the crutches and gave them to Andrew. Brian took Andrew's arm as he hobbled forward.

When they returned, Andrew sat in the straight-back chair in front of the card table. Brian lifted the casted foot and set it on another wooden chair. Then he slipped a pillow under the cast.

Brian went into the bathroom and came out a few minutes later rubbing his hands on a towel. He took a seat opposite Andrew.

Liz folded the napkins and set them next to the glasses at each setting. "How are the accommodations?"

Brian frowned. "The elevator is broken, and we were unable to get a room on the ground floor."

"Be grateful. The second floor is safer and better. The ground floor is busy, noisy, and dangerous."

"I don't like my patient going up and down uneven stairs on a slippery floor with crutches. Outside of that there are no other hazards. As long as his leg is elevated, he should be fine."

Liz looked puzzled. "Why do you men need to go downstairs? He has a bed, food, and a bathroom right here."

"I'll let you figure out what's missing." Brian chuckled.

Someone knocked and called, "Excuse me, master."

Liz opened the door to a young cocoa-skinned lady dressed in a blue uniform. She balanced a giant tray on her head. Taking the platter from the girl, Liz carried it to the table. She unloaded the plates and handed the tray back to the server, who left. Liz sat down between Andrew and Brian.

"How about it, Liz?" Andrew reached for her hand.

Liz clasped Andrew's hand and extended her right hand to Brian who took it. She bowed "Lord Jesus, thank you for bringing Andrew back to us. Help him heal. Thank you for this food and bless our conversation and time together. Amen."

Warmth flowed into his fingers from Liz's as she prayed. Andrew reluctantly let go of her hand. Breathing in Liz's floral scent, he sighed in pleasure. When the time was right, he'd tell her how much he cared.

Liz cut a bite of meat. "How's room service?"

"There isn't any. The lady who brought the food is used to me and brings it every day. The generator comes on when the power is cut. There's water all the time, but it's the rainy season." Brian sipped his beer. "There's a giant television in the main lobby always turned to the news and a smaller set in a side room which plays sports all day. There's a bar which is open most of the time."

"Oh, I get it." Liz set her fork down. "There's no television in the room."

"Smart lady." Brian grinned.

"Something's been on my mind." Liz swallowed a bite of meat. "Did they figure out who tampered with the plane?"

Brian glowered. "A renegade officer from a neighboring country got wind that the plane would be flying close to the border. He didn't know anything about HOW and thought the plane was part of a political group opposing his government, so he only intended to disable the aircraft."

"What happened to him?" Liz took a sip of water.

"Nothing. He claimed he never wanted anyone to get hurt." Brian finished his beer. "His relatives paid a bribe to the officials, so it was covered up."

"Thank God Andrew wasn't killed." Liz put her hand on her heart.

After they had finished eating, Liz stood and collected the empty plates. "I can see you're tired and so am I from the long taxi ride. I'll say goodbye now so you can rest."

After Liz left, Andrew fretted. His mind wasn't as sharp as it was before the accident. The doctor assured him all his memory would come back in time. Amnesia and a prolonged high fever were responsible for most of his forgetfulness. He would wait until he could remember everything before telling Liz how he felt about her.

***

When Liz and Henry returned home, a policeman, Mr. Bellolare, and his village chief, dressed in his official clothes for a judgment, were sitting on a log under the mango tree.

Henry kept her head averted, but Liz smiled at the visitors. "Good afternoon. What brings you here today?"

"We have come to escort Henry to her wedding. If you refuse to release her, give me one hundred thousand francs. It equals the two months that she has been working with you. We are appealing to your decency as a Christian."

Liz squared her shoulders and looked him straight in the eyes. "I will not give you any money. You are wasting your time to keep coming here and demanding this. Henry is not for sale. She is not a piece of property. Henry is a grown woman of twenty-five who worked her way through nursing school."

"I do not treat her like a piece of property," Mr. Bellolare growled. "You have not seen the last of me. I will return with the most powerful warlord in the country."

Henry shuddered.

Mr. Bellolare took a step closer to Henry and lifted his fist as if to strike his daughter, but Liz moved in front of Henry. Dropping his hand, he turned away from the ladies and yelled, "This white lady is annoying me. I will teach her a lesson she will never forget. Let's go."

After they left, Liz and Henry went into the house.

"My father would have struck me if you hadn't stepped in front of me. Thank you, Sister Liz."

Liz set the tea kettle on the burner. "It's best to stand up for what you believe in. You mustn't run away from challenges or one of these days you'll face something worse. Remember, greater is He that is in you than He that is in the world."

She smiled at Henry. "God will give us the victory."

CHAPTER FORTY-FIVE

As Liz approached her house a few days later, she gasped at the destruction. Tears filled her eyes. The door was smashed, the screens slashed, and the windows broken.

Liz lived in a friendly community. She had never seen the need for steel doors and iron bars across the windows, but many Americans living in big cities had them. She hated a metal door, but maybe she needed one now.

"I told you my father is wicked." Henry whispered. "He's responsible for this."

"Maybe so, but there is nothing we can do except get it fixed." Liz brushed a tear off her cheek. "Let's go inside and see what's missing or broken."

The couch, cushioned chairs, dining room table, bed, and stove were untouched. Liz opened the cupboards to check the cups, saucers, and plates, but everything was there. Even her towels, linens, and personal supplies seemed to be in place.

"Nothing's taken or damaged inside the house." Liz shrugged. "Do you think anyone in this village would have plywood to cover the front doorway until I can get it repaired?"

"We could ask the pastor. He knows everyone."

They hiked down the trail and found the pastor at home. After greetings were exchanged, Liz asked. "Have you seen my house?"

"Yes. It's terrible." The pastor leaned closer. "The head deacon is putting in a ceiling and will let you borrow a piece of wood to cover your doorway."

"Henry's coming with me to the city to buy an iron door and supplies for the repairs."

"You'll need a cement doorframe to hold the steel door in place. I'll call the church mason. There's only one size, so the door will fit the frame he makes."

"Please ask the mason to put in the cement doorframe today. Then the deacon can cover the opening with the wood, so it'll be ready when we return."

***

Andrew relaxed in a cushioned chair with his casted foot on a pillow. He'd read all the books he'd brought with him, gone downstairs and watched football on the television, and played chess with Brian. There wasn't much more he could do, except look forward to seeing Liz.

When Liz came into the room, his heart beat faster. Seeing the tiny-built lady with Liz, he wondered who she was.

"Andrew and I were discussing what we should do today." Brian stood and offered Liz his chair.

Liz asked, "How is your walking-cast holding up?"

The dark-skinned girl furrowed her brows. "How does the cast walk?"

"Henry, it doesn't walk." Liz giggled. "It's a solid plaster with a heel on the bottom of it, so the person can walk around."

Andrew rubbed the healed gash on his forehead wondering if the girl's name was Henry. He'd seen her somewhere but couldn't place her. The doctor assured him all his memory would return in time, but when? Spending each week alone with only Brian, as nice a guy as he was, didn't help Andrew's memory.

Andrew frowned at Liz's bowed head and asked, "What's wrong?"

With a glassy stare, Liz looked at him and then sobbed uncontrollably. "Someone broke down my front door, ripped all the screens, and smashed the glass panes. I came to town to buy an iron door and supplies to repair the damage."

Andrew reached for her hand, but Liz pulled it away and whispered. "No. You must have forgotten."

Forgotten what? He had no idea what she was talking about.

Liz turned to the African lady. "I enjoy living in the village with the people." She wiped a few tears off her cheek.

He took out his handkerchief and handed it to Liz.

She dried her eyes. "Security in the city is necessary, but now it looks like I need it in the rural village."

Brian asked, "Do you have any idea who did it?"

Henry crossed her arms and growled. "My evil father and his witch doctor friends did this because I won't marry the heathen man he has arranged for me."

Andrew shook his head wondering what that had to do with Liz's house. Maybe he'd lost more of his memory than he realized. His brow wrinkled. "How are you going to carry an iron door?"

"I'll hire a truck."

"Stan has one and is on the way over here." Andrew reached for his wallet on the dresser.

"We couldn't drive all the way to Liz's house, make the repairs, and come back in one day." Brian picked up Andrew's shoe.

Andrew stuffed his billfold in his pocket. "We can't leave Liz defenseless."

"Brother Andrew read all the books he brought, so he's a bit bored." Brian shrugged.

"I'll look in the mission library and bring a few action and suspense novels the next time I come." Liz smiled.

"Sounds good." Brian moved clothes from a chair, which he offered to Henry. "He's itching to get up and do something or go someplace. I'm not sure it's wise to go from doing nothing to major house repairs."

"Andrew doesn't need to carry an iron door and steel window frames. I'll ask the men in the church to help with that. The biggest challenge is getting everything to my house."

"We go downstairs a couple times a day to watch the news." Brian grinned. "So getting in the truck shouldn't be too strenuous."

When Stan came into the room, he listened to the plan. Then he pulled out his cigarettes, glanced at the ladies, and put them back in his pocket. "I intended to take Andrew for a ride. I thought he might have cabin fever."

"You men can put a mattress in the back of the truck so Andrew can keep his leg elevated on it." Liz reached in her bag. "I've made a list of the supplies."

"Read the list to us." Brian smiled.

Liz took out a pencil. "A mason is putting in the concrete door frame today. I'll need a standard-sized metal door, eight steel window frames with bars, twelve meters of screening, twelve meters of wire fencing and a hundred and eight glass panes because each window has sixteen panes."

"These additions to your home will protect you." Andrew looked again at the African lady, who kept glowering at him. He had no idea what he had done wrong.

Liz blew her nose. "Henry, do you want to come?"

The girl nodded.

"I'll bring the truck to the back exit." Stan picked up the mattress from the spare bed and left.

Brian grabbed his bag. "I completed the carpentry on my retirement house and enjoy woodworking projects. This will give all of us something interesting and helpful to do."

Liz took one of Andrew's arms while Brian supported the other as they descended the stairs.

By the time they exited the hotel, Stan was waiting for them. Brian and Stan helped Andrew onto the mattress in the back of the truck. Liz and Henry sat in the cabin with the others. Liz opened the partition window to the back.

Stan drove to a metal works shop and parked. Everyone got out and walked to the back of the truck. Stan lowered the tail gate. "How are you doing?"

"Lonely." Andrew handed Brian a stack of bills. "Liz, I'm paying for the supplies."

"Brother Andrew, it's my home, so it's my responsibility." She took a seat on the tail gate.

"Liz, I love you."

Henry's jaw fell open. She put her hands on her hips and asked, "Have you got permission from her parents?"

Andrew wiped the sweat from his brow. Why would a strange lady ask such a personal question? He wished he could remember who the woman was.

Ignoring the female, he looked at Liz. "I love you and want you safe. I heard you paid for the search party."

Liz's eyes widened. "Who told you?"

"Stan didn't think it was a secret."

She sighed. "I was going to tell you when the time was right."

Brian patted Liz's shoulder. "Let Andrew pay for the repairs. Otherwise he'll worry and won't be able to sleep. Surely you want him to have a good night's rest."

"I give up." She laughed.

Stan and Brian left to purchase the metal grids and door. Henry and Liz sat with Andrew on the tailgate. He kept his mouth closed, too afraid to say anything more and antagonize the African lady.

A few minutes later the men returned empty-handed.

Liz asked, "What happened?"

"They don't have what we need." Stan shrugged. "They suggested a place across town."

It took the rest of the day for them to purchase the grids, netting, glass panes, and iron door. After stacking them in the backend of the truck, Brian glanced at his watch. "We've had a long day, and it's too late to drive to Liz's."

Stan lit a cigarette. "Tomorrow is a national holiday and I'm free."

"Let's go ahead and have supper together and turn in early. Then we can get a good start tomorrow. There shouldn't be any traffic at six in the morning." Liz's eyes twinkled. "Henry and I will go to the mission guesthouse tonight."

"Great idea." Andrew winked at her.

Henry's mouth fell open. She scowled and shook her head at him. Andrew cringed. Everything he did was wrong according to Henry.

After they were back in Andrew's room, Brian elevated Andrew's foot. "I'll go down to the kitchen and get supper. What would you like, Sister Liz, Sister Henry?"

"Sister Henry and I like chicken, but I'll go down with you."

"Getting food is my job. I'll go." Henry turned to the door.

"I always order the meals, so they know me." Brian opened the door. "I'll need to sign for it."

They left.

"Maybe I should sit in the back with Andrew tomorrow." Liz started moving books off the table. I'm a nurse and can minister to him."

Stan chuckled. "What kind of ministering are you planning to do?"

"Suppose he gets a cramp or starts a fever."

"Isn't it forbidden for you to be alone with him back there?" Stan asked. "If not, it ought to be against the law."

Her eyes grew large, and she covered her mouth. "You're right, but I was only thinking of the patient."

"Sister Liz, I was joking." Stan chuckled. "If no one knew that you and Andrew were alone together in the back of the truck, it wouldn't offend anyone, would it?"

"No, it won't, but God's watching. If we remember that, it should keep all of us in line." She exhaled loudly.

Stan laughed. "I think the whole chaperon idea is hilarious."

"Stay in the back with me, Liz. Brian is good company but I want to spend more time with you."

"We'll keep the sliding window open between the cabin and back. That way you men can chaperon us." Liz said.

Stan nodded. "Let's be sure to do that."

The door opened. Brian, toting a large basket, came into the room with Henry, who carried a giant platter on her head. Henry and Liz set the table and served supper.

While they were eating, Liz turned to Henry. "I think you and I ought to stay in the back to watch Brother Andrew in case he gets sick."

"There's not enough room, Sister Liz. There's hardly enough room for Brother Andrew on that mattress with all the supplies we bought. It's best we keep talking to him through the window."

"That's best." Liz chuckled.

***

From his place in the truck bed, Andrew watched Stan back up to Liz's front door which was covered with a large sheet of plywood.

When the tailgate came open, Andrew slid to the end. "That's a lot of damage."

Liz handed her bag and house key to Henry. "I'll run to the pastor's house to call the men to help." Liz turned away and jogged down the trail.

Stan shook his head. "She doesn't waste time, does she?"

"No, she doesn't." Andrew picked up his crutches.

A few minutes later, Liz returned with a local man. "This is the mason who put in the cement frame for the iron door."

The worker peered into the back of the truck. "If you put all this on the house no one will ever break in. I'll help unload and put the new door in for you."

Brian lugged a cushioned chair outside for Andrew, and Henry brought a wooden bench for his casted foot.

Stan unloaded a giant metal box from the back of the truck. "We'll have to knock out the broken window frames first. Then we can set in the new ones and cover them with screening."

Brian pulled out a tape measure to check dimensions. "The generator's small, but it'll recharge the tools quickly to get the job completed."

They removed the old windows and set in the new frames. Using the staple gun, Stan covered the windows with screen and netting. Brian drilled holes along the outer edges of the original frames. He positioned an iron grid over the outside of a window and slid the bolts through the openings to the interior while Brian affixed the inner steel backing to the steel frame. Within a couple of hours, the men had the window frames, screening, and netting in place.

Andrew smiled. "Sister Liz will be safe."

Liz carried a tray of fresh lemonade to the men.

Reaching for the drink, Andrew saw a spitting cobra a few feet from Liz. If he yelled, the snake might attack, but he had to warn her. So he pointed and whispered loudly. "Liz, look out."

The serpent writhed and snapped open its mouth revealing its fangs. Its wiry tongue darted out. Stan grabbed Andrew's crutch, leaped forward, and pounded the serpent several times.

Brian reached for the tray in Liz's shaking hands. "Sit down, Liz."

Sweat poured from Andrew's brows. He'd almost lost Liz. What if something happened to her? He wanted to make certain his memory

257

was completely restored before he proposed, but what if it never returned? With moisture in his eyes, Andrew smiled at Liz. "Stay seated and rest a moment."

Henry came outside carrying a machete. "My father and his witch doctor friends did another evil deed to us." Using the tip of the blade, she lifted the snake and dumped it into a cluster of nearby bushes. "You men saved Sister Liz's life. A spitting cobra spews venom into a person's eyes and causes blindness. Its bite is deadly."

At the mention of her father Andrew remembered who Henry was.

Brian sat next to Liz on the doorstep and handed her a goblet of lemonade. The glass shook so much in her hands, the drink spilled. Liz steadied the tumbler with both hands and brought it to her lips.

Andrew slid his chair closer to her. "Liz, are you alright?"

Henry scowled. "She is Sister Liz."

Andrew remembered another time Henry rebuked him.

Tears slid down Liz's cheeks. "Thank God you saw the snake."

After everyone had finished drinking, Henry collected the glasses and went inside.

Stan pointed to the mango tree. "I sat on that log so many times waiting for Liz, I kept wishing it had been more comfortable. Wouldn't it be nice to have a bench around that tree for your guests?"

Liz's eyes sparkled. "I've wanted one for a long time. I tried explaining it to a local carpenter, but he looked at me like I was crazy. Who could make circular wood?"

"It won't be too difficult. We can work on it this week. It'll give us a new project to do over our Christmas break." Brian went to the huge mango tree and jotted measurements for the circular wooden bench.

Henry came outside. "Lunch is ready. I made spaghetti."

Liz stood. "We'd better go wash up and eat while the food is hot."

The men carried their tools into the house, set them on the floor, and took turns in the bathroom. When they were seated at the table, Andrew prayed.

After lunch they installed the glass panes. Then Brian and Stan helped get Andrew settled in the back of the truck.

Waving to Liz, Andrew took a deep breath and held it. He closed his eyes and saw the two of them together in Africa serving God. As soon as he was back on his feet, walking without assistance, and the rest of his memory returned, he'd propose.

But how long would that take?

CHAPTER FORTY-SIX

After a six-hour taxi ride to the city, Liz was happy to find Andrew and Brian eating in the hotel dining room.

Andrew pushed himself out of his chair to stand. As he gripped the table for support, it shook. "Have a seat. Where's your assistant, Henry?"

Liz sat next to Andrew. "She's buying supplies."

Andrew reached under the table and took Liz's hand. She relaxed as he rubbed his finger across her thumb and palm.

"You look frazzled." Brian poured her a glass of water. "Would you like something to eat?"

The waitress came to the table and asked, "What would you like?"

Liz smiled. "I'll have whatever these men are eating."

A few minutes later, the server brought a plate of beef stew and a bottle of water.

Seeing Henry come into the hotel restaurant, Liz waved to her. Henry came to their table. Brian stood and lifted the large washtub off Henry's head. She sat down in the chair that Brian offered her.

"Sister Liz, something awful has happened to Mercy."

Liz dropped her spoon. "What is it?"

"She's in the hospital with cerebral malaria. I met her father in the market and he told me."

"What hospital?" Liz asked.

"She's in the large government one. Mrs. Isaiah is a good mother and didn't wait until her baby wanted to die."

"What does that mean?" Brian asked.

"Many parents wait until a child is almost dead before going for help," Henry sighed. "Then it's often too late."

Liz looked at Brian. "Can you save this food for me?" Then she turned to Henry. "Do you want to come with me to the hospital to see Mercy?"

"Yes, but what about our purchases?"

Liz stood and asked, "Can we leave these with you and pick them up when we return?"

The men nodded.

Andrew said, "I'll pray."

"Pray they were able to get the malarial treatment to her in time."

***

Andrew closed his eyes and suddenly recalled how Liz had stared down a lunatic in the market. Later, they had been lost on an abandoned road when they rescued little Mercy.

An hour later, Liz and Henry returned.

Andrew put his book away and waved to them. "How's Mercy?"

"She's getting medication and a drip line. Thank God her mother took her to the hospital when she did."

Brian carried a bag as he approached them. "Andrew told us how you and he rescued the infant from a herd of forest hogs. It's hard to believe someone threw away a helpless baby to be eaten or trampled by wild beasts."

"It happens in our country if the relatives are superstitious and believe the child is cursed." Henry said.

"Liz, while you're visiting Andrew, I'd like to look at the tourist shops, but I'm not sure where the best ones are located." Brian glanced at a list.

Henry tilted her head. "Are you talking about souvenirs?"

"Yes."

"I know where lots of good ones are near the market." Henry said.

Liz asked. "Would you show Brother Brian the way?"

"You are an old man with gray hair." Henry wrinkled her brow. "So I better come with you to help."

Liz's lips twitched. "In our country, Henry, it's impolite to call someone old."

"It's a great honor here." Her assistant reached for Brian's bag.

He swung it behind him. "I'll carry my own sack. You're not my servant."

"All women must serve men. It's the law."

"It's not my rule."

"If I don't take your bag, people will glare at me for letting an old man carry his load. Strangers will yell at me for not respecting you."

"My two daughters are older than you are, so maybe I am ancient." He handed Henry the bag.

She set Brian's sack on her head. "Let's go. The tourist stores should give a fair price because they respect old people. Since you're a white man they might think you're rich and try to cheat you. I'll make sure no one takes advantage of you."

Brain mumbled. "I guess us old men need all the help we can get."

Liz grinned. "Remember, it's a great honor to be an old man, especially an old wise man."

Shaking his head, Brian followed Henry. "We shouldn't be gone long."

"Take your time."

Andrew laughed the loudest. "Now I remember everything."

CHAPTER FORTY-SEVEN

Liz lifted the cinnamon rolls out of the oven and set them on the table. She caught a whiff of the tantalizing aroma. Pulling off a small bite, she popped it in her mouth.

Andrew hobbled into her house and sat down. "It smells wonderful. My mouth is watering."

Stan and Brian set their tools on the floor and came to the table.

Liz handed each of the men a cup of fresh coffee. "Have a seat." She served them the cinnamon rolls.

Brain took a sip. "After our snack, we'll get started on the wrap-around bench."

"The pieces of wood are similar to a giant jigsaw puzzle. We put them together at the hotel, so they'll fit perfectly." Stan bit into his roll. "These are delicious, Liz."

"They're fabulous." Andrew grinned. "Did you make them from scratch?"

"Yes."

After Stan and Brian left, Liz started dinner. She mixed flour, egg, and water and rolled out the noodles. She dropped them in boiling water. Then she stirred the sauce simmering on the stove. The aroma of tomatoes, onions, and oregano filled the warm kitchen.

Andrew set his cup down. "After I became a Christian I wanted to see you again but didn't know where you were. I thank God I found you that day in the market."

"I'm glad we met again, too." Liz layered the lasagna with cheeses and sauce and put it in the oven.

"After the crash, when the natives shared their limited supplies with me, it made me realize how selfish I've been. So I re-dedicated my life to the Lord."

"I'm so pleased." Liz adjusted the oven temperature.

"As a pilot I've helped people get medications, vaccines, and establish a source of clean drinking water in needy areas. God is now leading me into fulltime ministry." He took a deep breath. "Will you pray about working with me?"

She hesitated before saying, "Yes." His suggestion disturbed her. Did he only want to work with her in a ministry? Turning back to him, she asked. "What kind of work are you considering?"

"A job in Africa."

"If you were an independent pilot, available to all missionaries and expatriate volunteers, you could evacuate anyone in need and fly supplies, equipment, and food to workers in hard to reach places."

"Would I need my own plane?"

"Yes, but that will cost a lot of money." Liz shook her head.

Andrew laughed. "That's not a problem. My great-great-grandfather founded one of the largest lumber companies in Oregon, so I can buy my own plane." He took her hand. "Why did you pay for the rescue?"

"Everyone was about to give up and stop looking for you, I believed you were alive. I offered to pay for a search team." Liz stared at him. "I'm not rich but worked hard and saved most of what I earned. My dad's a mechanic, the son of an immigrant."

Andrew smiled. "I've enough money for both of us and to support a ministry. I love you, your willingness to sacrifice for others, and the way you fit in anywhere, making everyone around you comfortable."

"I love you, too." Liz grinned, but he hadn't proposed.

The aroma of lasagna reminded her to check it. It was done, so she turned off the oven.

"The food's ready. I'll call the guys." She went outside. "This new bench is beautiful. Dinner's ready. There's time to get washed up before you eat." She turned toward the trail and waved to the approaching figure. "Henry, I'm glad you came. How is the pastor's family?"

"The children are feeling better. The pastor's wife was glad I helped." Henry followed everyone into the house.

After they were seated and had prayed, Liz set the pan of lasagna on the table.

Stan picked up his napkin. "There weren't many cars on the road this morning."

"Once the people reach their homes for Christmas they stay there until after New Year's." Liz sliced the lasagna. After serving the men, she handed a bowl of noodles and sauce to her assistant.

"Thank you." Henry took the bowl. "I can't eat slimy cheese."

Andrew furrowed his brows. "Are you talking about mozzarella?"

"What's a mat'za?"

"Never mind, Henry. I'll explain later." Liz giggled. "I can't eat your slimy green sauces."

The men coughed and choked.

Andrew took a bite, chewed, and swallowed. "This is the best lasagna and homemade French bread I've ever had."

"I baked a pie with imported apples for dessert."

Andrew grinned. "I can hardly wait."

After the men had eaten second helpings, Brian leaned back and patted his stomach. "I'm stuffed. Can we have coffee and pie later?"

"Yes." Liz helped Henry clear the table.

Then she handed each of the men a gaily-wrapped jar of nuts, a box of homemade cookies, and a blue plastic bag. "Merry Christmas. Thanks for your help."

Opening the bag, Andrew took out a shirt and held it in front of him. "Thanks Sister Liz. This should fit perfectly."

The other two men agreed as they looked at their own shirts.

Liz handed Henry a package, which she opened. Yards of expensive cloth tumbled out. Henry gasped, "It's so beautiful. I'll have the seamstress make the prettiest outfit for church."

Andrew gave Liz two wrapped boxes. Taking the presents, she wrinkled her brow. "Where did you get Christmas paper?"

"I had someone buy it for me in England."

Sliding her fingernail under the tape, Liz opened the smallest box. A necklace with matching earrings sparkled on a black velvet cushion. Liz lifted the earrings out of the container, admired them in the light, and put them in her pierced ears. "These are gorgeous, Andrew. Thank you." She held the necklace around her neck and leaned back toward Henry. "Will you clasp it for me?"

Henry furrowed her brows. "These are probably the five dollar ones. They won't turn green in a few months like the fifty cent ones do."

Andrew laughed. "If they turn green, I won't buy anything from them again."

Liz stroked the diamonds imbedded in silver. They were far too expensive. What was Andrew thinking? A gift like that confirmed his serious intentions.

She picked up the other present. "This is heavy." She unwrapped an ebony jewelry box and ran her fingers along the hand-carved monkeys on the side. "I love it."

Brian picked up his packages and stood. "We have to put a few finishing touches on the bench."

Stan and Brian left. Liz and Henry washed the dishes while Andrew drank another cup of coffee.

When the wrap-around seat was finished, Brian called, "come and take a look."

They went outside. Liz sat down on the new seat. "I love this, and so will my visitors. Thank you so much. Each of you men deserve a whole pie, but I only have one. Are you ready for a piece?"

"After we put the tools away, we'll be there."

As she rose, Liz turned toward Mr. Bellolare and two large sorcerers coming on the trail. Feathers stuck out of their hair. They carried spears and knives. Strange slashes of paint covered their faces.

Mr. Bellolare scowled. "We have come to take Henry back with us."

"Sister Liz, I won't go with them." Henry whispered.

Stepping in front of Henry, Liz locked eyes with Mr. Bellolare. "Henry is a grown woman and can make her own decisions."

The two sorcerers walked around Liz, grabbed Henry's arms and started dragging her away. She screamed.

Brian, still holding the hammer, and Stan, clutching the drill, walked up to the witches. Stan turned on the drill. It buzzed loudly and everyone jumped. Brian shook the hammer and growled.

Liz yelled, "Leave Henry alone and go away."

Henry's father turned to Liz and raised his fist.

***

No one moved or spoke. Andrew breathed easier when Henry's father lowered his fist and took a step backwards. Andrew suddenly remembered that Liz often ran into danger.

Liz raised her hands, palms outward as if trying to stop a truck. "Henry is not going with you."

Turning to face the witch doctors, Liz shook her finger at them like a mother shaming her child. "Let go of her, right now."

Andrew recalled Liz's impulsive acts in the past, which had nearly gotten them killed. That was who Liz was and it didn't change his feelings for her. When he married her, he hoped to convince her not to dive into peril.

Everyone silently maintained their positions and glared at each other.

Andrew's balance wasn't good, but he could protect Liz from Henry's father. The witch doctors were giants, but Stan and Brian would back him up in a fight.

"Do what the lady says." Andrew ordered. "Let go of Henry."

Mr. Bellolare turned and faced Andrew. "Are you speaking for Sister Liz?"

"Yes, I am."

"How can you speak for her?"

"She will soon be my wife."

Brian gave him an "I thought so" type of look.

Henry's father jabbered in another language. The sorcerers released her and stepped away.

Mr. Bellolare bared his teeth and then scowled at Henry. "I have no use for an ungrateful daughter. Stay with the white lady, but I will do nothing more for you." He spat on the ground. "The white lady's husband and brothers will have to take care of you now."

Andrew's lips twitched, but he kept his mouth closed.

Henry's father left with the witch doctors.

As soon as they were out of sight, Liz doubled over with laughter.

Henry smiled, too. "Thank God. My father will never bother us again."

"Liz, I worry when you rush into danger." Andrew hopped to the step in front of the door.

She grinned. "It's time for coffee and apple pie."

In the kitchen, Henry put the kettle on the fire. "Congratulations Sister Liz, Brother Andrew. We need to announce this in church."

"Announce what?" Liz asked.

"Your wedding."

Brian shook Andrew's hand. "Congratulations."

Andrew beamed.

***

After the men left, Liz was still troubled because Andrew hadn't proposed. He suggested they have a ministry and work together. Then he announced that he loved her.

"What's wrong?" Henry asked.

"Brother Andrew didn't ask me to marry him."

"It's not his place. Your parents should tell you what you should do. If your parents are not Christians, then you'll have to decide."

"Where I come from a gentleman always proposes to a lady."

"What's propose?"

Liz fell to one knee and grabbed Henry's hand. "My darling Sister Henry, I love you and want you to be my wife. Will you marry me?" She jumped up. "That was a proposal."

"Brother Andrew is not a gentleman so he is not required to propose."

Liz's heart lurched. Had he touched Henry inappropriately?

"Why do you say he is not a gentleman?"

"A gentleman is someone who courts you. Brother Andrew never courted you. He declared you publically, so he became your proper fiancé, not a gentleman."

Liz bit her lip. "He hasn't asked me to marry him."

"Brother Andrew is a strong man, and he is brave. He stood up against my father. Then he announced to everyone that you would be his wife. This is how he does things."

"Maybe so, but most American ladies want a real proposal." Liz shook her head. "I'm not sure what to do."

Henry scowled. "Marry him."

CHAPTER FORTY-EIGHT

Liz was surprised to see Brian without Andrew at her front door several weeks later.

After serving Brian coffee, Liz asked. "How's Andrew."

"He's fine and sends his regrets for leaving unexpectedly."

Liz's heart plummeted to the pit of her stomach. She couldn't believe that Andrew had left.

"The cast was due to come off next week, so he left early to visit his elderly parents in the States." Brian smiled. "I've enjoyed my job and appreciated the money. I'm sure going to miss everyone. I almost hate to leave and go back to my empty house."

"You're welcome to come again and stay as long as you want."

"I'll keep that in mind." He handed her an envelope. "Andrew wanted me to give this to you."

Liz took the envelope. "Thank you."

After Brian left, she read the letter. "Dear Liz, Can you meet me at the airport on Saturday, the eighth? Love always, Andrew."

* * *

In the taxi on the way to the city, Liz turned to Henry. "I'm sorry becoming a missionary seems to be difficult."

Henry sighed. "They told me I couldn't be one because I'm a lady. They only accept a married woman who accompanies her husband."

"Would Bible College qualify you?"

Henry snorted. "They told me ladies were not allowed there, either."

"You are a government-trained nurse. That should qualify you."

"They weren't impressed. They said if I had a husband they would think about letting me be a missionary."

Liz sighed, "Let's stop at the church headquarters and talk to the president."

After they arrived and exchanged salutation, Liz said, "This is Miss Henry Bellolare. She has been my faithful assistant. I would like to send her to Bible College so she can be a missionary. I'll pay her fees for the year."

The president lowered himself into his chair. "You can't do that, Sister Liz."

"Is it against the law?"

"Ladies are not permitted to attend Bible College. We make an exception for a few married women who will accompany their husbands to the mission field." The church president took a deep breath. "I've heard all about this young lady from your village pastor. He reported that she is stubborn and disrespectful. He would not recommend her to be a missionary."

Trying hard not to sound sarcastic, Liz asked. "Is there anything in addition to marriage that you require for your missionaries?"

The president sighed. "She could return to the village and submit herself to the pastor. He would put her on a two-year probation. If he saw a change in her that demonstrated respect for her elders and a quiet, submissive spirit, we would reconsider her."

When they left the church headquarters, Liz prayed. Then she smiled. "I think God has given me a solution."

Henry turned to Liz. "What is it?"

"I can send you as my assistant to Chief Tiolare's village for a few months. I'll pay your expenses. You won't be an official missionary, but you could tell them more about Jesus and teach them how to read the Bible. After three months, we'll talk about what to do next."

Henry beamed. "Thank you. Can I leave now?"

"We should sit down and set some goals to work on. We need to discuss some of the problems you might have."

"What problems?"

"I'll think about it, make a list, and we'll talk later."

"Do people make a list of problems?"

"Some people do." Liz sighed. "A long time ago there was a lady who was called to go to China. The mission board rejected her, but she worked as a maid cleaning toilets, bathrooms, and houses. She saved all her money, paid for her own way to China, and become a famous missionary. She had a lot of problems, but God took care of them. We'll talk about them when I get back." Liz handed Henry a list of supplies as Liz climbed into a taxi for the airport.

***

When Andrew saw Liz, he wanted to run and throw his arms around her, but his leg wouldn't cooperate. So he gripped his cane and limped toward her as fast as he was able. "I've missed you."

"I've missed you, too." She took his free hand. "How is your leg?"

"My ankle is stiff and uncomfortable, but I thank God I'm alive and have both legs to get around. If I do the prescribed exercises, I'll have full use of my foot in a couple of months. I won't need a cane, shouldn't have a limp, and will be able to fly again."

"That's good news." Liz asked, "How are your parents?"

Andrew's heart tightened. His parents hadn't understood or accepted the fact he was marrying a nurse and planning to live in Africa.

"They're fine."

"I prayed they'd believe on Jesus."

"Keep praying. They're upset over my decision to stay here and work, even though I was given a desk job with HOW until I get enough flexibility in my foot to fly." Andrew leaned on his cane. "Have you eaten?"

"No."

"Would you like to go to 'The Falls' restaurant?"

"Give me a few minutes. I look a mess, but I was afraid of missing your arrival, so I didn't take time to get cleaned up." Liz headed to the ladies room.

Andrew's heart pounded faster. She was an adorable mess and he loved her. A lopsided barrette fastened a twisted clump of hair behind her head. The chaotic style was another aspect of her charm. A radiance shone beneath the soot on her face, reminding him of the first day they met.

His parents threatened to disinherit him from their millions and refused to give him great-grandmother's heirloom ring. He'd prayed and hoped they would have agreed to meet Liz. If they had, they would have loved her, too.

None of that mattered. Liz and he loved God and each other. They were committed to each other, with or without an antique ring.

Liz returned with a washed face and wearing makeup. She had combed her hair and changed her clothes. She looked lovely.

"I can't collect my truck until I check in at headquarters."

"It looks like we'll have to rent one of those decrepit taxis you don't like." Her emerald eyes sparkled.

"At least we'll have it all to ourselves." He'd missed those green eyes, but he had missed her more.

During the taxi ride they sat close together on the back seat. Andrew held her hand.

When they reached the restaurant, a waitress escorted them to a table. Andrew pulled out Liz's chair and sat down across from her. He asked for a large bottle of water.

The server returned with the drink and took their orders of beef in gravy over noodles.

Andrew reached across the table for Liz's hand to pray. Taking a deep breath, he calmed his racing heart before he prayed.

Every woman deserved a proper marriage proposal. He had practiced getting down on one knee and up again without help. His foot was stiffer after the long flight. So he exercised his leg and ankle under the table while waiting for their food.

When the waitress brought their meals, Liz picked up her fork and took a bite. "Thank you. I'm glad you suggested this."

At the end of the meal, Andrew stood. Using the table for support, he stepped closer to Liz and dropped to one knee. He took a small, square box out of his pocket and opened it. "I love you. Will you, Elizabeth Connor, do me the honor of marrying me? I promise to love and cherish you every day of our lives together."

"Yes. Yes. Yes. I will." Liz took his hands and pulled him to his feet.

He slid the ring on her finger. It wasn't yet noon and no one was in the restaurant, so he put his arms around her and kissed her.

Then she flung her arms around him and kissed him. He'd enjoy a lifetime of her spontaneous impulses.

"I love you." She lifted her hand and stared at the flat cluster of glistening diamonds that dominated the ring. "It's magnificent and I love it."

He handed her another gift.

Liz took the silver-wrapped package and opened it. She lifted out a brown leather Bible and ran her fingers along the gold edges. "This is beautiful."

"I wanted to have your name engraved on it, but I wasn't sure what name you wanted to use. Look inside the cover."

Liz opened it and read out loud. "Every day of our married life we'll read and study God's Word together, seek His will and pray. Love forever, Andrew." Her eyes moistened. "You can print Elizabeth Connor Thomas on the cover."

"Let's set the date. Where would you like to go for our honeymoon?"

"I love surprises. Anywhere with you will be perfect." Liz rubbed the diamonds on her finger. "We'll live happily ever after." She threw her arms around him and kissed him.

Life with her would always be an adventure. A little Mercy brought them together and God's mercy would keep them.

THE END

Made in the USA
Charleston, SC
20 July 2015